INSATIABLE DESIRE

"I want more," Archibald said, kissing Jane. Caressing her bare shoulders, he pulled her closer.

"But there isn't any more!" Jane said, astonished. "Can you imagine anything better than what we've been sharing?"

"Yes," he said, "I can."

"So you're throwing me over," Jane said sadly. "You've had your way. You know my body. You can move on to the next woman."

"No," he said. "I want you."

"You have me."

"No, I do not," he said. "But perhaps there's hope. Lady Averham, will you marry me?"

Jane gasped. Never had she dreamed that so perfect a lover could make so perverse a proposal. . . .

Four in Hand

by

Margaret Westhaven

A SIGNET BOOK

SIGNET
Published by the Penguin Group
Penguin Books USA Inc., 375 Hudson Street,
New York, New York 10014, U.S.A.
Penguin Books Ltd, 27 Wrights Lane,
London W8 5TZ, England
Penguin Books Australia Ltd, Ringwood,
Victoria, Australia
Penguin Books Canada Ltd, 10 Alcorn Avenue,
Toronto, Ontario, Canada M4V 3B2
Penguin Books (N.Z.) Ltd, 182-190 Wairau Road,
Auckland 10, New Zealand

Penguin Books Ltd, Registered Offices:
Harmondsworth, Middlesex, England

First published by Signet, an imprint of New American Library,
a division of Penguin Books USA Inc.

First Printing, January, 1993
10 9 8 7 6 5 4 3 2 1

Copyright © Peggy M. Hansen, 1993
All rights reserved

 REGISTERED TRADEMARK—MARCA REGISTRADA

Printed in the United States of America

BOOKS ARE AVAILABLE AT QUANTITY DISCOUNTS WHEN USED TO PROMOTE PROD-
UCTS OR SERVICES. FOR INFORMATION PLEASE WRITE TO PREMIUM MARKETING
DIVISION, PENGUIN BOOKS USA INC., 375 HUDSON STREET, NEW YORK, NEW
YORK 10014.

1

LADY AVERHAM had not yet completed her morning toilette when there came a knock at the door of her bedchamber.

Her abigail, brandishing a hairbrush and looking very fierce, stalked immediately to answer the summons and conferred in a low voice with the person in the hall—the third footman, her ladyship surmised from the squeaky adolescent tones.

"Well, Pauline? What is it?"

The maid gave a Gallic shrug. "These interruptions! It is the Comte de Foxburgh, madame. He makes the visit."

Lady Averham nodded thoughtfully. It was much too early for a morning call. "I'll go down at once. His lordship would never disturb me so early if it were not important. And you must remember, Pauline, we British have no counts. Lord Foxburgh is an earl."

Another shrug. "He has a nun with him."

"A nun? What on earth . . ."

"Of the Benedictine order, madame," Pauline elaborated in the bored tones of a perfect servant.

Her ladyship was mightily intrigued. That her late husband's close associate should visit her was nothing wonderful. Foxburgh had been most attentive ever since his arrival in Vienna. That he should bring a nun with him, though, and at such an odd hour of the morning! "This I must see. Throw my hair together any which way, Pauline."

"But naturally." And the dresser continued in her interrupted task, though she did not hurry.

"Don't pout, Pauline. I know you will never settle for less than perfection."

"No more will madame."

* * *

In the entry hall Lord Foxburgh was indeed waiting in company with a black-clad sister. His thundercloud expression brightened when he saw Lady Averham.

"Good morning, my lord." She extended a hand and allowed her friend to salute it. "And *Grüss Gott, meine Schwester.*" She gave a special smile to reassure the nun, for the good sister seemed ill-at-ease. In fact, Foxburgh appeared to be suffering from the same malady.

The Earl of Foxburgh, a tall and rawboned man in middle age, was indeed in an agitated state, though only an old friend would have noticed. When he spoke, his Scots burr came through clearly. "Dear Jane, I have a boon to beg of you." Glancing about him at the liveried retainers who seemed to fill the hall, he added, "May we go somewhere to talk in private?"

Jane nodded, recognizing in surprise a nearly frantic note in the earl's voice. She led the way into an ornate reception room, all plasterwork and gilded furniture, a room much in the style of the Viennese baroque chambers at Schönbrunn or the Hofburg. Before the warmth of the giant *Kachelofen,* whose painted tiles represented the meeting of Venus and Adonis, was grouped a cozy circle of ornate chairs. Jane placed herself in one of these, motioning her guests to take adjacent seats. One of the servants was dispatched for wine and biscuits.

"How may I be of help?" Though Jane's words were for Lord Foxburgh, she was directing her friendly and inquiring glances at the nun, who did appear nervous and shifty-eyed for one of a calling which usually dictated serenity. What could a nun be doing outside the cloister, and in company with a Scottish lord?

Foxburgh cleared his throat. "Jane, I come to you with a particular problem. A most particular problem. This," and he made a careless gesture in the direction of the holy sister, "is my daughter."

"Oh, my dear." Jane reached out to clasp the nun's cold hands. "Do forgive me for assuming you were not English, Sister . . . Scottish, I mean to say." She thought quickly. Never had a whisper reached her of the Foxburghs deviating from the established kirk of their native Scotland. The earl's daughter must have converted to the Catholic faith in defiance of her upbringing. Immediately

Jane's heart went out to the girl. She studied the thin, pretty face and traced some resemblance to the hardy Foxburgh in the high cheekbones, the light blue eyes.

"She's not a nun," Foxburgh said.

"Not a nun? But . . ." Jane glanced at the young woman in the habit, who was beginning to look very stormy.

"You find us in a rare predicament, Jane." Foxburgh sighed. "My fine daughter arrived in Vienna but a week ago yesterday. This morning I was told I would find her fleeing the city in this nun's garb, which she bribed someone to get for her. Thank heaven for servants. A few coins will buy the most closemouthed."

Especially in Vienna, where informing had been elevated to a fine art, Jane thought in a moment of humor. She took a closer look at the girl. "Why did you do it, my dear?"

"Because it would be much safer to travel in a nun's habit than in the clothes of an ordinary female, of course," the young lady snapped, eyeing Jane as though she were an imbecile.

"I meant to ask why you felt you must leave Vienna," Jane elaborated gently. "You have but just arrived." She paused. "You must be Lady Flora MacGowan. Your father has always spoken of you with great affection. I feel as though I know you already."

Foxburgh, thus recalled to his duties, made gruff apologies for neglecting the formal introductions.

"Oh, heavens, Foxburgh, you are allowed some leeway in your position as a concerned father."

Lady Flora scowled and folded her arms, dislodging the crucifix on her breast.

Her father continued to explain their situation. "The child has some maggoty notion that I've brought her here to the Congress on purpose in order to marry her off. It never would have occurred to me to bring her here, and as for thinking Vienna would get her off my hands when London hasn't! I'm not such a fool." Foxburgh gave Jane a special private look which informed her that he indeed cherished such hopes. And with a daughter so little given to obedience or proper behavior, what parent would wholly blame him?

"You did not bring her here? Yet Lady Flora is here." Jane was still mystified.

"Only out of dire necessity," Foxburgh said. "But the fact remains, Jane my dear, I cannot keep her with me in the Herrengasse if she's to be running off at every turn. And as for disciplining her as she deserves—a fine notion I'd give of the British delegation if it were found I was keeping my daughter locked up in her room. I was hoping . . . I know you have two daughters of about Flora's age. The companionship of other females is what she needs. She leads a solitary life at home in Scotland."

"But I have no quarrel with my life there," Lady Flora put in. "I see no need to mince about at parties and balls. This foreign rigmarole will be as deadly as my London Season—more so. I wish to go back to Alpin Castle. Now."

"And I tell you that is impossible," her father replied. "You canna stay alone in the plaguey castle." Turning to Jane, he finally explained, "Her companion has gone and taken ill. The woman had to be sent to a spa for doctoring, and so her brother Archie brought Flora along here. There was nowhere else to send her. The child wouldn't have come on her own, you may be sure." After this aside, he faced Flora once more. "I am trying, with the best will in the world, to get you an invitation to stay with Lady Averham and her family. You might at least refrain from showing her what an obstinate lass you are."

Jane spent no more than a moment in regretting the change in her domestic arrangements which the sullen Lady Flora MacGowan would no doubt necessitate. In her heart she knew that the girl would be happier in the Averham household than knocking about in her father's quarters while he chased hither and yon on business for the British delegation. Flora would doubtless make one escape attempt per week if she remained with him—and what if such an attempt succeeded, leaving a young girl open to the dangers of crossing Europe by herself?

"Will you stay with me?" Jane asked, smiling. "I would need to have your promise, naturally, that you wouldn't run away again, for I won't engage to lock you up, nor do I wish to have to explain myself to your papa."

The silence in the room grew heavy while Flora stared

stubbornly at her hostess, at the floor, at her father. Finally she sighed deeply and turned to Jane. "You have my promise, Lady Averham. Word of a MacGowan."

"Which I can assure you is sacred to the lass." Foxburgh passed a relieved hand over his high forehead. Then he glanced sharply at his daughter. "Swear also on Saint Columba," he directed.

Looking mutinous, Flora did so.

"You will be the greatest of help to me, Lady Flora," Jane said in an effort to dispel the tension. "My own girls are too much on their own, I think, and a young lady of your social standing will be the perfect example for them."

Jane had meant the reference to rank to be a compliment. She didn't expect Lady Flora to rise from her chair, rosary flapping, cheeks aflame.

"Rank!" the girl cried. "How I detest it. How I despise it."

"I begin to see that you do have a problem, my lord," Jane murmured to Foxburgh.

"If you will do this favor for me, Jane, I will count myself forever in your debt," he said softly. Louder, he spoke to Flora. "Keep your tongue between your teeth, lassie. Her ladyship cares nothing for your outbursts. She thinks," and he addressed Jane again, "that I want to marry her off to a title. Nothing, of course, could be further from the truth. I'd marry her to the devil himself to get her off my hands, and I've never read his name in the peerage."

"Oh, my lord, you don't mean that," Jane admonished, for she could tell that Flora had heard the last words, however quietly muttered, and was mortified under her bravado.

"I ought to explain myself, Lady Averham," the girl said with dignity, sitting back down. "I care very much for my own rank. There is something quite fine in the breeding which only generations can bring. I simply do not wish to see my own identity buried under a husband's title. I won't. I am an heiress in my own right—Father can't take that from me, no matter how I plague him—and Alpin Castle belongs to me."

"It is a minor property, a drafty hulk perched high on a crag on the coast of East Lothian," Lord Foxburgh explained. "Her grandfather left it to her. He was fond of the mite."

Flora glared at her father and folded her arms again.

"Flora will doubtless find life with my family somewhat different. The house is drafty, to be sure, but we haven't the advantage of a coastal climate here in the Johannesgasse. How you must miss the sea, my dear." Jane patted Flora's hand.

"I do." Flora averted her eyes and edged away.

"Then you'll really do it, Jane?" At the lady's nod, Lord Foxburgh grasped her hand and kissed it soundly. "I'll have the chit's traps moved in here today. You'll be much happier, lassie, mark my words," he told his daughter, "and we'll see each other often. Archie and I will visit you here, and there are parties by the score planned for this autumn."

"Parties. Oh, how heavenly," Lady Flora said in glum sarcasm.

Jane cast an assessing look at the girl and decided that Flora would do much better if allowed a moment to cool from the distress of her flight and subsequent capture. With an eloquent nod to Lord Foxburgh, she led him to the door of the large room. They met the servant coming in with refreshments on a tray. Foxburgh intercepted the man and poured himself a glass of the light Rhenish wine, which he downed while standing in the doorway. Then, pressing Jane's hand between both of his, he murmured his thanks once more and was gone.

She thought he looked perceptibly lighter in spirit from the back. A more carefree set to his shoulders . . . Lady Flora was bound to be a handful.

Straightening her own shoulders, Jane went back into the room to confront a certain nun.

Jane, Lady Averham, had been widowed for nearly three years. In that time she had become accustomed to thinking and acting for herself, tasks which her late husband had never believed proper for a female. Though she managed her own property quite well, and had had the courage to remain in Vienna, where diplomacy had brought the Averham ménage some years before, she still felt, at times, that she bowed too easily to other people's wishes. Jane traced this directly to her marriage and the

years of saying yes when she meant no. Plainly put, and
Jane was one for plain speaking, she let her friends walk
all over her.

Foxburgh was an old family connection and a personal
friend of some years' standing. It followed that if he
wished to saddle Lady Averham with his capricious
daughter, he would succeed. So he had done without any
trouble. But Jane had her own inner resources when it
came to dealing with the notion that she had been co-
erced. She brought herself to believe, before the day was
out, that inviting Lady Flora into her home had been her
own idea.

When Flora's things arrived, Jane called her two
daughters into the stately guest chamber she had assigned
the young woman. They surprised Lady Flora just com-
pleting her change from the nun's garb into a morning
gown with the aid of a red-haired young abigail as sullen-
looking as herself.

"You may go, Jeannie," Flora said, exchanging a look
with the maid.

"Aye, my leddy. Ye call if needful," Jeannie returned.
Tossing her bright curls, she flounced from the room.

"I do hope she gets along well with the rest of the
staff." Jane looked after the girl in concern. "My own
abigail is French, but she speaks English. Then we have
a French cook who speaks nothing but his own tongue,
and the rest of the staff is mostly Viennese."

"Jeannie wants to go home too, and is vexed that I've
made her promise not to go quite as I promised you,"
Flora said. At Jane's nod of approval, she added, "She
was to have joined me in St. Pölten. We didna . . . didn't
leave together because we wished to avoid suspicion."

"What a lovely voice you have, my dear. If I were
you, I wouldn't strive to lose your accent. It is quite a
charming quality and will make you an original."

Flora scowled, and Jane somehow knew that the girl
would let no whisper of a Scots accent pass her lips again,
at least in her hostess's hearing.

Jane gave Flora a sweeping glance, taking in her appearance, from the long straight flaxen hair which hung
down her back to the expensive morning gown with its
plaid sash—the MacGowan tartan, no doubt. Lady Flora
was nineteen, Jane had learned from the note her father

had sent along with the trunks. She had had one Season in London and had rejected all suitors. If Jane could possibly contrive to marry the girl off, she would be doing Foxburgh the greatest of favors.

Given the young lady's striking looks, Jane didn't think the task would be too onerous. And if Flora meant to begin her visit at the Averhams' by being disagreeable, there was every incentive to settle her as soon as might be.

Besides, she was likely not ill-mannered. The girl was young and still overset. Perhaps new friends would help. Jane motioned to the two girls who stood at the door of the chamber. "Come in, darlings. I must introduce you to our guest.

"Lady Flora MacGowan of Alpin Castle," she said, using the archaic-sounding Scots style she assumed Flora would prefer, "may I present my daughters, Phyllida and Chloe Bellfort."

"But, ma'am." Flora stared at the two young ladies, then at Jane. "I expected little girls."

Jane laughed, a warm and musical sound. "I will take that as a compliment, as I trust Chloe will. I still call her a little girl." With affection she ruffled the hair of the shorter miss.

There followed three curtsies of varying distinction, as Flora presumably remembered herself, and Jane's daughters followed the visitor's example. Jane watched critically and saw nothing to deplore in Flora's grace or technique. She had been well-trained by someone.

Jane's elder daughter, Phyllida, a slender and pale young lady with auburn hair and eyes of hazel green just like her mother's, smiled shyly as she rose from her graceful reverence. As for Chloe, small, round, and dark, she bobbed up and down like an apple in water—but she was only thirteen. She had plenty of time to perfect the movements.

"Phyllida is seventeen," Jane said to break the silence which followed the introduction. "She is to make her first appearance in society this autumn. Now, shall I leave you young things to talk? I have some letters to write."

"May we have tea and cakes sent up, Mama?" piped Chloe.

"Certainly, my dear. I'll take care of it. Flora wouldn't

take breakfast or luncheon, and I'm sure a little bite to eat would make her feel most at home. But don't forget that dinner is in two hours.''

Jane went away, trusting that a good coze with her dear daughters would make Flora lose that stiff air. The child looked as though the next stop was to be the guillotine.

The second her mother had left the room, Chloe bounced onto the bed and exclaimed, ''How exciting to have you here, Flora! You are such a beauty. I'm certain you'll fill the house with suitors.''

''What a very odd thing to say.'' Flora looked more closely at the dark-haired plump young girl.

''You mustn't mind my sister,'' Phyllida Bellfort said, positioning herself on a bench at the end of the bed. ''She is determined that someone in this house shall be a romantic heroine this autumn. She knows she can't count on me.''

''I would put my money on your mother,'' Flora said with a thoughtful air. ''She is so very lovely. I don't believe I've ever seen such beauty. I was astonished to find her the mother of grown girls, but I suppose she married very young.''

Chloe giggled. ''Imagine one's mother being young.''

''Mama is beautiful, isn't she?'' Phyllida said. ''Everyone in Vienna sings her praises.''

''My father,'' Flora said darkly, ''is probably in love with her.''

''Mama? But she's ancient!'' Chloe shrieked. ''Certainly past the age for romance. Is your papa really in love with her? I suppose it's possible. Lord Foxburgh is quite old himself.''

''Chloe, Chloe.'' Phyllida shook her auburn head. ''What will Lady Flora think?''

''Please call me Flora.'' Once the friendly words were out, Flora wondered what had possessed her. She had no desire to make friends of these chits. Strange Continent-bred creatures. She couldn't put her finger on it, but there was something odd about both of them, something besides the indefinably foreign cut of their clothes. An air of having seen more than Flora had; worldliness, that was it. This impression set her back up, though she had never wished to view anything but her beloved corner of Scotland.

Flora hadn't listened carefully to her father in the carriage on the way to the Averham house in the Johannesgasse, but she had gathered enough to know that though both Lady Averham's daughters had been born in England, they had been reared in harum-scarum fashion wherever their diplomat father's work had taken him. Flora was a true Scot. She thought the English foreign. But these young ladies were something worse.

"Thank you, Flora. You must call us Phyllida and Chloe." Phyllida was accepting the privilege of Christian names with an innate grace. She poked at her sister.

"Thank you, Flora," Chloe echoed.

"By the way, I don't think you have to worry that Lord Foxburgh is in love with Mama," Phyllida added. "He was a friend of Papa's, and we've known him all our lives, but . . . I simply don't think so. Wouldn't he have done something about it if he were fond of her? Our father died three years ago."

"I suppose you have a point there." Flora began to pace the room. Her long slender fingers worked nervously at the end of her sash.

Phyllida couldn't hold back a sigh. "Oh, Flora. How I do envy you your fingers."

"My fingers?" Flora glanced at them but saw nothing out of the common way.

"They are so long," Phyllida explained. "Look at mine."

Flora did, but could note nothing to despise in the small white hands Phyllida was examining so severely.

"Short fingers," the girl explained with a shrug. "My greatest trial at the pianoforte, though I do try to remember that it is only another obstacle to surmount."

"Oh." Flora still looked puzzled.

Chloe, with a giggle, explained that her sister's only love was music. "That's why we don't expect many suitors to come here on her account," she added.

Phyllida gave a serene nod. "Indeed not. We must leave that to Flora."

"And I'm not likely to wish any of these foreigners to call upon me," Flora said with a severe look at young Chloe.

"Oh, if that is your only objection, there are Englishmen aplenty arriving every day to work with Lord Castlereagh's staff,'' Chloe said importantly.

''And not a Scot among them, I don't doubt, except for my own brother.'' Flora shook her head. ''Why Archie should wish to mix with foreigners, I'll never understand.''

The other girls exchanged glances, beginning to see that Flora's definition of ''foreigner'' was somewhat narrow.

''Well!'' Chloe sighed deeply and flounced about, mussing the feather bed. ''I shall simply have to make excitement for myself. I fully intend to be a woman of the world, you know,'' she told Flora.

''So I see. But might it not be a bit too soon, lassie?''

Flora's words hung in the air. Chloe looked indignant; whether it was the sobriquet of ''lassie'' or simply irritation at the reference to her youth, Flora could not tell. ''We'll see about that,'' she said with a toss of her head.

''Your mother will have her hands full someday with that one,'' Flora told Phyllida.

Chloe's sister gave an eloquent shrug. ''Indeed, I believe she has them full already.''

Flora stiffened perceptibly, then looked more closely at Phyllida. The pale, lightly freckled young face showed not a hint of awareness that something had been said which might be interpreted as a slight on her guest.

Flora decided to give the girl the benefit of the doubt. She expected to have enough to take offense at in this house without flaring up at every little word.

When Jane was settled in her boudoir before her writing table, having sent for her own pot of tea and a couple of the cakes which made a stay in Vienna so perilous to the figure, she thought with fondness of her children.

Phyllida lived for her music. From an early age she had exhibited a decided talent for the pianoforte, an inclination Jane had indulged with the best masters and finest instruments. Indeed, Phyllida's attachment to the world of music was one reason Jane had chosen to stay in music-loving Vienna after Lord Averham's death. Now, though, the girl was old enough to look up from the ivory keys and focus her attention on the world of young men. Jane herself had been married for a year at Phyllida's age. While she didn't wish an early marriage for her daughter, she did think it past time for Phyllida to admit that the opposite sex existed.

As for Chloe . . . Jane smiled. Chloe would grow out of her puppy fat and become a stunner, a tiny dark beauty in the style of the late Lord Averham's mother, whose Gainsborough portrait Jane had much admired. That time was not yet arrived, and Jane's soft heart went out to the child, who by virtue of her youth must miss most of the thrilling activities of the autumn. The question was, would Chloe take her exclusion tamely?

Jane's own imagination was caught by the idea of all the upcoming festivities. Truly, it was most convenient for Bonaparte to be languishing on Elba at precisely this moment in time. Phyllida would never get another such chance to meet so many eligibles as the scores who were converging on Vienna to help settle the fate of Europe.

Jane's prejudices were not so firmly set that she would not consider a foreign-born gentleman as a husband for her daughter. Phyllida might even prefer someone from the Continent, since she had spent more than half her life at one foreign diplomatic post or another. But in any case, Englishmen would be plentiful too. Jane had heard that Lord Castlereagh's staff included many presentable young men from fine families.

As for Jane's own future, though she was unsure—just a little—as she prepared to make her first appearance on the scene as a matchmaking mama rather than a desirable woman, her heart thrilled at the thought of entertaining the many friends who would be in Vienna. She even hoped that somehow she might make a difference in the negotiations. A woman could often be of help in ways the men could not fathom: by contriving clever seating arrangements, by charming the right gentleman, by suggesting the right topic of conversation.

Quite excited now, she set down her Sèvres teacup and perused again the first letter in the pile she had to answer. This was a missive she had not expected to get, but was more than pleased to reply to with the invitation the writer petitioned for.

Jane's lips curved upward. Thank heaven the house had plenty of bedrooms. She would indeed have more than enough lives to manage this autumn.

2

"JANE IS A LOVELY WOMAN; the loveliest woman I've ever seen. I admire her purely as a friend, you understand." Lord Foxburgh spoke gruffly, and his normally ruddy face took on a deeper hue.

His companion's blue eyes sparkled, and he laughed. "I should hope you would say such pretty things of any lady who would take on Flora. Lady Averham must either be very kind or very mad. As to her looks, though. Do tell me the truth, Father—is she even passable? A middle-aged widow with a grown daughter can't be the paragon you so gallantly style her."

"You have much to learn of the world," Lord Foxburgh informed his son. The two sat at their ease in overstuffed chairs in the salon of the earl's ornate, if slightly cramped, residence in the Herrengasse. The city was filling fast for the Congress, and Foxburgh had been lucky to secure one floor of a vast town palace which was now bursting to the seams with Russians, Englishmen, and Germans of various small electorates and principalities.

Archibald MacGowan, Foxburgh's younger son, was recently arrived in Vienna to serve in Lord Castlereagh's office. Due to the pressures of diplomacy, he and the earl had not seen each other in a long time and were taking a leisurely approach to reacquaintance over a prized bottle of Scottish whiskey, Archie's gift to his sire.

Archie laughed again at his father's words, shook his head, and lifted his large feet onto a puffy, squat piece of furniture which was probably designed to hold them. "I'm learning more of the world each day," he said, forgetting the issue of Lady Averham, "but I'm hardly a boy."

"No, you're not." The earl looked at his son in frank appraisal. Archie was tall and lean, the epitome of Scots

vigor. The strong planes of his face put Lord Foxburgh
in mind of his own twenty years ago, and the slight rud-
diness of the skin, the crispness of the blond hair, all
recalled to the earl's mind his own features. Foxburgh
had never been a modest man; now that his hair was
going to gray and his face was lined, he still considered
himself with justice a fine figure.

Archie, now—he was someone to brag on, both in
looks and in character. A younger son with nothing to
do, he had early evinced an interest in his father's concerns and had grown up by his side at diplomatic posts
around Europe. On attaining his majority some years before, he had begun to build a career of his own. Now he
was a trusted member of Castlereagh's staff in his own
right—no parental privilege about it.

"Son, I'm proud of you," Foxburgh said with a cough.
"You've done well."

"I hope I shall continue to do so, Father. Now, tell
me more of Flora's latest start. Think of getting herself
up as a nun! Are you sure you haven't taken too much
advantage of this Lady Averham? My little sister is a
handful. She nearly slipped through my fingers more than
once on the journey here, she and that maid of hers. Can
Lady Averham handle—?"

"You may be sure we exacted Flora's promise that
she'd make no further flights," Foxburgh said. "Swore
on Saint Columba, she did. I'm satisfied she'll stay in
Vienna. And Lady Averham is clever as well as beautiful.
She may even contrive to marry the lass off."

"You'll grow old waiting for that day, sir," Archie
said, shaking his head. "Flora is sworn to marry only a
man lower in station than herself. Wishes to control her
husband, or some such flighty notion. She confided her
plans to me on the journey here. Inane project! She'd do
better to remain a spinster, for I swear she'll end by
throwing her cap over the windmill."

"But not until she's one-and-twenty. Until then she's
bound to obey me. The girl's only nineteen. Think you
that she can wait two years to marry?"

"I've waited ten years longer than that myself," Archie said with a laugh. "But lasses are a different matter.
I'll tell you what I shall do, Father. I'll visit her tomor-

row at Lady Averham's. The Johannesgasse, did you say? Do you think I'll be made welcome?''

''By whom? Your sister? I believe she'll be glad of a friendly face. As for Lady Averham, she may be even gladder. She's got her own daughter to get off this autumn. You, my son, are a prime target, thanks to the glamour of your career. I can tell you that from my own experience.'' In the years since his wife had died, Foxburgh had indeed been pursued, on the Continent and in England, by sundry ladies hoping not only for the title of countess but also for the excitement that attached to a life in the ranks of diplomacy. His son had no title to offer; but a title wasn't everything.

''I never thought I'd wish to quarrel with my choice of profession,'' Archie answered with a mocking shake of his head. ''I shall take my chances, though. What is the name of Lady Averham's daughter?''

''Can't remember. She's not out yet, and the last time I saw her she was only a wispy little thing. But if she takes after her mother, you can bet she'll be a diamond of the first water.''

''I'll risk it.'' Archie held out his glass. His father filled it with more whiskey, and the talk moved on to other matters. Many political nuances of the coming Congress merited their consideration, and many stories of friends in Scotland had to be exclaimed over before they were finally ready to go to their beds.

Jane arose next morning wishing that the day would bring something extraordinary. An eternal optimist, she dressed accordingly, in her finest new morning costume. The beautiful and worldly Duchess of Sagan, one of the great ladies of Vienna, had recently given Lady Averham a recommendation to her own dressmaker, and Jane was especially pleased with the gown she put on, of amber muslin. The cut displayed her figure to best advantage, and the color turned her hazel eyes to a warm golden brown.

As Pauline put the finishing touches to her costume, Jane looked wistfully into the mirror. She didn't yet feel as she believed a matchmaking mama should feel, and she knew she didn't look the part. Would a collection of floppy caps help her image of herself? She had never

liked to cover up her hair, and thus wore the merest scraps
of lace in her upswept auburn curls, a solution which
gave the suggestion of a proper matron's cap without its
cumbersome qualities. But would this be enough for a
grown girl's mama?

Her eyes were large and gave her a rather innocent
look even in her maturity, she thought critically as Pauline applied the customary touch of blacking to her
lashes; and her cheeks, enhanced by the smallest whisper
of rouge, still blushed on their own when she was embarrassed or took too much wine.

"I must not be remiss," she stated in sudden determination, thinking with a twinge of Phyllida. She brought
her fist down on the dressing table. "I shall go into dark
colors, Pauline, and stop painting. As for this morning,
bring me a large cap of some sort. Perhaps you have one
of your own that I may borrow."

"Madame is feeling unwell?" The Frenchwoman narrowed her sharp eyes and scrutinized her mistress's image. "It would be an abomination to shroud oneself in
the costumes of old age. Beauty is a gift from God."

"You are so religious, Pauline," Jane said with a sigh.
"I am no longer to be an attractive woman. You must
know that. When Phyllida comes out, I come out as my
daughter's mother. For her sake, I can't afford to appear
ridiculous."

"My point *exactement*," murmured the abigail with a
dark look. "And madame thinks nothing of my feelings,
of my reputation as the first ladies' maid in the city? If
it becomes known I dress madame to look a fright—"

"Give over, my dear, I don't really wish to look a
quiz," Jane said with a relieved laugh. Pauline was indeed the foremost dresser in Vienna, in taste as well as
experience. "But tell me—you have seen even more of
the world than I. Will a woman of my years be accepted
as a young lady's mother if I continue to dress as I have
always done?"

"Madame cannot hide her gifts from the world," was
Pauline's judgment, uttered in tones of great severity. "It
is to put a cabbage leaf over a rose. Pah! Madame will
not be so foolish. Mademoiselle, she must look to herself. She will be her mother's equal one day. Not yet, but
the time will come."

"I do worry about that." Jane studied her reflection frankly. "Will she have the happy experience I so want her to have? At Phyllida's age, I, too, was a thin and pale little creature. We are late bloomers in my family."

"Such as every wise man prefers."

"Do not say anything about fine wines, if you please," Jane replied, laughing. "I am already too aware of the march of time. Children are such a reminder of mortality, Pauline." She paused, still looking into the mirror, but no longer seeing herself. "I love my daughters so much."

"All the world knows that, madame."

"And I wish them to be happy. If only the right man for Phyllida will appear at one of these parties!"

"But if the early marriage is not the girl's desire?" Pauline spoke with the wisdom of one who spends much time with the domestic staff and knows the real situation of a household.

Jane shuddered, thinking of her own case. "Early marriage has nothing to say to it. Social poise is the lesson she must learn this autumn, Pauline, along with the knowledge that there are many men to choose from." Knowledge Jane had never had a chance to glean at Phyllida's age. "But of course she is bound to marry before long. Marriage is every young lady's wish, and Phyllida will be no different once she is pried from her pianoforte and stands up to dance with an attractive young hussar. Or perhaps a prince or a count. There are no limits on a young girl's dreams this year in Vienna, Pauline."

"As madame says," Pauline muttered.

Jane glanced sharply at her waiting woman. Pauline was French, of course, and that must excuse a wealth of pessimism.

"The bronze slippers, madame?" the maid asked smoothly.

Jane nodded, unwilling to belabor the point. Phyllida would find happiness this Season in Vienna. Jane somehow felt it in her bones.

At breakfast Jane observed that Flora seemed a little less depressed than usual. The girl was taking her second warm roll, and she had also cleaned up the oat porridge which she had confessed she really preferred to break her fast. Jane had dealt with the shocked refusals of her French cook, the result being that a porringer was at Lady Flora's place every morning.

"May I be excused, Mama?" Phyllida pushed back her chair. She had taken only half a roll and a cup of chocolate.

"Why so soon, dear? Breakfast isn't only a matter of eating. There are social obligations as well. Do stay and talk to Flora and me. And Chloe, of course." Jane included her younger daughter for politeness' sake, though Chloe's main object at any meal was food and not conversation. The child looked up from her fourth *kipferl*, nodded blissfully, and reached for a plate of fruit.

"But there's the new Beethoven piece," Phyllida protested in a pleading tone. "It arrived only yesterday. Please, Mama." Her eyes grew wide and filled with tears. Phyllida was nothing if not impassioned on the subject of music, and especially that of Herr van Beethoven.

"Don't make her stay on my account, ma'am," Flora put in. "We shall do very well together, the three of us."

Jane nodded, and Phyllida instantly hurried out of the room, pausing only to plant a feathery kiss on her mother's forehead.

Jane's sigh as she watched Phyllida speed forth was not only for her daughter's musical preoccupation but also for her slapped-together morning toilette. The muslin gown was not one of the new ones Jane had ordered, and the shawl draped carelessly around the old dress, a necessity for warmth in these huge rooms, had seen better days. In fact—Jane took a second look just as Phyllida and the shawl whipped out of sight—wasn't that the cover from the small pianoforte in the schoolroom? The girl was impossible.

"I did wish to talk to you, Lady Averham," Flora said with a sweet and completely uncharacteristic smile.

Jane was immediately on her guard, and she noticed Chloe looking suspiciously at their guest from behind a shrinking bunch of grapes. "What is it, my love?"

"I've been thinking over the terrible position my father has placed you in," Flora said earnestly. A glance at Chloe, and then a shrug, said eloquently that she considered the younger girl to be no impediment to her speaking on this sensitive issue. "He gave you no chance to refuse to take me in, and I must be a vast amount of trouble for you.''

"Why, you're no trouble at all. We love the company,'' Jane assured her.

"How can that be so, ma'am? I can see, now that I've been here a few days, what a busy woman you are. You have callers from morning till night.''

"You hardly trouble me there,'' Jane said. "You've yet to come down to join my friends. And I know you would enjoy them, Flora. This is such a grand chance for an English—no, of course I mean a Scottish girl. So isolated as we are on our island, we rarely have the opportunity to meet those of other cultures, other countries. Why, yesterday Metternich stopped to pay his respects. And we had my dearest friend, the Countess Zlotska, and that sweet man from the Danish delegation, and the dear old Prince de Ligne, and a host of others you would find fascinating.''

"You must not be insulted by this, dear Lady Averham, but aristocrats are aristocrats no matter what their country. Where can I meet the common people? Not in your drawing room.''

"Can you meet these common folk at your father's?'' Jane queried with a little smile.

"No, but I have it in mind to board out in the country until Father's tasks are over, or until I can convince him to hire a new companion for me and send me back to Scotland.'' For the first time in Jane's acquaintance with her, Flora spoke eagerly, and her eyes were alight with interest.

"And you think Lord Foxburgh would agree to that?'' Jane was sorry for it, but such naiveté was best crushed at once. "Don't you know, Flora, that your father is determined to see you enjoy yourself in the society you were born to? And so you ought. You would be an ornament to any gathering, and if you would but deign to listen, you might find that much of interest is being said. All people of our station are not the same, you know.''

Flora looked skeptical, as only a person in her teens can.

Jane had the sudden insight that if Flora did stay with her, she would not long have to worry about feeling or acting too youthful for her venerable position as the

mother of a marriageable girl. Lady Flora did have the
knack of making one feel a hundred years old.

The door opened, and a footman looked in, bowed,
and started to say something. Whatever he had meant to
convey was forestalled by a pretty, diminutive young lady
in a simple traveling costume who rushed past him and
knelt at Jane's side.

"Dearest, most gracious lady," said this person in
charmingly accented English, "how grateful I am to
you."

Jane stood up, taking the young woman's hand. Flora
and Chloe looked on, astonished, from their different
corners of the table.

"Can this really be little Petra?" Jane let go the girl's
hands and held out her arms. The young woman went
into them for a hearty embrace.

"My dears." Jane turned to address the others. "This
is Petra Schmidt, my goddaughter. She will be staying
with us for a few weeks—months, I hope. At any rate,
until Christmas. Everyone says the Congress will be over
by Christmas."

Petra's dark eyes sparkled, and she added, "Please
God, it will not be over before I catch a husband. That
is how you say it, not so, madame? Catch a husband?"

"Indeed, yes." Jane laughed.

Petra drew off her bonnet and cloak, and closer in-
spection revealed her to be a dark-haired little creature
with an elegant figure. Her merry face was lovely in an
elfin way.

"Lady Flora MacGowan, may I present Miss
Schmidt"—Lady Flora bowed coldly— "and this young
lady is my younger daughter, Miss Chloe Bellfort. Phyllida, my other daughter, is somewhere about." Jane
hoped that the belated formality would mollify Lady
Flora. The girl had looked shocked and displeased at
Petra's blithe admission to being in Vienna with matrimonial designs.

Petra, as the household soon found out, moved with
the speed of a small whirlwind. Before anyone knew quite
what had happened, she was sitting at the table opposite
Flora and pouring herself tea from a nearby pot. Though
the house was as clean as a regiment of scrubwomen

could make it, the impression in Petra's vicinity was somehow that of dust settling.

"Now, do tell me, madame," she said in a cajoling tone, "do you think I would have a chance at the Prince de Ligne?"

"My child, he is over eighty! And though he's still more than willing to admire beauty—indeed, one does hear some stories—he is no likely candidate for matrimony."

"Pity." Petra sighed and heavily sugared her tea in the Austrian manner. "Well, there will be someone else, or you will be wrong about him, madame. Many a man of that age has made a fool of himself."

"You would actually consider marrying an old man?" Flora said in horror, "For security, no doubt." In the faint lift of her nose was apparent the life of ease which made such a motive contemptible.

Petra seemed to understand this, Jane thought in relief, for the young woman's eyes lost none of their sparkle, her smile none of its good humor as she returned, "Your ladyship must forgive me. I have my way to make in the world, and I must be practical." She laughed. "With Lady Averham's kind invitation, here I am in Vienna, in the most glorious Season, about to be surrounded by all the most eligible gentlemen in Europe." She held out her arms, as though to embrace the city and every one of the men she dreamed of. "Would you have me waste my time?"

"You've barely taken off your bonnet, dear. You can wait until after breakfast," Jane said.

She noticed that Chloe, seated beside Petra, was looking at the girl in undisguised admiration. Well, so much the better. The lively Chloe could get little resembling companionship from her vague older sister or their icy Scottish guest. Perhaps Petra would be more forthcoming.

Jane turned the subject to Petra's wardrobe and announced her intention of making her goddaughter the gift of a few dresses. Petra objected with just that degree of vehemence which suggests that the next offer, or at the outside the one after that, will be accepted.

Jane, pleased at the girl's practicality, retaliated by wondering if they could possibly afford to wait for the

latest noted couturier who was shortly to arrive from
Paris. Petra visibly wavered in her next objections.

Flora, whose wardrobe was more extensive than she
felt it needed to be, what with her previous Season's ball
dresses and the new things her father had pressed upon
her on her arrival in Vienna, was bearing this conversation with considerable contempt when suddenly her face
lit up with an honest, affectionate smile as the door
opened yet again.

Jane turned, curious to see who or what could bring
that expression to Lady Flora's discontented face.

She found herself looking into the bluest eyes she had
ever imagined. Charming features, yes, but the eyes were
only the beginning. The tall fair-haired gentleman who
was bowing and making his apologies for disturbing the
ladies at their meal was extremely well built, with a
handsome strong-jawed face. His shoulders were magnificent, his smile warm and intimate. He was dressed in
the most elegant of morning clothes.

Jane rose and extended her hand. The man took it and
favored her with a look so melting, so eloquent with admiration that she nearly shivered. Her hand, she noticed
with a strange detachment, was being raised to his lips.
He kissed it, and she really did shiver then.

"Lady Averham," he said in a thrilling, slightly Scottish voice, "you make me ashamed. How could I ever
doubt my father's word?"

She blinked at this odd remark. "Your father?"

"I was insolent enough, naive enough not to believe
him when he said you were the loveliest creature in Vienna." He kissed her hand once more. "I doubted such
perfection could exist."

"Really, brother, I'm sure Lady Averham is too clever
to be taken in by your nonsense," Lady Flora said at this
point in an acid voice.

Jane came quickly down to earth. She had been allowing herself to be charmed, and in front of the two girls
under her care as well as her own daughter! She must
learn conduct before she attempted to teach it. The visitor's identity was before her in a flash, thanks to Flora's
words. Yes, Jane remembered hearing that the Earl of
Foxburgh's younger son was on Castlereagh's staff . . .
younger. His handsome features somewhat roughened by

weather, his eyes lit by a knowing gleam, he hardly gave the impression of callow youth. Young he must be nevertheless, younger than she.

"Mr. MacGowan?" She tried to invest her smile with all the maturity, all the detachment her first reaction to him had lacked, and endeavored while she did so to drag her mind as well as her eyes from his physique, especially his thighs, which she could well imagine . . . and what did she mean by a lewd thought like that? Jane gave herself a desperate mental shake, blushing as deeply as she ever had in her teens.

"Archibald MacGowan, at your service, ma'am," he returned with a bow. Jane thought he was looking at her cheeks in speculation, or amusement, or something. "Pardon me again for bursting in upon you without letting a servant announce me, but I wished to surprise Flora. And my sister is right. I must ask you to forgive my sallies. For only a moment I thought, you see," and at this he leaned closer, "that we were alone."

Jane laughed, glancing about at the three pairs of interested eyes on them—four pairs, if one included the footman who had followed MacGowan into the room—and said, "You will find, Mr. MacGowan, that in this house one is rarely granted that much privacy. I have three . . . four young ladies to shepherd this Season, you know."

Chloe looked gratified to be included in the number, and Petra, Jane noticed, was gauging Archibald Mac-Gowan with all the practicality of one who meant to waste not a moment longer than necessary on each candidate.

Introductions to the young ladies followed. Jane felt an irrational rush of relief when Petra, evidently concluding that an untitled younger son was unworthy of her consideration, wiped the calculation from her pretty face.

Jane voiced her regret that Phyllida was not in the room, and Mr. MacGowan said all the proper things about wishing to meet Miss Bellfort soon. He was as gravely polite to Chloe as he was to Miss Schmidt, which attention caused him to rise even more in Jane's estimation. Having accepted Jane's invitation to a seat at the table, he consented to take a cup of coffee with the ladies before the breakfast party dispersed. He fitted right in with the family, much as Petra had done. Before long he was being brotherly to Chloe and Petra as well as to Flora. In his attentions to his hostess could be remarked a definite difference, an attraction which Jane hoped was merely idle gallantry.

Well, she would soon show him by her serene behavior that she was a mother first this Season. Jane took deep breaths, forcing herself back to reality. She had never before felt so vulnerable, so desirable in a man's presence. She had never expected to. And certainly not this autumn, when her mind should be on Phyllida and the other young ladies. Yes, she must think of Phyllida. . . . As for MacGowan, he probably had this effect on every woman. Some men were simply too attractive for anyone's good.

Having thought herself into a sort of calm, Jane observed MacGowan through narrowed eyes. He might spell danger to her, but his attractions could serve a useful purpose. Yes, he would do. He was only a younger son, to be sure, but so handsome and lively, and with such a ready wit!

Something in his manner, too, promised great physical satisfaction for his woman. That something had nearly made Jane forget herself and her mission, but his allure was really most fortunate. Jane had seen too much, lived through too much to think lightly of the physical aspect of a young lady's marriage.

She was certain that Phyllida would be charmed by Mr. MacGowan; and that she, as a diligent mama, could do no better than to encourage a match in this direction.

3

ARCHIBALD MACGOWAN was eminently suited to his position on Lord Castlereagh's staff. When he wished to, he could appear as carefree as any other young man in the delegation. Yet, in common with the other equerries and aides, he was well able to concentrate: to work long into the night deciphering messages, planning strategies, and burning evidence.

The Viennese secret police, headed by the emperor's efficient Baron Hager, tended to see Archibald Mac-Gowan, who lived with his father and spent hardly any time on business, as a most frivolous fellow.

He would have been pleased to hear this. In pursuit of the idle appearance which would make him most useful to his superiors, he had come to Vienna prepared to spend his time and money on opera girls and to carouse more than he cared to—all from a patriotic motive, to be sure.

He had even expected to enact an elaborate charade, to pretend to be engrossed in some female and to use the cover of an infatuation to ferret out information no one would suspect him of having the energy to get or the concentration to remember. He and Castlereagh had discussed this, undecided as to whether MacGowan should choose one of the Russians or some Austrian lady as the target of his attentions. He had quite looked forward to keeping his head when all around him would think he was losing it.

Now, of course, those plans meant nothing. There would be no pretending now.

MacGowan was rather surprised to find himself wandering under the chestnut trees of the Prater at midday, directly following his first visit to Lady Averham's. He hardly saw the festive park, lushly green still and crowded with the perpetual holidaymakers who were thronging to Vienna.

He did reach out a hand in surprise to a lilac blooming at the side of the walk. A symbol of spring. The foolish flower didn't know it was autumn, then. It was as confused as he was, confounded by a glimpse of the sun's full glory when it was least expected.

"Jane," he whispered, seeing not the bloom, but the lovely face, the tempting figure, the speaking hazel eyes which had so entranced him. And she had been attracted to him. He had known that with all the confidence of a handsome man who had never yet questioned his power over women. Why, then, had she suddenly changed, grown cold before he had ended his visit?

"Cold" wasn't precisely the word to describe the alteration. She had been friendly as ever. She had never fallen down in her courtesies to him. But that intensity he had felt at their meeting, the woman reaching out to the man—that had been missing. No, not missing precisely, but buried so far beneath the surface as to be nearly invisible.

Could he have offended her in some way? MacGowan sighed, pulling the flower from its stem and thrusting it on impulse into his lapel.

Perhaps his first impression of Lady Averham had been at fault. She would prove to be stupid on better acquaintance, or her beauty, at second sight, would not hit him with the force with which it had this morning.

He had to find out. Smiling, he reflected that he would be visiting his little sister more often than he had intended. And Flora, blast the girl, had taken in at a glance his attraction to her hostess. She wouldn't be fooled into thinking that he had blossomed, after a lifetime of near-indifference, into a paragon of brotherly affection . . . yet Flora was self-centered. Perhaps she would not notice . . .

"I say, my good fellow. Why are you looking like a mooncalf?"

MacGowan started at the words and pulled himself with difficulty back from a fantasy involving himself, Lady Averham, and some hotly tangled bedsheets. A fashionable widow was perfectly fair game for a liaison. But how the devil did one make love to a woman who had four young ladies in her charge? The Averham house was large, but the problems of such an association—his young sister in another room, no less!—caused every finer feeling to revolt. Yet he knew there must be a way. There were chalets in the mountains, discreet inns . . . even locks on bedroom doors.

"I say, MacGowan! Are you jug-bitten at this time of day?"

Archie's eyes finally focused on the speaker, one of the most genial and lighthearted equerries of the English team. The young man's apple cheeks and curly head gave him an unsettling likeness to Cupid; his cheerful and vacuous expression deftly hid a keen and incisive mind. In his early twenties, he was still enthusiastic enough about all around him to be more than penetrating on certain subjects.

"No, Thompson." MacGowan smiled at his young friend's insight. "Not jug-bitten, but drunk on something." He breathed in deeply of the heady scent of lilac.

"A lady, I'd wager." Thompson offered a sage nod. "Here, forget all that until the evening and say how d'ye do to Averham. He arrived only today."

"But . . ." MacGowan looked in confusion, then dismay at a handsome, dark young man who, he only now noticed, was standing beside Thompson. A man of about his own age; an intelligent-looking and aristocratic specimen. "I understood she was a widow."

The dark fellow smiled broadly. "Aha! You must have met Lady Averham. Don't be cast down, for she's my sister-in-law, not my wife."

"Oh." MacGowan felt a surge of relief which was surely not warranted. He had barely met the woman.

Lord Averham was looking at him keenly. "You have indeed met Jane, then, and been taken with her. I'm not surprised. She can have that effect on one. Could have the same on me, I don't mind telling you, but we were practically brought up together. She'll always be a sister to me."

MacGowan gave a tight nod. He had not even begun to consider how he could keep his proposed affair with Lady Averham a secret, and already speculation was rampant! He would have to be careful; so careful. A dalliance with an opera singer was one thing. A love affair with the most beautiful woman in the city would be quite another. He had no wish to sully her reputation. And what exactly was her reputation? He would have to find out in some discreet way. More discreet than he was being now. . . .

"Lord Averham, may I present Archibald MacGowan, one of our best men." Thompson, apparently seeing his Scottish friend about to drift away again, made haste with the introductions. "Averham is to pay a purely social visit to his family, you know, MacGowan." This was spoken only after the three men had moved out from the trees into an open stretch of parkland. "There's no telling what he might turn up that could be useful to the negotiations."

"One hears that my sister-in-law has an *entrée* into the very cream of Viennese society," Averham added with a wise nod.

"And you're to live with her? To live in her house?" MacGowan asked a bit too quickly. Already his mind was pursuing the delicate issue of how he was to commence his dalliance with her ladyship under her brother-in-law's nose.

"Wouldn't be proper, I'm afraid." Averham shrugged. "Jane is chaperoning a pair of young ladies this autumn, along with my nieces. And even if she weren't, I'm afraid tongues would wag, I being a bachelor, she such a lovely woman. People are always ready to see things the wrong way."

"Yes." Especially in Vienna, MacGowan added silently. So much of the gossip here seemed to be true. And with every action being reported to Baron Hager, no one could afford to cause an eyebrow to rise except on purpose.

Archie didn't mention that one of the young women Jane was chaperoning was his own sister; that would have entailed too many digressions from his true interest. "So," he went on, his eagerness to know anything and everything concerning Lady Averham overriding his private vow of discretion of a moment ago, "you were brought up with Lady Averham, were you, my lord?"

Averham laughed. "Not quite; merely a figure of speech. She was barely sixteen when she married my brother, and I was thirteen. Two young creatures knocking about in a baronial hall. I fear she had more in common with me than with my brother, who was much older than she. We even shared a tutor for a time.''

''Shared a tutor?'' put in Thompson. ''Singular.''

''We did, though. Until my brother found out and put a stop to Jane's visits to the library during my lessons. Felt it wasn't seemly, I suppose, for a baroness and mother-to-be to be taking instruction in dry subjects in company with a schoolboy.''

MacGowan had a sudden vision of the young Lady Averham, barely old enough to be a wife, being torn from the only pastime which made her new life bearable. A melodramatic version of events, no doubt. Still, his heart went out to that young girl.

''How did she happen to marry your brother? It sounds as though they weren't well-matched, if I may be so bold.'' Archie's gruff tone was reminiscent of his father at his most Scottish. Realizing this, he grinned. ''Forgive me. I have no wish to pry into your family's affairs.''

''Why not?'' Averham was evidently an easygoing sort. He grinned back. ''It's no secret. One of those typical marriages, I suppose, the kind the poets deplore. I've suspected more than once that Jane deplored it a bit herself, but she's always been the perfect lady about the matter. The truth is that she was sold to my brother. Came from a rich family—the Farrowstones of Herefordshire, old untitled stock—and the parents bought a title for their only daughter along with the Averham influence for their sons, who benefited greatly. And my late brother, you must know, had no objection to the settlements they made.''

''Your brother had an eye for beauty too.''

''Not a bit of it,'' Averham said.

Archie repressed a sudden desire to call the man out, and Thompson visibly started.

The surprised, indeed indignant looks on the faces of both his auditors were probably what prompted Averham to explain himself. ''Jane was not the sort of woman who bloomed in her early years. It took her some time to become the stunner she is now.''

Mollified, MacGowan said, ''So your brother married for money. I am sure he repented his action and rejoiced in his luck when he found what a treasure he'd acquired in her ladyship.''

Averham shook his head at this, but he caught himself, perhaps sensing that he had already been less than discreet in front of strangers. The family confidences came to an end, and the trio began a conversation about the diversions to be found in Vienna. A grand ball at the Hofburg was only a few days away.

"It's exciting, that's what it is,'' Thompson exclaimed with his habitual youthful enthusiasm. "We talk of parties, but every king in Europe will be coming to them. Thrilling days and nights are ahead for us, even if it only seems at the time to be another dance with a lady.''

Another dance with a lady. MacGowan's heart lifted at the prospect of taking Lady Averham into his arms for a waltz. A waltz would be a fine beginning.

"You're floating off again, MacGowan,'' Thompson said in that irritating cheery tone. "What the devil is up with you? I say we drop into that little *Weinstub'* over there. You might as well be foxed if you're to act it.''

"I would be happy to stand you a drink, MacGowan,'' Averham added with a friendly nod. "Damn, but it's good to hear English voices again after that trip across the Continent.''

In another mood, MacGowan might have quipped that he was not English, but Scottish. Thompson looked surprised, no doubt that his friend would let such an opportunity go by.

No matter, MacGowan thought with a sigh. He couldn't seem to concentrate on male companionship, on the exciting events about to unfold before him in Vienna, on anything but a beautiful pair of hazel eyes, a warm, entrancing smile, and a figure . . .

"I could use a drink.'' He smiled in acknowledgment of Averham's offer.

"You look as though you could at that,'' the baron responded. "Perplexing species, the ladies. I never go near them if I want to think clearly.''

"Excellent advice, I'm sure, my lord,'' MacGowan said. The two men followed young Thompson to a table under some bright trees and spent the next hour or so in furthering what promised to be a pleasant acquaintance.

* * *

A couple of mornings later, Phyllida Bellfort closed her eyes in reverence as her hands lifted from the keys. She was trembling with the emotion Herr van Beethoven's new composition had stirred within her.

"If only I could meet him," she murmured, dashing a tear from her eye.

"Who?" Her sister, Chloe, was playing spillikins near the instrument and seemed quite oblivious of the fact that something momentous had just occurred.

"The composer," Phyllida snapped.

"Oh. Him." Chloe wrinkled her nose. "Everyone says he's deaf and walks about scowling, gloomy as anything. You wouldn't really wish to meet him."

"You don't understand genius, do you?" Phyllida said with a lofty air. "Do you not know how grand it would be, how splendid, to worship at the feet of a genius?"

A moment passed in silence. "I would rather be one's mistress," Chloe then said in decision. "Though if Herr van Beethoven is really as deaf and stodgy and old as one hears, I believe I ought to hold out for someone more interesting."

Phyllida sighed, shook her head, and met the amused eyes of Petra Schmidt.

"You had better not be a mistress, Chloe. Marry the genius instead," was this young lady's sage advice. Seated upon a sofa, she was engaged in attaching lace to a gown. Petra was always busy with some practical matters, the Bellfort girls had noticed first in vexation, then in reluctant admiration.

"I don't know. I can't decide. Mama's friend the Duchess of Sagan married twice, but I heard her say that husbands are too expensive and that from now on she'll only take lovers."

"Chloe!" Phyllida let out with a gasp. "How did you hear any such thing?"

The younger girl shrugged. "I happened to be in the window seat in the small reception room when the duchess chanced to visit Mama, and the curtains happened to be closed, and I couldn't very well interrupt them when they were talking, could I? It would have been quite unseemly."

"Quite." Phyllida passed a hand over her brow.

"In any case," Chloe went on, "what do you really

think, Petra? Would it be best for me to hold out for the position of wife? From what the duchess said, I believe it might be better simply to take the lovers in the first place and avoid the divorces.''

Petra appeared to consider this carefully, while Phyllida, still trying to instill some decorum in her younger sister, said, "Kindly remember you are English, my dear, and that the laws of our land grant divorces to the man—not the woman—and then only by a private act of Parliament. How can you talk so? If Mama could hear you . . .''

"She might agree," Chloe said with a shrug of plump shoulders. "Mama is a woman of the world.''

"And she might send you to your room for ten years for announcing your intention to be a doxy. Why, what if Flora had been with us just now? You know how stodgy she is. She would have fainted, or at the very least set you down abominably for even voicing such shocking thoughts.''

"But Chloe was right to ask our advice," Petra spoke up. "She is young. How else is she to learn? I think, my dear," and here Petra addressed Chloe, "that you must have a great deal of money secured to you before you try any such thing as taking lovers without the protection of marriage.''

"I have a great deal of money, I'm told, but I'm afraid it's a dowry," Chloe said with a sigh.

"Do you wish to come with me to my room?" Petra spoke to Chloe, but her sharp eyes were on Phyllida's strained face. "Your sister might play on in peace, and we could do your hair *à l'impératrice.*''

"Might I try on your new ball gown?" Chloe demanded.

"Well . . . yes.''

Phyllida looked gratefully at Petra, who obligingly winked at her as she shepherded an excited Chloe from the room.

How had they ever got along without that girl? Phyllida thought in admiration. Petra always knew what to do.

Then the elder Miss Bellfort spun back to the keyboard and began on yet another rendition of the new sonata by her hero Beethoven.

* * *

Petra and Chloe walked down the corridor with the linked arms of easy friendship. "I think I have identified the spy," Petra whispered into the younger girl's ear.

"You have?" Chloe's eyes gleamed with excitement, and she took furtive looks about her. They seemed to be alone, but she had always thought this huge house the very sort to be riddled with secret passageways. Someone could be listening to them from behind that stuffy portrait of a bewigged Hapsburg . . .

"It's the new footman," Petra said.

"Johann?" Chloe spoke too loudly. She gave another frightened glance around, but when no servant popped into view, she relaxed. She and Petra looked at each other and giggled.

Both girls were aware, though they had not precisely been told, that Austrian agents were being introduced into all the great houses in Vienna. The Emperor Franz was said to be most exacting about his network of secret police, and most interested in all details of the many foreign guests in his capital. It went without saying that he would leave no stone unturned in his zeal to uncover information. Even Lady Averham's house was bound to be watched, though she, as the mere widow of an English diplomat, had no official reason to be trading in secrets.

"I say," Petra murmured, "that we give him something to talk about to his masters."

"Do you mean feed him lies?" Chloe asked in delight. "What sort?"

"Oh, any sort. Whatever most amuses us at the time." Petra's eyes were glinting with mischief.

"Oh, Petra." Chloe gave her new friend's arm a squeeze. "You are the greatest sport. Much better than Phyllida. She would never approve."

"She hasn't much sense of humor, poor girl," Petra said. "It comes of concentrating on music, I think. Come, now," and she opened the door to her room, "you will look delightful in my ball gown, my dear. We are nearly of a size, you know, and our coloring is remarkably similar."

Chloe, elated to hear her plump and still-undeveloped self described as of a size with the elegant Petra, passed into the room with a quick step and soon lost herself, not only in the glories of grown-up finery but also in lighthearted plans to tell Johann what he might well wish to hear. Could Mama's maid Pauline be thought to be a spy for the French? And what about Petra herself? She might have come to Vienna to spy out secrets for her government.

"Exactly where do you come from, Petra?" Chloe asked as she tried to refine this idea.

"Switzerland," Petra said. "I'm half-English by blood, though."

"Switzerland!" Chloe ignored the part about Petra's half-English heritage—how boring, for oneself was English. And Switzerland had to be the dullest place in Europe. "Well, perhaps it would be best if we stuck with Pauline. Or . . . we should not cause trouble for anyone in the house. Pauline can be a bear, but I'd hate to have her really overset. And I'm afraid she would be quite overset if the secret police arrested her."

"I should think so," Petra said with a giggle. "You are right, of course. We must do nothing to upset things greatly. Why does no one in this house see how proper you are? It is most clear to me. Let's simply leave strange notes in cipher torn up in the wastebasket."

"That would be best, I'm sure." Chloe sighed in contentment. "Can't you see that stick Johann rooting through the wastebaskets and pasting letters back together?"

The young ladies mulled over the idea of the letters while Petra undid Chloe's dark hair from its simple braids and piled it on top of her head, frowning in concentration as she deftly pinned and coiled.

"What will the letters say?" Chloe bounced in her excitement, dislodging a curl.

"For that let us wait," Petra decided with a wise nod. "We are bound to think of something terribly funny."

Jane, all unaware that her younger daughter and her goddaughter were plotting such domestic horrors, was sitting peacefully in her study. She brushed her cheek with her quill, put the pen back into the inkstand, wiped it clean, but came no closer to writing out the bills she had sat down to pay. From the adjoining room came Phyllida's piano-playing, a stirring sonata which Jane recognized as the new one by Beethoven, Phyllida's latest passion. As the second movement started, a dreamlike, intimate piece, Jane tried her best to think what a fine husband Archibald MacGowan would make for her elder daughter.

Discreet inquiry had revealed that MacGowan was liberally provided for. An inheritance from his grandmother made him independent; though, as Foxburgh's favorite son, he would surely never be deserted by his family. And he had a brilliant career ahead of him, a future Jane contemplated with a little stab of envy. She adored being a woman, but she sometimes chafed at the restrictions placed on her. The world of politics was so exciting, and all a female could do was meddle, giving dinners and dropping comments here and there.

But such thoughts were not at all productive. Jane returned her mind to MacGowan's qualifications as a husband. One could tell merely by looking at him that he was a fiery young man, one who would know instinctively how to pleasure a woman. Oh, yes, one could tell . . .

A wave of some sort passed over Jane, and she shuddered, fighting to concentrate on another fact about MacGowan. He was twenty-nine.

A man younger than she, a man not yet thirty. Any thoughts aside from the most maternal would be improper. As for feelings, the kind of overwhelming passions Jane's sophisticated friends made so much of, they were clearly absurd when applied to a man younger than oneself. A man, moreover, who would be ideally suited to one's daughter.

Phyllida must have passion buried deep inside her, or she could not play so very well, Jane thought resolutely, rising from her writing table in sudden determination. She passed into the other room and surveyed her firstborn with fond eyes.

Phyllida's lower lip was caught between her teeth, as it usually was when she was excited about what she was playing.

The movement ended. Jane had learned, over the years, not to interrupt her daughter in mid-note. The girl's eyes would cloud over immediately, and she would wear an injured expression for the rest of the day. But Phyllida had been trained, in the interests of family harmony, not to cavil at an interruption between movements of a sonata.

"Phyllida," Jane said at the precise moment that the last note died away.

"Yes, Mama?" Her daughter looked up, her face radiant with the joy of her music.

"You really must come up with me to your bedroom and look over your gowns. The Hofburg ball is tomorrow night, for heaven's sake. Even Flora has chosen her gown, and for all I know, you're planning to wear the comforter from your bed." Jane looked disparagingly at Phyllida's drab morning gown, a muslin which had seen better days and which any other young lady would have long since given to her maid to cut up for handkerchiefs.

"Oh. But, Mama, I'm right in the middle—"

"I heard you finish the sonata once, dear, and it is delightful. But other things than music must come first while you're making your bows in society."

Phyllida gave a loud and injured sigh.

"I mean it, dear. Come with me now to your room. Once we complete this tiny little project and confer with Pauline about your hair, you may play for the rest of the day and night for all of me."

"Truly?" Phyllida's eyes lit up, and she followed her mother with a quick step.

Choosing Phyllida's attire for the ball was really no great task. Jane had had several ball gowns made up for her daughter, in colors which would suit her delicate complexion, in the latest and most flattering styles. She was not surprised, somehow, to find the gowns still in boxes next to the wardrobe in Phyllida's room. Phyllida's abigail, taking full advantage of the fact that her young mistress cared nothing for clothes, was a slipshod creature, but Jane considered this inconvenience well worth the fact that the maid, Liesl, was the only one in the city who could find the myriad garments and hairpins Phyllida was always dropping about the house and forgetting.

Jane looked through the dresses briskly, holding each of them up in front of her daughter's slim and drooping figure, throwing the rejected items on the bed for Liesl to deal with. A pull at the bell brought the young maid running, extravagant apologies falling from her lips, and she scurried about in the background as Jane picked up an apple-green gauze. "Yes," she said with narrowed eyes, "this is the one."

Phyllida giggled. "You mean to advertise to the world that I'm a green girl, Mama?"

With an answering chuckle, Jane said, "I never thought of it that way, but what more proper for your debut? So many of the young ladies will be wearing white, you know. It's only right that my daughter should stand out."

"But, Mama, you will stand out so yourself, you won't need me. I fade to a shadow beside you."

Jane stood quite still, gazing earnestly at her daughter. "My dear, are you afraid of being judged by me? My looks are more flamboyant than yours, to be sure, but I no longer have the charm of youth."

"And I'll look exactly like you when I get to your age. Yes, you've explained all that, Mama, but I simply . . . I'm not ready." Phyllida hung her head.

"You are seventeen," Jane said. "At your age I was married and had you. Now—" she lifted a hand and went on quickly at Phyllida's stricken look—"I don't wish an early marriage for you, dear child. You must come out for one reason only: to begin to look about you, to know more of the world. You must not marry the first man you see. Though," and here Jane smiled mysteriously, "the first man you see might well be the best candidate. One simply never knows. And that is the charm of society."

"Yes, Mama," Phyllida said with an eloquent shrug.

Jane was too wise to allude directly to Archibald MacGowan. He and Phyllida had met on the occasion of his second visit to his sister. They had shaken hands and murmured greetings under Jane's watchful eye; but that was all. She had hoped that meeting the perfect man would jolt Phyllida out of her distraction; but Phyllida had gone back to her music after only moments in the young man's company, and MacGowan had devoted himself to Jane for the rest of the call.

That was folly, of course, but he was doubtless merely trifling, as all men did. Jane frowned, remembering how his eyes had lingered on her as they spoke, in a remarkably easy manner, of this and that—nothing she could remember, nothing that had seemed important at the time. Still, she felt that she had ended that visit knowing more of him than she did of any other person. Wishing she might know much more.

"Oh, heavens," Jane murmured, passing a hand over her forehead. She and MacGowan could have nothing between them. He would be so perfect for Phyllida. If not as a husband, than certainly as a dancing partner and a charming example of the men to be met with in the world. *Think like a mama,* she sternly admonished herself.

"Mama?" Phyllida looked up, and Jane was struck by the concern in her daughter's eyes.

Jane reached out her arms and embraced the girl. "Dearest, you must pardon me if I seem a little too zealous to see you settled. It's not at all necessary for you to make an early marriage; please remember that you will be made to do nothing against your will. I've simply caught the fever from Petra. She is so right when she says that there are more eligibles in Vienna now than ever have been collected in one place."

Phyllida looked at her mother in astonishment, as though she had just been told that more snowflakes, or cricket bats, or houseflies were collected in Vienna than ever had been before. "Men, you mean? What could that have to say to anything?"

"Well, who can tell?" Jane gave Phyllida's cheek a pinch. "Give it time."

4

THE HOFBURG, the ancient fortress in the heart of Vienna, home of the Austrian royal family and seat of the Holy Roman Empire, was blazing with lights and colors as it had done on nearly every night this autumn. Through the majestic reception rooms, some newly decorated by the artist Isabey, strolled kings, princes, dukes, duchesses, gentlemen and ladies not owning titles, and even people of more common descent.

"What do you think, my dear?" Jane asked Flora, pausing to take in the lively scene.

"Foreigners," Flora grumbled, looking down.

Jane hid a smile. She suspected that the haughty Lady Flora MacGowan was secretly impressed by the varied society to be met with in only a glance around. Perhaps, thought Jane, this Congress where wastrels rubbed elbows with kings was the dawning of a new age of freedom from social boundaries. A strange fancy to have about a gathering which was meant to reestablish the divine right of kings; to take the map back to what it had been before the French wind had swept through Europe.

Smiling at this flight of fancy, she stopped mulling over the meaning of the Congress and returned to her personal concerns. For tonight and all the nights to come, her priority must be the girls under her care.

Phyllida, Jane could tell, was apprehensive on this evening of her first ball. As she, Petra, Flora, and Jane entered the vast *Redoutensaal,* the young girl had surveyed the crowds of gaily dressed people with an expression of vague displeasure. She would much prefer to have been left at home with her pianoforte and the quiet house to herself, but Jane had not seen her way clear to fulfilling her daughter's wish. It was time for Phyllida to come out, and come out she would.

Jane moved among the throng easily, confident that she was looking her best. For this she had to thank her maid, Pauline, who had won their skirmish before the ball. In truth the abigail had not had to fight very hard. Jane had no real wish to hide behind the identity of a chaperon. Not tonight.

Rather than being done up in dowager style, she was clad in her most becoming new costume. A clinging robe of bronze satin with a delicate lace underskirt set off her vivid coloring and brought out the fiery lights in her auburn hair. She couldn't wait to see Mr. MacGowan—for Phyllida's sake, of course. Surely he would be here. Would his blue eyes light up with that peculiar, unmistakable admiration when he saw her—no, of course she meant when he saw Phyllida. She couldn't wait to see him. And she knew, in the bottom of her heart, that her eagerness was not solely for her daughter's sake. Jane took a couple of steadying breaths. She would not make a fool of herself over that man.

The pretense of calm was almost as good as the thing itself. Jane nodded and smiled, saying a word here and there as she recognized some one of her numerous acquaintance. She kept the girls near her. They would be scared to death if they were lost in this crush; at least Flora and Phyllida looked as though they would be.

Jane hoped that Petra, who had turned aside to greet a Swiss lady she had glimpsed across the room, would find them again without incident. Petra was so capable that Jane often found herself forgetting that her goddaughter was younger than Flora and needed as much care.

They hadn't a prayer of finding chairs among these multitudes; Jane headed for the next best thing, a vacant space out of the main walkway.

"Madame la baronne." A familiar voice reached her ears, and she smiled sunnily as an aged man dressed in formal finery approached.

"You are delectable as always," this gentleman exclaimed. "And flanked by these beauties, you will be the Venus of this assembly. Venus and the Graces. But should there not be three of them?"

"Why, yes, Prince," Jane replied, showing her dimples, "but the third Grace has fallen behind for the moment. Ah, here she comes now."

The old Prince de Ligne followed Jane's look and gazed on the small dark beauty charmingly attired in diaphanous white. "Another goddess!" he exclaimed, kissing his fingers. "Madame, they do you credit, all of them. But that one in white—you have my compliments, dear lady. Your generosity is truly angelic."

Jane gave him a long look. "And your discretion, Prince, is truly generous." She glanced at the two girls beside her. Flora, of course, betrayed no interest in the prince's remarks about Petra, but Phyllida looked startled.

The prince gallantly changed the subject, addressing Phyllida. "Mademoiselle Bellfort, I trust you are looking forward to your first dance. Ah, if it were only possible for me to oblige you!"

"Looking forward!" Phyllida exclaimed, eyes widening in horror. "To a dance?"

The old man shook his head. "Dear young lady, if that is your feeling, I fear you will have to accustom yourself to much displeasure."

"I hope we all will," put in Petra, who had arrived in time to hear the last exchange. She cast Phyllida a merry glance. "Dancing will be great fun. You'll see."

Phyllida shuddered.

The group of four lovely ladies was nothing if not conspicuous, even in a crowd of diamonds, and, Jane being so well-known in Vienna, many men could claim an introduction to her charges. A dashing young hussar appeared before long and solicited Phyllida's hand for the next dance. Jane knew him, or his family, and sent her daughter off with a satisfied smile, which Phyllida answered with a frightened stare.

As soon as Phyllida's green skirts had fluttered away, the Prince de Ligne drew forward a darkly handsome muscular young man who had been hovering near the group for some time. This newcomer had a small mustache and slightly slanted eyes which proclaimed Magyar blood.

"May I present Monsieur Bronsky," the prince said with a smile. "When we first glimpsed your party, *ma chère,* he begged me to introduce him to the most beautiful ladies he has ever seen, and though he is a bit of a rogue, I couldn't refuse his plea."

"His highness was indeed most kind, madame, to grant me such a pleasure," the young man said in a charming voice whose accent was hard to place, as were many accents now that Vienna was so crowded with every nationality. He made a great show of bowing over Jane's hand. Then he seized Flora's and raised it to his lips in a lingering, practiced way.

Flora favored him with an appraising look before he was forced by politeness to turn his attention to Petra, who gave him short shrift and devoted herself to the prince, an attitude at which Jane had to smile. She was not used to seeing young females ignore handsome young men in order to flirt with octogenarians.

Petra did seem to have been born with the rare talent of making a gentleman in his eighties feel young again. She lavished attention on the Prince de Ligne, whom she had met recently at her godmother's house, and he received her overtures in good-humored courtly style.

Jane watched this with a wary eye, wondering if Petra could really be as practical as she seemed. Surely she was not thinking to encourage the prince into matrimonial designs! Many young girls were fond of older men, of course; that was nothing new. But an age difference of sixty or more years was surely most unusual. Ah, well, the Prince de Ligne was an aristocrat of the old school, a worldly man who had seen more than Petra could yet imagine. He could take care of himself.

Jane found herself distracted from her goddaughter's behavior when Bronsky addressed her.

"May I have your leave to dance with Lady Flora, madame?" he asked, his dark eyes almost pleading.

Jane shot her charge a look of query and was surprised at Flora's tight nod of acquiescence. Lady Flora MacGowan consenting to dance with a foreigner! Most surprising. "You may, sir," Jane said, dazed.

How odd to see Flora allowing a young man's admiration, but so it was: after her first cool stare, she even favored the exotic Bronsky with her smile. As the couple walked away to the dancing, Jane did not know what to think. Flora had never taken advantage of the opportunities which had offered at Jane's house, and many suitable young men had been calling in the past few days to pay their respects to the pretty Scot. What could she see in this Bronsky?

"Who is that lovely blond girl?" a voice asked near Jane's ear. "Is she one of your charges, Jane?"

"Robbie! What . . . how can you be here? Oh, how delightful!" Completely taken by surprise, Jane threw herself into the arms of her brother-in-law. Darkly splendid in evening dress, his gray eyes twinkling with fun, Averham was a most welcome sight—and absolutely unexpected.

"Yes, I've come to Vienna." Averham drew Jane away from the prince and Petra in order to pace a little way along the ornate room. "I'm on a social visit merely; I have so many friends who have duties here."

"That sounds about as likely as what most of the gentlemen are saying these days," Jane remarked in a dry tone. "Well, whatever your mission for the government—don't poker up at me, everyone is on a mission for some government these days—my daughters will be thrilled to see their uncle. And you will stay with us, of course. Why didn't you present yourself the moment you arrived in Vienna? I'll have to be very cross with you, my lord Averham. As head of the family, you were remiss in your duties."

"Forgive me, Jane. But you must realize I can't stay with you. You have a houseful of young ladies, or so they say. I could hear the tongues wagging even before I entered the city walls, and so I decided not to satisfy the gossipmongers. And I thought it best to settle into my lodgings before coming to see you. Well? You haven't answered my question."

"Question?"

"I asked about the fair-haired young lady. Who is she?"

"Lady Flora MacGowan," Jane said with an assessing look across the dance floor. Flora was at her best in a pale rose costume she had brought with her from London. But was the cold and disdainful young woman really smiling again at that doubtful young man Bronsky? The situation would bear watching. "She is staying with me. Her father is Lord Foxburgh."

"Yes. I've met her brother here, I believe, and Lord Foxburgh I've seen in London. There is a certain family resemblance among Foxburgh's clan. Well, if she's staying with you, you can surely present me to her as a most suitable partner. You will know how to puff up my qualifications.''

"You, Robbie, smitten at first sight? I find that hard to believe," Jane said. Her joke was automatic, for, her own recent experience fresh in her mind, she did not find the notion of an attraction at first sight hard to credit in the least. Even so small a thing as Robbie's casual mention of Lady Flora's brother had set Jane's heart to hammering, and she wished, even while knowing it impossible, that she could think of some way to bring up again the all-consuming subject of Mr. MacGowan.

"I wish to dance with a flaxen-haired beauty. Is that so hard to understand?" Averham laughed. "For all I know, the girl's as stupid as she can stare."

"She's not," Jane told him. "Take care of your heart, then, if you mean to keep it." She spoke on a note of raillery, wondering if Flora's chilly manner could really melt any man's heart. Her beauty, though, was considerable . . .

"Thank you for the warning. Ah, here she comes. Who is the evil-looking fellow with her?"

"Someone the Prince de Ligne introduced. A dancing partner, no more." Jane wondered if she had been lax already in her chaperon duties. Should she not have demanded Bronsky's pedigree before releasing Flora to his care, especially since Flora had taken the unprecedented step of allowing his attentions?

Well, what was done was done, and Jane consoled herself that she was thoroughly aware of her brother-in-law's character and antecedents. She would be happy to pass Flora to his care, and she would try hard not to crow at the suitability of it all.

"Lord Averham, how do you do?" Flora inclined her head in her usual stiff way at the introduction.

"I am delighted to meet you, Lady Flora. Will you give me the honor of the next dance? I warn you," and Averham's eyes lit with humor, "I can be very hard to turn down. You'd best get this over with if you don't want me trailing at your heels all evening."

"Well." Flora glanced sideways at Bronsky. And why consider him? Jane wondered. As Flora's chaperon, she would most definitely have to make some inquiries concerning the dangerous-looking young man.

"Your answer, Lady Flora?" Averham grinned as though to show he was already beginning on his program of persistence.

"Very well." Flora shrugged her slim shoulders. "Thank you, Monsieur Bronsky, it was a pleasure," she added, turning to her last partner. She gave him her hand. Jane stared.

Bronsky was fulsome in his parting compliments. Jane examined him, exasperated. He was a dashing foreigner, but Flora had shown herself immune to dashing foreigners. Besides—a light of mischief appeared in Jane's eyes—by Flora's strict Scottish lights, the English Lord Averham would be a foreigner too.

"And now, Lady Flora, I believe it is my turn," Averham said, a slight note of reproof evident in his voice. "Take my arm, please."

Startled, Flora took hold of the offered black sleeve, and the pair headed for the dance floor.

Jane looked after them. If only Robbie would fall in love with Lady Flora, and she with him! Theirs would be a most suitable match, and love might do wonders for the child's disposition.

Jane was beginning to parry the compliments of Bronsky, and to wonder at his impertinent questions about Flora, when a hand landed on her shoulder.

"I must speak with you, my lady," Archibald Mac-Gowan said in a low, urgent voice. The merest hint of Scotland glinted in his tones.

How odd, thought Jane, turning swiftly to greet him, that she had never before thought a Scottish accent was alluring.

MacGowan was at his finest in dark evening clothes. Beside his blond splendor, Bronsky faded away to nothing. The other man did have to be given credit for some insight, though. Evidently seeing that he was *de trop,* he instantly took his leave.

MacGowan had never noticed that Bronsky was present until the fellow made his farewells. He was staring at the lady of his desires, trying unsuccessfully to keep his eyes from a thorough scrutiny of Jane's figure. She was so beautiful in that gown. How much more lovely

would she be out of it! He looked her full in the face.
The expression of her large hazel eyes was most revealing
in that one moment before she veiled her glance and became a proper lady. Yes, the spark was there. She wanted
him; he would wager on it.

Yet his research had not borne out this opinion. All
Vienna extolled Jane as a paragon of every virtue; a
woman who had never given in to passion. He would be
mad to try to seduce her, the thoroughly respectable
widow who was playing duenna to his sister; but how
idiotic would he consider himself if he did not seize this
chance? She had only to say no; he would take her refusal
like a man.

"I'm grateful to that fellow, whoever he was, for
knowing when he's not wanted," he said, speaking more
roughly than he intended. He took Jane's arm in a firm
grasp and led her through the crowd, heading for a wall.

Jane had noticed earlier that there were some small
alcoves, lodging places for bits of statuary or stray chairs.
MacGowan headed for one of these; though still in public, the place had a touch more privacy than could be got
in the middle of the crowded room.

"Did you wish to dance?" Jane smiled up at him once
she was standing inside the little alcove. She ought to
feel intimidated by this attitude, she backed up against
the wall, he looming over her. But there was nothing of
trepidation in her mind. She fought to preserve a normal
manner, not to show the attraction which was unseemly
in a woman of her years, but his nearness was working
hard to finish her composure. The touch of his hands—
on her shoulder, on her arm—she had never experienced
anything like the excitement those simple gestures raised
in her. He must not guess, of course. "I'm not planning
to take the floor tonight, but my daughter would be delighted—"

"Jane, Jane." With no further ado MacGowan leaned
forward and whispered into her ear. "Let's not have any
more of that nonsense. You know I have no interest in
Miss Bellfort. We mustn't hurt the girl by pretending that
I do. It's you I want, you I must have."

Jane gasped. Never had she expected this to be so
quick. She had even thought that, by a determined concentration on Phyllida's needs, she could forestall the

moment forever. Yet here it was: direct, inevitable, and so very welcome.

"I know." She looked right into his eyes, fully aware of what he was saying and what it would mean to her ordered life.

Once she met his eyes, she was lost. Her maternal plans evaporated along with all sense of decorum. How simple it was. For years she had secretly congratulated herself on her immunity to the passions which drove her sophisticated friends. Now she came in for her share, and she could not wish it otherwise. Not that wishing would do her any good. She was this man's for the taking; it was as simple as that.

Perhaps later, she thought in an odd detachment, she would examine this phenomenon. She had been a model of rectitude all her life. Yet here she was—she, who had never betrayed her husband and had easily remained true to his memory in the face of myriad attempted seductions, was calculating the easiest way to get this man into her bed.

"When?" she whispered. "Where? I have so many obligations right now—the girls . . ."

"Leave it to me." MacGowan, looking almost too serious, too sober to be an eager lover, lifted her hand to his lips. His words, though, made the matter clear. "You mean more to me than you know. You obsess me; I think of nothing, of no one else."

"I think of you too," Jane said softly, cursing the inventors of gloves. How she longed to feel his mouth on her skin.

She had of course, been taught the proper forms from childhood. No woman would ever admit to more than a passing interest in a man to whom she was not married— even in that case, there were many limits. And in the sophisticated, cosmopolitan society in which she had been moving in late years, a certain brittle subtlety was still the rule. She was distantly aware of not playing her part in some age-old game. Flirtation. Slow seduction. She brushed off these duties like snowflakes; they seemed unbearably silly. He knew; she knew; no pretense was possible. Games would waste precious time.

"If only I might kiss you now," MacGowan said, still

in that serious tone. "I would make you forget those worries, whatever they are."

"Worried? I?" Jane tried for a worldly smile, the smile of the woman he doubtless thought she was, a sophisticated creature to whom this kind of encounter was nothing out of the ordinary.

"Those girls. That's it." MacGowan was evidently not taken in by her pose. "You are conscientious; you are good and kind. But you worry for nothing. No scandal will attach to your household. I'll find a way. I promise you." Once more he kissed her hand, then held it to his cheek for a telling moment. "It won't be long."

"It can't be long," Jane said, then could have kicked herself for being so transparent. Honesty was one thing, a blatant show of desire quite another.

"Dance with me," were his next words, muttered in a harsh, demanding tone. "They're playing a waltz."

"Good. Yes. I mean, no. I must not unless I see my charges properly taken care of."

MacGowan, whose view of the room was so much better due to his greater height, took a look around. "Your daughter is going off on the arm of a young man whom I know. Mr. Thompson, of the British delegation, an eminently respectable fellow. Your brother-in-law is keeping my sister on the floor, evidently overcoming her objections to a second dance. And as for Miss Schmidt, the Prince de Ligne must have decided to escape. He has just sent her on her way with the Comte de la Garde-Chambonas. A bore, but a respectable one not far past thirty."

Jane sighed in embarrassment. "The girls have had to fend for themselves while I—"

"While you discussed family matters having to do with Flora . . . with Flora's brother," MacGowan finished her sentence with a smile. "Have you ever done much acting, Lady Averham?"

"No." Jane wondered a little at the return to formality, then remembered that it was necessary to preserve appearances.

"You will have to start now, then. Join me. Dance in my arms, my dearest Lady Averham, and behave with perfect propriety. For my part, I promise not to ravish you in the middle of the floor. What do you say?"

The humor in his tone struck Jane as precisely the proper thing. Anyone who might overhear his remark would surely take it as a joke.

And had it been a joke after all? The last moments could have been a dream; indeed, she couldn't believe any of it had really happened. If it had, then she had gone from respectable widow to abandoned lover within the space of five minutes. One glance at MacGowan cleared things up somewhat. She had not known blue eyes could burn, but so his seemed to do when they looked at her. Whatever one might call what had just occurred, it had been no dream.

As MacGowan took her into his embrace and proceeded to keep his promise of a respectable waltz, Jane schooled her expression into a distant friendliness. Her face was all she could answer for, though. She felt the rest of her body go eagerly into a warm little world where only MacGowan's arms mattered. She could somehow tell that he felt her surrender, and she was glad of it.

The strange speaking she and MacGowan were doing so effortlessly would save a multitude of words, words so universal, so basic that they could not but be hackneyed. And Jane had no wish to remember this rare experience in terms of clichés.

5

HER FINGERS TREMBLING, she opened the note. *Tonight* was all it said, the single word scrawled in a bold hand. There was no signature.

Tonight! Already. But how?

"Thank you, Johann," Jane said, glad that her voice was not shaking as badly as her hands.

The footman nodded and went on his way down the corridor after eyeing the note in what Jane was certain was a longing manner. She had long since identified Johann as Emperor Franz's spy; she was seeing to it that none of her papers was left lying about. Not that she had ever had anything to hide, to be sure. Until now.

Jane mounted the stairs to her suite, willing herself to remain calm, wondering. Incredible though it seemed, she was about to embark on her first liaison. How had it happened? She was still not certain. He had said he wanted her, and her defenses, feeble at best, had crumbled in an instant. Every finer feeling insisted she was weak, that it was contemptible to be crushed under the weight of a sudden attraction. Why, then, did she feel empowered by her decision?

It *was* her decision—the first such choice that she had ever been allowed to make. She was driving her own destiny after so many years of mild acquiescence to others' desires. She wanted MacGowan, and he wanted her. They would have each other. And that, amazingly, was all there was to it.

Her own part of tonight's mission was clear; she must do nothing, must go about her usual routine. If she held herself in readiness, if she prepared, she must seem to be doing nothing out of the ordinary.

But what qualified as ordinary now in Vienna? The night before had been the Hofburg ball. Jane had heard that the poor empress, not in the best of health, had been carried fainting to her rooms when the festivities were over. It was by no means the first time. The unfortunate young woman could evidently not keep up the frenetic pace, yet she tried mightily. Everyone in Vienna was doing the same.

This evening was to be devoted to an event which even Phyllida was looking forward to with delight: a performance of Herr van Beethoven's opera *Fidelio*. Jane had promised that all her brood might go—even Chloe, whose task it was to appreciate the music as part of her education. That young miss would be taken straight home after the performance rather than attend the supper party which awaited the others. The Averham household would share the box of the Countess Zlotska, Jane's intimate friend. The evening was settled in every detail.

How, Jane wondered, could MacGowan manage to take her off and bed her in the midst of all this activity? Did his one-word message signify that she ought to make some excuse and stay at home tonight? No, he would never expect her to fall down in her duties to the girls. Phyllida would be distraught, Petra disappointed, and Chloe appalled if Jane decided to stay away from the opera. Even Flora might be a little miffed.

Jane could hardly send the girls alone. Marya Zlotska, dear though she was, could not be termed a proper chaperon for a flock of innocents.

Yes, her duty was clear. She would attend the opera and keep her eyes open. MacGowan was highly intelligent and most resourceful. He would find a way. This very night, since he had said so. This very night.

Jane had never known before that desire could be a palpable thing. She grasped the banister to steady herself, then continued to her room to pick out the most blatantly seductive of her evening dresses.

"The girl Jeannie was seen to go out on an errand today," Pauline said later, as she did Jane's hair. "I thought madame would wish to know that she was carrying a secret note."

"A secret note!" Jane's eyes opened wide, and her mind went at once to the note she had received. It was safe in her bosom. She hadn't been able to bear the thought of destroying it, as any sane woman would have done, but had had the urge to preserve it as she would any and all messages from MacGowan. Where to hide it had been her problem. Being a woman of open and unsecretive habits, she possessed no sliding drawers in desks or false legs on pieces of furniture . . . She forced herself back to the conversation at hand. "How do you know that the note was secret, Pauline? Surely Jeannie may carry messages for her mistress, or even for herself, without our making a piece of work about it."

"One knows it was secret," said Pauline severely, "because the clumsy girl dropped it out of her sleeve when she was passing through the servants' hall, and whipped it back out of sight. Madame knows me too well to think that I would use such an adjective did I not have cause."

"Forgive me." Jane was properly contrite. The maid obligingly inclined her head. "I wonder. Lady Flora has never had secrets before that I know of. I do hope she's not thinking of running off. She gave me her word she would not. Perhaps it's the maid, having an intrigue with somebody."

Pauline shrugged. "Perhaps. But that one has no words but English—and even that a strange dialect. Whom could she find to intrigue with in this city?"

Jane had no idea, and she declined to guess at this point. She made a mental note to have a word with Flora; to ask the girl if her maid had grown truly reconciled to life in Vienna and in the Averham household. If Jeannie were to do anything foolish . . .

"Heavens," Jane said, giving herself a shake. The servants could take care of themselves. "I simply cannot concern myself with every soul in this house. Not tonight."

"Not tonight. As madame says," Pauline replied in her usual serene and soothing tones. She looked startled when this perfectly reasonable rejoinder earned her a sharp look from her mistress.

Petra and Chloe had decided to make their toilettes together; that is Petra had invited Chloe into her room to watch her dress. Chloe, whose wardrobe was simple, had been dressed for hours for her first visit to the opera. She had to be satisfied that the sash to her white muslin gown was satin and in her favorite shade of cherry red. Her dark hair was dressed in the usual simple braids, and her ornament was the only one she possessed, a plain locket which contained a miniature of her parents.

She sat on Petra's bed and sighed with envy as the older girl put on a diaphanous creation of pale lilac. All of Petra's gowns were gauzy and soft and showed much more of her figure than did Phyllida's or Flora's dresses. Of course, thought Chloe, her assessing eye lingering on her friend's bosom, Petra had more to show than did either Phyllida or Lady Flora.

"Well." Petra, whose ways were modest at home despite her bold public manner with elderly princes, employed no dresser and had told Jane she didn't need one, indeed preferred to see to her own needs. When necessary, a housemaid would be called to button her into some recalcitrant garment, but with the lilac net this hadn't been necessary. She fastened the last tape. "I believe I shall do."

"Oh, you're so lovely," Chloe exclaimed. "I would look most beautiful in that shade too. I must remember it for later, when Mama lets me dress in colors. Lets me dress at all," she amended her words, fingering her fine India muslin in disdain. Nothing was more mortifying to her mind than the thought of appearing in public in the garb of a child. She knew that her soul was that of a passionate heroine, a *grande amoureuse* in the French style. (Chloe had never seen Paris, but she had heard stories.) Who would notice this, though, when the soul was buried beneath a figure which might kindly be described as a bit plump; a face which hadn't lost its child-like round contours; a wardrobe which would have done for a six-year-old?

"You must not fret, Chloe. Your time will come. As a child I was remarkably like you, and today you are kind enough to call me lovely."

"You couldn't have been like me."

Petra gave her little friend a considering stare, then nodded in decision. "I'll prove it to you." Crossing the room, she opened a drawer and brought out a small wooden casket. Chloe bounced off the bed and followed. While Chloe hung over her shoulder, Petra drew forth a miniature set in an oval frame. "I am the one on the right."

Chloe stared. The portrait was of two children of indeterminate age, both wearing white frocks, both with serious expressions. On the left was a thin child with reddish hair. The girl on the right was a plump, squab little creature with nothing to recommend her but a pair of large, expressive eyes. "That is you? You don't say! Who is the other girl? She looks familiar."

"A foster sister. And I *do* say." Petra whipped the picture back into her box and snapped shut the drawer. "Now, think no more of your looks, but put your mind on enjoying the opera. Lucky girl! It is said to be fine, and I will be much too busy to think of it."

"What will you be doing?" Chloe asked curiously. "We are all going to the opera, you know. Didn't Mama tell you?"

Petra picked up her skirts and began to waltz about the room. "I will be getting down to business, *ma chère*. Last night I was made to understand that there is really no getting at the Prince de Ligne. He would be ready to dally; fancy that, a man of his years! But for an establishment I must look elsewhere. And so I shall. Tonight."

Chloe nodded sagely. Petra was her heroine. If Petra said she was going to do a thing, it was as good as done.

"You are so much more fun than Phyllida," Chloe said with a sigh. "She's been filling my ears all day with nothing but her raptures on hearing this opera. She played the overture so many times I nearly became ill."

"Phyllida has her passion." Petra shrugged. "And lucky she is that her circumstances do not demand of her what mine do of me. She has no need to make good her time here. She is being foolish, I say, if she wastes these months. But it is not my business."

"And what of Flora? She really seems to hate young men. I wonder why she sent off a note to that Bronsky fellow she met last night."

Petra's eyebrows lifted at this. "What? Lady Flora has sent a note to someone? To Bronsky, that odd creature we met last night? How would you know this thing?"

Chloe drew herself up. "I have my ways. Do you know that she sent her Jeannie off with the note, and the silly creature dropped it? This interested Johann, and he waited his chance and picked her pocket before she could leave the house. He replaced the note, naturally, without her seeing it.''

"Are you on such terms of confidence with our house spy, then?" Petra asked.

"He didn't tell me, silly. I saw him do it," Chloe said. "I sometimes feel I am destined to be a spy myself." She took a moment to contemplate the lovely vision she would make, as graceful and full-bosomed as Petra, going masked to dangerous encounters, flirting with heads of state on missions for her government—any government. Chloe didn't feel particularly English. She would simply choose the noblest cause . . .

"And how do you know the name was Bronsky, if you didn't see?"

"Simple." Chloe was rather proud of the next bit. "I was luckily in my cloak, because Anna and I had just come in from our outing to the park. I simply sped out of the house after Jeannie and saw the person she spoke to, a street sweeper. He was quite a small boy, poor thing. I gave him a copper or two to tell me where the strange foreign woman wished to be directed to. And when I found out the direction, which is quite near here, I went along and was in time to see Jeannie disappear into a certain house.''

"And you went and inquired at the house?"

Chloe gave an indelicate snort. "Much luck I would have had with a project like that! Mama won't understand what a safe place Vienna is, and she would have had fits if I'd gone that far. And you had better believe she would have heard of it; Mama has almost as many spies on me as the emperor has on everyone else. I ran back into our house and sent Anna to inquire who lived in the place. She returned with a half-dozen names, and I simply picked out the one which sounded most likely.''

"Since you had heard us discussing the ball at breakfast," Petra finished the tale. "Admirable, my dear! But you know, it is still a guess." She paused. "A good one, I admit. Flora danced with Monsieur Bronsky, and she seemed much taken with him. I was above anything shocked when she actually mentioned his name this morning; I never would have thought to hear her talk of any gentleman.''

"That was my opinion," Chloe said. "This spying is so easy it's . . . it's contemptible. Oh, Petra, have you decided yet what tricks we are to play on Johann?''

"I have an idea," Petra said with a twinkle. She sat down on the bed near Chloe in a whisper of soft lilac. "What would be the most shocking thing Johann could bring to his masters?''

"I can't guess. That one of us is a spy, I suppose."

Petra nodded soberly. "I propose that Johann be the spy.''

"But he is." Chloe cocked her head in puzzlement, a gesture which gave her a resemblance to an alert bird.

"Yes. And he will bring them letters in code, saying that someone in this household has discovered the most shocking thing: that Johann is a spy. We can easily think up a cipher, and I'm certain the secret police can as easily interpret whatever we invent. And we will write several letters, making him a spy for . . . I think only for the four great powers. No need to go farther afield than that. First Russia, then Prussia, then England, and for our finale we shall write that he is suspected of spying for Austria. Since of course he is for Austria, there will be delightful confusion.''

"Oh, what a perfect joke." Chloe clasped her hands. "Petra, you are a genius.''

"I fall lamentably short of that, my child," Petra said with a shake of the head, "but I cannot approve of this infiltrating of people's private homes. Why, what if we wished to do something shocking? We wouldn't be able to get away with the smallest indiscretion without the most proper Emperor Franz reading about it at his breakfast table.''

Later, at the opera, Jane's mind was filled to bursting with the prospect of "doing something shocking." She barely heard the multilingual chattering of the crowd, let alone the opera, which made her daughter sigh and droop over the railing of the box in rapturous longing. She saw only in a blur the uncommon brilliance that surrounded her. Royalty was everywhere; not only the emperor and empress of Austria, but those of Russia smiled and nodded to their admirers from a velvet-draped box. Lesser luminaries took positions of lower prominence. In Countess Zlotska's box, Jane and her brood had a good view of the spectacle. But Jane's inner turmoil was such that she could not be dazzled.

"You preoccupy yourself, my dear," the countess said, leaning toward Jane to tap her softly with a feather fan. Countess Zlotska was a lushly dark woman of about forty who always dressed in an opulent style at odds with the wispier garments in current Viennese fashion. "If I didn't know you better, I would say there was some man in the question."

Jane tried to dismiss that comment as nonsense and wondered if she quite succeeded. Was her smile perhaps a little wooden, her eyes a little too feverish? And she couldn't seem to stop her gaze from roving around the theater. Where was MacGowan?

"Your brother-in-law, now," the countess said in a low tone, dark eyes slanting across the box to where Averham was conversing with Lady Flora. "There is a man! Do you English have no remedy for those tiresome problems of consanguinity? Though no laws of church or state have ever prevented a woman from having her fun."

"Masha! You know I have no interest in Averham." Jane was shocked at the mere idea, and looked it.

"Ah. You mean him for your little charge. Do you think she can catch him?"

"I doubt if Lady Flora would deign to try," Jane said with a sigh. She was much afraid that the Congress would end with Lady Flora still unattached. Jane was sorry for Lord Foxburgh, who so evidently wanted the girl off his hands; but somehow she was even sorrier for Flora.

Lord Averham was indeed finding heavy weather in his pursuit of the flaxen-haired Scottish beauty. Lady Flora, dressed in her favorite white with plaid ornaments—the MacGowan tartan—began the evening by calling Averham's compliments to her looks "nonsense." Then she would simply not be drawn into witty conversation, no matter what the provocation. Averham had a witty conversation all by himself while Flora nodded mildly, glanced away, and examined her jewelry.

But logic has little influence on the heart, Averham

considered with a rueful smile. Such behavior from Flora
was the very thing to make him determine that she was
the most fascinating of young women. As an eligible peer
he had never been treated as less than a matrimonial
prize, and to experience the rare thrill of a young lady
who had no use for him he would bear with many an
incivility. He found himself staring at her stern profile,
her severe blue eyes. What kind of a man was she looking
for?

The answer, when it came, was most unwelcome. Averham saw those chilly eyes light up when a certain young
man entered the box, bowing and scraping to all. It was
that fellow he had noticed at the ball. The one who had
danced with Flora before he had.

"Bronsky, I believe you know Lord Averham?" Flora
was brisk and businesslike when the young man approached her and seized her hand.

Bronsky murmured something about a pleasure. Averham grunted and eyed askance the other man's tight
hold on Lady Flora's gloved appendage. *He* had not been
allowed to take her hand, even in greeting. She had been
fiddling with a bracelet, and the moment had passed.

The spirit of rivalry, until then dormant in Lord Averham's breast, beat its wings loudly.

"I was delighted to hear from you, my goddess,"
Bronsky said to Flora; low, but not so low that Averham
didn't hear it.

The baron started. She had been communicating with
the unsavory fellow? This was surely not in the common
way for a proper young lady.

Flora looked significantly at Bronsky, then at Averham, but said nothing. Then, when Bronsky continued
his raptures at her goodness for granting him the privilege of—whatever the exact communication had been—
she spoke sharply. "I merely wished to let you know
where we would be this evening. Bronsky, you must not
become conceited on the subject."

This was better. Averham relaxed; but there was still,
for his taste, too much of familiarity in Flora's manner
to her foreign admirer.

"Do you know," Flora said to both men, or to neither,
depending on the intimacy one might require in a con-
versational setting, "I had expected to see my brother

here tonight. I've already waved to Father, in that box across the way, but I wouldn't have thought Archie would miss the event. He likes music,'' she explained, as though that were a rather shameful weakness.

''What sort of music pleases you, Lady Flora? Must it be bagpipes or nothing?'' Averham asked in a teasing tone.

Flora looked daggers at him—dirks, no doubt. He immediately made a smooth and contrite apology that was worded in such a way that she must accept it or look surly.

He suspected that Flora would not have hesitated to look surly in his eyes, but that she wished to appear a bit more conciliating for the benefit of her foreign admirer. A challenge indeed.

Newly charmed, Averham kept up his close observation of Lady Flora. He had never known before what an abrasive personality could do for a young woman.

Petra, seated at the other end of the box with Chloe, had been surveying the house with the thoroughness of a general before battle. Lord Foxburgh, Flora's father, was most genially leering at Miss Schmidt's deep décolletage from across the way. Petra had met him at Lady Averham's and found him . . . well, she had found him to be a new friend's father, and as such, impossible to think of. Why, she wondered, had she had no trouble in thinking of the aged Prince de Ligne?

''This is more difficult than I thought,'' she whispered to Chloe.

''What is?'' Chloe, eyes nearly blinded by her first sight of the Congress at play, wasn't really listening.

''My decision,'' Petra said with a sigh. ''I have not yet made it, and I fear this evening will be wasted.'' Merely to try her power, she smiled at Lord Foxburgh. The Scottish peer obligingly bowed. Even more intriguing, he stood up and appeared to make his excuses to Lady Castlereagh at his side. Would he come over to pay his respects? Petra straightened, her interest piqued.

'Oh, look. Here is Mr. MacGowan,'' Chloe whispered. ''Mama means him for Phyllida, I hear. Do you suppose my sister will even notice he's arrived?''

But Mr. MacGowan didn't pause to greet Phyllida or

any of the young ladies, including his sister. As he entered the box he went directly to Jane, who was busily talking to Countess Zlotska.

Jane summoned up every rule of conduct she had ever been taught and managed not to throw herself into MacGowan's arms. His own manner was composed when his gaze lit upon her.

"Lady Averham," he said after the Countess Zlotska had given him her customary dressing-down, which she gave all the young men, for being so handsome as to be the death of her, "I hope you'll be indulgent. I'm forced to beg for your aid."

"My aid?" Jane looked up at him, bemused.

He had to tear his eyes away from her beauty. Never had he seen her look more lovely, more seductive than she did in that simple, nearly transparent gown of creamy gauze shot with gold, and to see her on such blatant display, knowing what he knew, nearly drove him mad. "Yes. I must have your help," he said in the clipped tone which such a statement would warrant. "You might have noticed earlier that I was escorting the Duchess of Sagan."

"Why, no, sir. We haven't glimpsed you all evening," Jane answered in surprise. What did this have to do with anything?

"The duchess has been taken ill; for some reason, she seems upset. She will not be comforted."

"It's Metternich, or that Prince Windischgraetz," was the Countess Zlotska's matter-of-fact diagnosis, delivered with a flap of her fan. "Or perhaps it's the czar. Too many strings to her bow, has Wilhelmine, and she is more sensitive than she pretends, poor thing."

"Ill! The poor dear lady!" Jane spoke to MacGowan, ignoring Masha's gossipy flights. "But what has this to do with me, sir? You must take her home at once."

"She is asking for you. I believe she wishes to talk as only one female can to another, and she speaks most highly of your sweetness, your listening ear, that sort of thing," MacGowan continued, looking hard at Jane. "Will you come, ma'am? I'm not much used to dealing with vaporish females." He managed to look as boyish as he did not feel; to give the impression that he had never had much experience of any sort with those mysterious creatures, the ladies.

"But I cannot leave my girls."

"Nonsense, my dear," said the countess. "You will go with Wilhelmine. I can bring your girls safely home. I shall have milord Foxburgh come and rescue us, in fact. Lady Flora's father will be a most suitable escort, though we have your charming brother-in-law also."

"Chloe is to go right home after the opera," Jane said, summoning up motherly concern. "She will tease to go on to the supper party."

"With my own hands I will wrest her from the carriage and march her into your house," Countess Zlotska said with a firm nod. Leaning forward, she whispered, "I depend on you to tell me tomorrow what is amiss with Wilhelmine."

"Oh, dear." Jane twisted her fan in her lap and heard one of the sticks break.

"Go, dear Jane. This young man depends on your goodness."

At this Jane did get up. "You will explain to the young ladies, Masha? I fear to broadcast Wilhelmine's predicament. Perhaps you could say . . . oh, you will think of some excuse, either that or swear them to secrecy on the matter. And tell them that I will likely be at home before they are."

"I doubt that," MacGowan put in. His hand was now on Jane's arm, and the pressure was firm yet caressing. "The duchess seems to require a lot of soothing. I wouldn't know, of course, for certain."

"Of course not. You are a man." Making little shooing motions, Countess Zlotska waved Jane and MacGowan away with a smile.

At the door to the box they bumped into Lord Foxburgh, on his way in.

"Why, Jane! I was just coming to pay my respects," the earl said with a bow. "You about to take her away, Archie?"

"You've caught me out, Father," MacGowan said in an odd tone. "There is a problem—ask the Countess Zlotska to explain it to you. It's a delicate matter."

"Delicate. Ah." Lord Foxburgh continued to observe the pair more keenly than Jane could like.

"I do hope you will forgive us, my lord," she said with a weak smile.

Foxburgh was more than ready to do so. Whatever he thought of their leaving the box together—and he was not certain what to think—he pushed it to the back of his mind and paid his respects to Countess Zlotska. He had soon completed this diplomatic project—which involved extravagant compliments, Marya Zlotska being of an exacting character—kissed his daughter's forehead in a paternal manner quite unlike his usual behavior, and transmitted an avuncular greeting to young Miss Bellfort. He was then free to turn to Miss Schmidt, who, most unaccountably, seemed to be attached to a schoolgirl. Ah . . . the memory came to him. That would be Jane's second daughter.

"Good evening, my lord," Petra said sweetly, giving the earl her hand. Beside her, Chloe eyed the encounter as intently as she knew how.

"My dear Miss Schmidt." The earl took a seat next to Petra. "I saw you across the theater and had to pay my respects. You light up even this brilliant gathering, madam."

Behind the man's back, Phyllida glared darkly at Petra. Lord Foxburgh's loud voice was interrupting the most beautiful aria of the whole opera.

"I thank you, my lord," Petra said softly. "Would you be so good . . . that is, I promised Miss Chloe that she would walk in the corridor before we must go home. Would you be so kind as to escort us?"

"Capital idea, lass," Lord Foxburgh said enthusiastically. "I'll fix it up with the countess."

Petra bowed in acknowledgment to Phyllida. Taking Lord Foxburgh right out of the box should satisfy her musical friend. And it would be charming to walk in the corridor with the English milord.

"You don't have to take me," Chloe whispered in a conspiratorial tone.

"Don't be silly, my dear," Petra returned. "It is a simple walk, no more."

Chloe confined herself to looking wise beyond her years when Lord Foxburgh, his mission with the countess complete, came back to their corner of the box with an eager step.

* * *

Jane did not pause to breathe until she and MacGowan were sitting in an unmarked *Fiaker,* which, she was not surprised to find, did *not* contain the Duchess of Sagan. "What have you done?" were her first words. She was longing for him to touch her, his hands were reaching out, but she simply had to understand. "Is the duchess . . . did you confess to her about this? About us?"

MacGowan managed to seize her hand and remove the glove; then he pressed eager kisses into her palm. "We had to have an ally. She understands. We can trust her. She is quite fond of you and instructed me to tell you that she will be pleased to receive your call tomorrow. I'm afraid she wishes to hear all about it." He gave a wry smile.

"By tomorrow," Jane said leaning toward him, "I might have a great urge to talk to some understanding female."

"Don't tell her everything."

She laughed, a strange, nervous sound to her ears.

And there was no reason to put off their first kiss any longer. Jane knew she should be amazed to find herself fitting into his embrace as though she had spent years with him instead of only minutes. Yet she was not really surprised at all. Then his lips were on hers.

Now she was surprised. How could mere kisses light such fires? She wanted more; needed more.

They returned to reason only when the carriage came to a halt before a dark door; what looked like the rear entrance to some grand building.

"Where are we?" Jane whispered when she had caught her breath.

"Better if you don't know. Come, now. Quickly." MacGowan ushered her out, wrapping a hooded cloak around her as she stepped down from the carriage. Jane was tingling. The kisses, the caresses, and now to be herded into an unknown house exactly as a doxy might be . . . why couldn't she feel insulted? She was only eager. She had never expected to walk the primrose path, let alone to gallop down it, yet she was doing nothing less.

Or someone was. Another Jane had come with MacGowan tonight, not the devoted mother or the diplomat's widow, but someone else, someone Jane had a violent curiosity to know.

That other Jane followed her lover-to-be up a dark staircase, down a gloomy corridor, and then MacGowan opened a door. He fairly pushed Jane inside, then leaned against the door and turned the key. There was a bolt too. He shot it home.

Jane glanced around at what she could see of an opulent bedchamber, not dissimilar to her own room in the Johannesgasse. A large and looming bed was heaped with crisp linen. A fire burnt in the huge tiled stove. Not a single candle was in evidence.

"We aren't to have lights?" she asked, feeling strangely disappointed.

"It's safest this way. No one must know this room was occupied tonight."

Jane nodded, standing still. Now that they were here and about to begin the business that had driven them, she felt strangely shy.

MacGowan came forward to put his hands on her shoulders. "Do you know, can you know how much this moment means to me? Please trust me, Jane. Trust me tonight."

"If I didn't trust you, I wouldn't be here," she said softly, looking up at him through the shadows. She untied the enveloping cloak and let it fall. And then she caught her breath as what she had been longing for began.

"You. I want to see you," she gasped when she was undressed, the seductive gown having come off as if by magic. She began to pluck at his waistcoat. Her fingers were suddenly as clumsy as sausages.

He had to undress himself, which he obligingly did, revealing a muscular body surprisingly bronzed—or was that only a trick of the wavering firelight? Before she could look her fill, he had her in his arms, was spinning round with her and falling with her, dizzy, onto the bed.

The laughter surprised her, coming at such a moment. So did her delighted response.

"How did I know?" she asked softly, reaching out to grasp his hand as they lay together in the aftermath of the first eager encounter.

"How did you know what?" he murmured back.

"I knew it would be good. I've never had this sort of an experience before, never taken a man to my bed on short acquaintance, yet I knew that it could happen with you and that it would be wonderful. How?'' Jane was extremely curious on this point. Now that it had actually come to naked bodies, to the same act she had once submitted to with her husband, she had no idea why she had rushed headlong into intimate relations with a stranger. How had she been able to foresee such a rare, such a beautiful experience, she who had never known such a thing before?

''I don't know how,'' he said. ''I felt it too. There's simply a bond between some people. We were lucky enough to recognize it.''

''There was such power in it,'' Jane said in wonder. She had never known that before, either.

He sighed.

As his chest rose and fell, so did Jane's spirits. Was he sorry already that he'd brought her here?

He must have felt her stiffen in alarm. Chuckling, he said, ''Do you know what that heartfelt sigh was for?''

''No.''

His arms went around her. ''You are already talking in the past tense. Yet I was hoping to find the words to convince you that it isn't over. You see, I had some idea that if we did this together, if we worked out our passion as soon as possible, it would be spent. That we would be free to go on about our business. But I trust you didn't have a single encounter in mind, Lady Averham, for this night has simply whetted my appetite for more. Much, much more.''

Jane had never been so grateful to hear anything. ''Has it, Mr. MacGowan?'' She realized that she had not yet called him by his Christian name. Not that she had ever called her husband by his, but this was different.

She hesitated, then spoke. ''May I call you Archie— in private?'' she asked shyly, wondering why she was having more difficulty asking this than she had in doing a thousand wordless, intimate things with him only moments before.

He laughed. ''I hope so. You are such a treasure, Jane.''

Then his embrace tightened, and she forgot all about the question of names and her own hesitation for another interlude in his arms.

6

WILHELMINE, the renowned Duchess of Sagan, lived in one wing of the Palm Palace in the Schenkenstrasse. Hers was a crowded and informal household despite her great title and substantial wealth. She had several young foster daughters who, though technically at Madame Brévillier's school, managed to fill the place with their exuberant presence. She was a great hostess whose salon attracted the most intelligent and discriminating of the Austrian party.

And then there were her lovers. Wilhelmine de Sagan had been divorced twice and was rumored to lead a nearly libertine existence—in short, to behave as men had been doing for centuries. Many censured her for such behavior, and some would not receive her, including the Castlereaghs, who were doing their best to see that what was most unyielding and upright of British virtues was displayed to Vienna this Season.

Jane had always liked Wilhelmine and admired her lack of hypocrisy. And now she felt a special bond with her.

When she received the English baroness, the great lady was puttering about in her bedroom in a tattered dressing gown, two slices of lemon bound up at her temples.

The duchess saw Jane looking at her head. "The lemon has something to do with the skin, or the mood—I forget exactly," she said, dark eyes sparkling. "I suffer from disabling migraines, you know—but of course you do, for the migraine was my excuse last night. The lemon is to fend that off as well. Now, my dear Jane, tell me all about it."

Jane blushed fiercely. This was a feature of her redhead's complexion which had much distressed her in her youth. But at her time of life, and especially after the past night's activities, she supposed she ought to be grateful to be able to blush.

"Oh, Wilhelmine," she said with a sigh. "You've been telling me for as long as I've known you that I should take a lover, should see something of life. What can I say? I must tell you, at least, how grateful I am for your help last night. I could kiss your feet."

"Ah, don't make me the recipient of your caresses," the duchess said, pouring tea. "It would be quite a waste. That young man is . . . well, if I did not lead such a busy life, you would not keep him long."

"I don't expect to keep him long in any event," Jane said with a shrug. Despite Archie's professions last night, his assurances that his desire for her ran deep and strong, she knew how love affairs were handled in her world. Perhaps she would be lucky enough for the liaison to last as long as the Congress did. Or perhaps not. Already, though society hadn't been gathered long in Vienna, people were changing partners in a frenzy, as though the weather which made unseasonable flowers blossom in the parks had transmitted its effect to humans.

"Enjoy the moment," was Wilhelmine's advice. "I can see that you enjoyed last night."

"Is it so obvious?" Jane took a worried glance into a large mirror across the room. She had never even considered such a possibility as her experience showing in her face. She had had breakfast with the girls, for heaven's sake. Had they seen something they shouldn't?

"My dear." Wilhelmine reached out to pat her guest's hand. "Do not look so distressed. I am a woman of the world. Don't worry about your young ladies. Females at that time of life are turned in, not out. They won't notice a thing."

Jane didn't know if she could manage not to worry, but she calmed down. What was done was done, and if the girls had remarked something in her manner, she would have to find a way to explain it. "It was so kind of you, so sweet and generous to leave the opera and pretend to be ill. And then later to send me home in your own coach, with your maid's attendance! You may be sure my porter was watching. I'll never forget it. I didn't even know you were acquainted with Archie." Jane finished her speech of thanks with a statement which was really a question.

"We met not too long ago, though I've known Lord Foxburgh for years," Wilhelmine said with a smile. "MacGowan mentioned you, in quite a casual way, and I'm afraid I jumped to a conclusion. I told him that you needed such a man as he, and that I would be at your service if, at any time, I could help. He took me up on that offer." She paused. "And as for my maid, it was no great distance to send her. You were here last night."

"Here! In the Palm Palace?" Jane cried.

Wilhelmine nodded mischievously.

"Fancy that!" Jane didn't know whether to feel chagrin at her exposure or gratitude that the whole matter had been handled in such a simple way. "Then I have even more to thank you for."

"No more thanks, if you please. We are women together in this dreadful world the men have arranged. We must help each other all we can."

Jane nodded, realizing that though Wilhelmine spoke with a note of raillery in her voice, there was real bitterness too. And Jane agreed. Why should she, because she was a woman, have to account for every moment she spent, or lose her reputation? She didn't have the choice of not caring for the falsities of society, of flinging her good name away, as had Wilhelmine and some others. She had to maintain some standards for her daughters' sake.

She couldn't keep thinking along such sober lines, though, on such a morning. More pleasant things insisted on occupying her mind. "Did you say before that he mentioned me?" The question was held out shyly.

Wilhelmine returned what was needed, a recital of her first encounter with MacGowan. She made much of his amusing Scottish accent and dwelt with experienced pleasure on his manly form. "His father brought him here, and I contrived to get him alone. A young man of that sort, I will usually manage to get alone. I asked him if he had met many of the ladies of Vienna, and he said you were the first one who had made much of an impression. He said it so stiffly, so Britishly, if you will, that I simply knew you'd conquered him."

"Fancy that!" Jane said for the second time in a very few minutes. "Yet I am so much older than he."

"Jane! He is no untried youth, but a man who knows the world. As for you, you are but a year older than I, and if you think I would have failed to attach him if he hadn't already been under your spell, you are much mistaken."

"Oh! I'm sorry." Jane sighed. "But here I am the mama of a grown girl, and one fast becoming a grown girl, and I simply don't feel as venerable as my position demands. Is it really true, Wilhelmine? Will we feel as young as we do now all our lives? I swear I felt sixteen last night. No," she amended her words, remembering a certain frightening wedding night many years ago, "not sixteen."

"Thirty-four," Wilhelmine said, sipping tea. "More than twice as good."

Leaning back against the carriage squabs for the short ride home, Jane fell to wondering what would become of her now. She had stepped, quite unthinkingly, into a world which for years she had looked at askance, and certainly from a well-regulated distance.

She scrutinized the grand house she had just left—the place where she had made love the night before. In the other wing of the Palm Palace lived the Princess Bagration, Wilhelmine's great rival in the feminine political world of Vienna. Catherine Bagration was a widow, as Jane was. She had taken innumerable lovers even during her marriage and was rumored to have set her sights on her cousin the czar this autumn. Looking up at the lady's windows, Jane wondered if she herself would soon lack all reputation. Why, respectable young girls were never taken to the Bagration's parties! What would it be like to give a party which one's own daughter ought not to attend!

No. Jane wouldn't imagine such a thing. Her affair with MacGowan would be an aberration. She simply couldn't see behaving in such an abandoned way with another man.

Then she caught herself. What had happened with MacGowan had been so strange, so unexpected: that instant attraction had been clear, as had instant knowledge of delights to come. How was she to know whether or not that sort of blatant lust would come to her in the future?

She rested her chin in her hand, wondering if she had opened herself to such feelings in some way by giving in to them once. What, pray tell, was she to do? How could she prevent herself from becoming truly abandoned . . . or was it too late?

Or—a much more pleasant thought—it could be that what she had found with MacGowan was too special to happen more than once in a lifetime. Much though she scorned herself for a hopeless sentimentalist, she was inclined to this view.

There was more than enough to think about. Yet two thoughts only forced themselves into prominence in Jane's mind: the two words she had spoken to MacGowan only a few days before, at the Hofburg ball.

"When?" she whispered, though there was no one in the coach to hear her. Alone she might be, but she was aching with desire quite as though he were beside her. "Where?"

Archibald MacGowan was meditating upon those same two words as he emerged from a highly secret meeting at the mansion in the Minoritenplatz that Lord Castlereagh had made his headquarters. MacGowan had his orders—nothing strenuous, merely to chase down the origin of some trouble being stirred up on the ticklish issue of Poland's future borders. MacGowan had comported himself in a businesslike manner, coming up with ideas, even impressing Castlereagh into saying that he was a deucedly clever fellow.

Little did his colleagues know that MacGowan's whole world began and ended in bed with Lady Averham. Though amazed that others couldn't pick up this fact by looking at him, he was glad to have hidden his new enthusiasm from the others of the British delegation.

Now, though his superiors would have been shocked, the question which filled his mind was not the future of Poland. How was he to meet *her* again?

It must be soon, and he must be the one to take care of it. One of the many things Jane had let fall last night had been her total inability to arrange secret rendezvous.

She had never done so in her life and didn't know how. He, on the other hand, was either naturally adept at the business or had had much experience, she had suggested in a moment of slyness.

He was chuckling to himself as he walked down the street in the sunshine. He suspected that his Jane was simply lazy on this issue, and the notion didn't displease him in the least. She deserved to be catered to and relieved of all mundane burdens. Was she not the most fascinating woman in the history of the world?

Besides, to give credit to her reluctance in the matter, he did fail to see how she could receive him in her boudoir or meet him at a country inn in the daytime, as many lovers were doing in these mad autumn days. How would she manage, with all those girls hanging on her sleeve?

He would have to be ingenious, and he would have to be quick, MacGowan was thinking as he turned into the Ballhausplatz, where he was to meet with some Austrian dignitary whose name he couldn't remember. He couldn't wait for long. Even practicality was on his side; he would be no use to the British cause if he were driven mad.

A vision of Jane as she had looked in the firelight, so enticing and sweet, so passionate and welcoming, rose up before him. In the middle of the Ballhausplatz! Incredible. Shaking his head, MacGowan quickened his steps, eager to get the coming business out of the way. Then he would search out yet another excuse to take Jane away from her responsibilities and into his arms.

The next day, in her opulent house in the Johannesgasse, Lady Averham was receiving callers.

Talk was all of the performance of the night before last. Herr van Beethoven's *Fidelio* was fast becoming the fashionable opera. The visitors noticed that even Miss Bellfort, who was usually so languid and uninterested in the world around her, listened with shining eyes and full attention to the Countess Zlotska's raptures.

Marya Zlotska, to be sure, had spent most of the evening at the opera in chatting and surveying the house, but the following days found her in full agreement with the greatest music lovers in the musical city. She had happened to read an account of the opera in the *Wiener*

Zeitung, and if high society was said to be enthusiastic, then she would prove herself one of the elite.

"Oh, ma'am," Phyllida said with a sigh, "how I should love to meet that man! So sad that he can hardly hear the music he conducts with such passion. He must be the greatest genius now living."

"But I hear the composer is practically a recluse, my dear. A deaf and dour middle-aged one, at that," the countess said with an odd little smile.

Phyllida sighed again. No one could understand that she didn't wish to meet Herr van Beethoven because of any social graces he might possess; she merely wished to view him at close range, to marvel at what he had done, and perhaps to thank him. The fever raging through Vienna had settled itself, for her, in that man's music. She could scarcely even persuade herself to play her old favorite Mozart these days. She truly believed Mozart was one of the greats, but his status as a late composer made him no comparison to one who still walked the mortal ways—no matter how dourly.

"Still and all," the countess mused, with an even odder expression, "it would be an extraordinary *coup* to become the mistress of such a man. To deal with a genius, dear Phyllida, would be difficult."

"I don't wish to be his mistress," Phyllida objected, blushing hotly, a defect of the complexion which she had inherited from her mother. "If I cannot see him close up, and I do not see how I can, I only wish to see him from afar and gaze at him. As I did the other night at the theater."

The Countess Zlotska considered this ambition with every appearance of seriousness.

Meanwhile, behind the countess's deep and solid armchair, Chloe was having an illuminating morning. Madame Zlotska was a woman of the world. Perhaps she was right. All Vienna seemed to be only too excited by Herr van Beethoven. Wouldn't it be the greatest of all beginnings to one's life as a famous heroine to be his mistress?

Chloe frowned as she considered the problem. Physically, she was hardly mistress material—yet—but Beethoven was said to be middle-aged, ugly, and deaf. Blind, she mused, would have been better for her purposes, glancing at what she could see of her figure. Still, someone of his type couldn't be too choosy. She was able to spend a good few minutes in rapt appraisal of a mythical future in which the great man dedicated symphonies and concertos to Miss Chloe Bellfort—the inspiration of his middle years.

Across the room, Petra took an amused glance at the small foot just visible behind the Countess Zlotska's chair. She hoped that Chloe was using her time well. The child did have definite talents for the game of espionage.

"Do tell me something about yourself, Miss Schmidt," Lord Foxburgh was saying heartily as he surveyed Petra through his quizzing glass. "I know virtually nothing. You are Lady Averham's goddaughter, and you are distractingly pretty. What can you add to that portrait, lassie?"

It still startled Petra to be called "lassie," to be reminded that the cosmopolitan Lord Foxburgh was indeed the very Scottish Lady Flora's father. She smiled as demurely as she knew. "Milord, I have no interesting traits. My childhood was quiet, and now you see me on my first venture into the world."

"Where do you make your home, my dear? I've told you about Scotland enough times; retaliate and give me some idea of your background."

"Switzerland," Petra said. "I was brought up there, in the country. And dear Lady Averham is my godmother because my mother once lived in London, where I chanced to be born."

Foxburgh nodded soberly; he had had the answer to his question, yet this young lady's explanation somehow gave a very mysterious effect. "And are your parents still living, Miss Schmidt?" He smiled. "You must not fear this is an interrogation. I merely take a friend's interest."

A friend! Petra's heart lifted at this proof of her success. "My mother is living," she answered. After a pause she added shyly, "I'm glad you call yourself my friend, sir. May I hope for the honor of being yours as well one day?"

"My dear young lady." Foxburgh felt a strange sense of comfort, as though he were sitting before a fire in his slippers with a bottle of good Scots whiskey at his elbow. "You are much too modest."

Petra lowered her lashes. "My lord, I fear that you will one day find that I am not at all what you think me."

Jane, busily charming a court of gentlemen, watched through narrowed eyes as Petra worked her wiles upon Lord Foxburgh. Ought someone to warn the earl against the matrimonially inclined young lady? No, that would be an impossible slight on his own powers of discernment. Jane resolved to put a word in Petra's ear if the girl became too obvious. She was in Vienna to catch a husband, and admitted it to all who asked; she might not wish, though, to admit it to Lord Foxburgh, at least at this stage of the negotiations. Petra was doomed to disappointment, of course. Foxburgh was unassailable, as many a lady could testify.

"Tell me something if you will, Jane," Robbie said, leaning back in his chair. Her brother-in-law was sitting next to Jane, to the great disappointment of a couple of Austrian hussars and a Polish prince who had chosen this morning to pay their respects to the lovely English milady. "Where is Lady Flora this morning?"

"She is gone out riding with her brother. They should return before long, and I hope they join us," Jane said with an admirable calm. Even the thought of MacGowan made her limbs go oddly languid. She certainly did hope he and his sister came into the salon, and not merely so that Flora might draw daggers with Robbie.

"Her brother. Excellent." Averham crossed his arms over his chest. "Well, next tell me this, dear sister. Are you finding your home indeed to be the exclusive British gathering place the wits call it?"

"Sometimes," Jane said, tipping her head to one side. She smiled at the non-English gentlemen who hovered near. She did wish that there was some subtle way of directing these gallant young men to pay their respects to her daughter; their compliments were wasted on her. "I also find that the gentlemen of this country are most kind. You can see there are no British here this morning, Robbie, except for you and Lord Foxburgh. I do tend to collect the British visitors on two or three mornings a week, though. Do you wish to make a note to come on those days to be sure of picking up whatever is said?" Laughter warmed her voice, and she smiled mischievously at all the gentlemen. They chuckled in appreciation.

"I expect I'll come every day, as Foxburgh seems to do," Averham said. "But I'd hardly try to ease my way in among the Britishers if I wished to ferret out information, Jane." He exchanged a look of masculine condescension with the Polish prince. "You forget, my dear, that I'm here merely on a pleasure trip."

Jane was forming some clever yet discreet quip in answer to this evident falsehood when the doors opened and Lady Flora entered, the train of her riding dress looped up on her arm. In her wake came two gentlemen, also in riding clothes. One, dark and handsome in a flashy way, in a coat which had seen a bit too much wear, was Bronsky. The other was Archibald MacGowan.

Jane had eyes for no one but MacGowan, and she forgot what she had been about to say and even who was with her. She had not seen *him* at all the day before. It seemed a lifetime ago that they had made love. Averham glanced at her in some curiosity as MacGowan walked briskly up to them.

"My dear Lady Averham, forgive us for appearing before you in all our dirt. My sister wished to go directly to her room, but I thought it would be only courteous to come in." He took Jane's hand to place a kiss upon it.

She stared at him, appalled and thrilled by his boldness; then realized that it was no boldness at all, merely simple courtesy. She was the only one in the room who would know what effect the touch of his lips on her naked flesh had on her.

MacGowan seemed to notice Jane's confusion, and he covered for her nicely. "Lord Averham!" He released his lady's hand to turn to Robbie. "I must tell you, sir, that I believed you would be here and thought my sister had better meet with you. She has told me that you have sworn to be persistent, and there is no use in her avoiding the issue, I say."

Averham grinned. "You talk sense, MacGowan. Is that why she immediately ran to the side of the Countess Zlotska as though they were the best of friends? I noticed she didn't say two words to the woman the other night at the opera."

"Chase her down, Averham," MacGowan advised.

"We met Bronsky, there, on our way into the Prater, and he's been with us ever since, sticking to her like a burr. A bit of competition, sir, will make for more sport."

Averham left, and, quick as a flash, MacGowan possessed himself of the vacated seat. One of the hussars looked madly jealous for the space of one instant; then he strolled away to a group of men who were conversing in a corner.

Jane brightened at this gallant's defection. That was one disposed of. How would she rid herself of the remaining hussar and the prince? Short of clapping her hands, or swatting at them, she had no idea what to do. Her training as a gracious hostess had included no correct forms for booting a gentleman from one's vicinity. She remained silent and didn't look at anyone, least of all MacGowan. She had made that dangerous mistake once already.

Luckily her newly insipid manner provided such a contrast to her former vivacity that the prince and the hussar soon wandered off of their own accord, to the pretty wife of one of the Swiss delegates who was talking animatedly to the Prince de Ligne.

"At last," MacGowan said under his breath.

"We are in public, sir," Jane whispered back.

"Not so public that we can't exchange words for one moment," he returned.

She looked at him helplessly. "Now I know why illicit lovers write letters which are later used against them. There is so much to say; so little time to say it."

He nodded; a muscle on his temple twitched, but there was no other outward sign of emotion. "I couldn't put what we have into words if I tried. There is so much that could never be described."

Jane nodded and spoke so softly that he had to bend toward her to hear at all. "There is so much more."

"So much more than what?" he asked with a tender smile.

She shrugged. There was really no way to explain the awe she had felt in his arms—not at his ardor, or even at her response, but at the mere fact of their being together, with each other, at that particular time and place. The wonder of the situation had overwhelmed her then, and it overwhelmed her now into silence.

"Well, perhaps you will tell me someday. Meanwhile, I have an idea for our next meeting," he said, still speaking low.

She looked at him in such eagerness that he was almost moved to laugh. But not quite. He would tease her later, when there was time.

"Does it involve trusting someone else with the secret?" she asked. "I am deeply embarrassed that Wilhelmine . . . I know we can trust her, but it was rather awkward to look her in the face."

"My prudish Englishwoman! You are doing nothing wrong, and I'm certain she told you so," MacGowan said.

"She did. Well, sir? What have you thought of?"

"I've thought of riding with you in the Vienna Woods. This morning's jaunt with Flora put the idea into my head. We could ride out with her and your brother-in-law. We might get in a bit of matchmaking while we're about it."

"Matchmaking? How will it serve us to be their chaperons?" Jane demanded in a normal voice. She was alarmed at the sound and instantly turned about, but the drawing-room chatter had effectively covered anything strange in her tone. She realized, with a wry smile, that they might as well have been speaking in regular timbres the whole time.

"For the details you must trust me. I haven't quite thought them up. But may I make the engagement? I assure you, this will pass for a clever maneuver on our parts to get those two into each other's arms." He followed her head, no longer whispering, talking in as offhand a manner as though he were discussing the weather.

"I'll trust you. You know that," Jane said. She would really have to try to be more clever in this matter of secret meetings. If she took Pauline into her confidence, something might be contrived. . . . Though she had suggested to MacGowan that he take the entire burden of planning and scheming onto his shoulders, she felt guilty in the event. All she had to do was place her trust in him, follow where he led, and enjoy herself in his arms. It really wasn't fair. "I'll be better," she added, meaning to try to convey some of these feelings.

"Better than perfection? Don't try, ma'am. You'll be the death of me," MacGowan said with a grin.

Jane hesitated, on the point of beginning some convoluted explanation, then gave up. She burst out laughing.

For the first time since MacGowan had entered the room, the couple had many pairs of sharp eyes upon them, prominent among these being the Countess Zlotska's and the Prince de Ligne's.

"Oh, dear," Jane said softly.

"Not to fear, my lady." MacGowan made an extravagant gesture. "You have merely been kind enough to laugh at one of my famous *bons mots.*"

"Are you famous for those, sir? I hadn't heard."

"No." He shrugged his shoulders, which Jane thought all the more grand and broad for having seen them unclothed. Leaning near, he whispered one last time. "I had never thought to come away from my experience with you with a reputation as a wit."

Come away! Jane's fascinated thoughts of his shoulders ended abruptly. She looked at him in sudden dismay, wondering if he were already planning to end the affair. She changed her expression instantly, hoping he hadn't noticed it, and exerted herself to be cordial and impersonal with her lover.

She must have succeeded. They were joined, after a few moments, by another of her guests who was attracted by her charming conversation, and the morning passed away in intelligent talk, the sort of talk which would have fascinated Jane were she not busily looking forward to the next time she and Archie could be together.

7

"OH, JEANNIE," Lady Flora MacGowan said, "how I detest parties. How they bore me. This is all so difficult."

"Oh, aye," muttered the maid in a tone which expressed sympathy yet also revealed, ever so slightly, that there were some folks who would not mind being in a position to be bored with parties. She fastened the last small button on her mistress's evening gown of pale blue *mousseline de soie* and wandered off across the room, shaking her head, in search of the matching shawl.

Flora regarded her reflection in the floor-length looking glass. With her cool flaxen hair and cooler blue eyes, she resembled an ice maiden in this gown. The ensemble was new. Lady Averham, while agreeing that Flora had plenty of dresses, many of which had not been worn during her recent Season, had nevertheless insisted that her young charge must have something from one of the fashionable French modistes who thronged the city. Lord Foxburgh had not objected; indeed, it had been as much his idea as Lady Averham's to display his daughter to her fullest advantage.

Flora thought little of clothes, and she was too frugal to be pleased that her father would waste his money on useless fripperies. But even she had been delighted with the outcome of the expedition. The couturier had seemed to understand and agree with the untouchable image the young Scottish lady wished to project, and Flora did not doubt that this gown would prevent a renewal of those tiresome attentions with which some of the silly young men from the British delegation persisted in troubling her.

"My leddy, I've another note from that Sassenach."

Jeannie, returning to Flora's side, dug into her apron pocket. "Forgot it till now."

Flora held out her hand for the missive, opened it, and scanned with a bored expression some extravagant professions of love, written in a clumsy English. Crossing to her dressing table, she placed the note inside a drawer, where it joined a stack of other, similar messages in the same handwriting. She narrowed her eyes. If she were the man, and Bronsky the woman, she would have more than enough material to compromise him.

"Why do ye allow it, my leddy?" Jeannie was nearly whining as she set a length of filmy gauze about her mistress's rigid shoulders. "It's nae comfortable for me to skulk about the streets, meeting that one. He's nae even got a servant to run his errands."

"I suspect he is dreadfully poor. Possibly even baseborn," Flora said with a shrug. "I'm sorry he provides no one for you to flirt with, Jeannie. You may flirt with himself if you wish."

"Gae on with ye, my leddy," Jeannie said with a toss of her curls. "I've enough on my plate with that Johann. Doesna understand a word of plain English, that one."

"Well, amuse yourself, but take care," Flora warned. "Remember we're in a savage foreign country—worse than England."

"Aye, but once you made me promise to stay, I didna think a bit o' fun would come amiss to pass the time."

"Quite so. But don't let this Johann take advantage of you."

Jeannie wrinkled her freckled nose. "Don't ye worrit yersel', my leddy. The house spy, he is. I thought I'd hae it over the housemaids by snaring him for my flirt."

"The house spy?" Flora's eyes opened wide.

"Oh, I ferget yourself dinna pay much heed to such," Jeannie said importantly. "Ye know, my leddy, he's the one looking for secrets for the king here."

"Emperor," Flora murmured in a thoughtful tone.

"They're all over the city, I hear tell. Spies in the households, I mean."

"It doesn't seem to be a very discreet system," Flora mused. "Tell me, Jeannie. Do you suppose your Johann would be willing to take on another assignment for a bit of pocket money?"

"Why, my leddy, what can ye wish in that line?"

Flora smiled serenely. "I believe it's time that my friend Monsieur Bronsky was investigated. I cannot proceed with my plans until I find out everything about him."

"Why not forget your plan, ma'am? Have that Lord Averham, her leddyship's brother-in-law. He's soft on ye, the house is all agreed on that, and rich and titled and all."

Drawing herself up, Flora said, "You know my feelings on the subject, Jeannie." And though the maid had a few more things to say in Averham's favor—his good looks had struck her when she had seen him in the street one day, and Jeannie had an eye for a good-looking man— her mistress would brook no further discussion on the matter.

Flora was a little distracted as she put the finishing touches to her toilette: a small diamond pendant and earrings, to continue the ice-maiden theme of the gown. Averham's attentions worried her more than she would admit. She could too easily see herself caught in his net. And then what would become of her? She would be an English baroness, and it was Scotland she loved and needed. She would bear innumerable children, as her poor mother had—or perhaps only one.

She, Archie, and their older brother were the only three surviving children of their family, but there had been twelve babies altogether before Lady Foxburgh had finally been carried off with childbed fever when Flora was six. The worst of it was that Mama had seemed to welcome the constant childbearing; a mental deficiency, Flora was convinced, brought on by the married state, and one which she herself had no wish to suffer.

A husband was necessary, that much Flora knew. Oh, she might cherish dreams of an independent single life, but when one was single one must always be wary. Marriage was the only sure way to stanch the flow of offers from gentlemen eager to trap the wealthy daughter of an earl. Flora had been nearly trampled by fortune-hunters during her London Season; and Father would surely drag her to every Season until she was off his hands. He was displaying her here in Vienna, wasn't he, as if she were a monkey on a leash? His air of innocence on the issue did not fool Flora in the least.

Yes, marriage was the way out of the trap. A marriage of convenience, in which she would hold the purse strings and thus direct her own future, was the most attractive option. She would have peace; and, most necessary of all, she would have the upper hand.

Head held high, Lady Flora MacGowan marched from her room, quite ready to depress the pretensions of the entire outlandish continent of Europe—not excepting one persistent English baron.

"And where do you go tonight?" Chloe was asking her sister as Phyllida's maid, Liesl, put the finishing touches to her young lady's simple coiffure.

"Oh, I don't know." Phyllida was bored by the mere thought of the evening to come. Her mind was going over and over the music she wished she could stay at home and play; her fingers itched to put in another hour at the pianoforte before she slept, but when she returned home it would be too late and would disturb the others. Unless, perhaps, she might steal away to the schoolroom instrument . . .

"If only I could go in your place," Chloe said with a deep sigh. "If we looked more alike, Mama might not even notice. She's been preoccupied of late."

Phyllida was roused to laughter. "Mama would have to be a deal more preoccupied to mistake you for me. And I'm afraid her distraction only means she is concentrating on marrying me off." Her laughter died at the thought. "And after she promised me she wouldn't."

"Is she still thinking of Mr. MacGowan for you?" Chloe asked, more than ready to collect the latest gossip while her sister was in a rare communicative mood.

"Yes . . . no . . . I don't know. He has no title, you know, and I always thought that Mama would wish me to catch a title. I simply pay no attention to anyone," Phyllida said, staring past the mirror into a more distant realm.

"How silly of you! You are meeting so many fascinating gentlemen."

Phyllida spoke in a dreamy tone. "Do you know, I have heard that Monsieur de Talleyrand, the French representative, employs a musician to play to him every night. He can't sleep, it seems, and the music serves as a background for his work. Oh, if only I had known about that position! It sounds like heaven. Such work would be paradise to me. For that, Chloe, I would have played one of the dramatic tricks you rave on about. I might have dressed as a boy . . .'' Phyllida dismissed Liesl's efforts with a wave of her hand and continued to gaze unseeing into her mirror. "Though one hears, to be sure, that Talleyrand has employed the same young man for years.''

Chloe took a disgusted look at her sister. "Good gracious, Phyl, this is such a waste! You don't want to be out at all, do you? You really would as soon chain yourself to your instrument.''

"So I've told Mama a thousand times, but she won't listen,'' Phyllida acknowledged.

"And I want all this so much!'' Chloe's dark eyes sparked in anger. "You are wasting Vienna, Phyl, and I can't bear to see it!'' With her accustomed drama, she twirled out of the room.

Phyllida exchanged a glance with Liesl. It had to be admitted: Chloe probably had a brilliant future ahead of her as the passionate woman she so desperately wished to be. She already had the gestures down perfectly.

As it turned out, the engagement for that evening was at the very house where Phyllida secretly longed to be employed: the Kaunitz Palace near the Averhams' in the Johannesgasse, seat of the French delegation. Jane and her trio of young ladies had received a special invitation from Dorothea de Talleyrand-Périgord, Talleyrand's hostess and niece by marriage, who had met them at her sister Wilhelmine's. The four were attended by Lord Averham, whose presence the young countess had specifically requested. One could not have too many handsome men at one's parties!

Jane, in a pomona-green watered silk which suited her to perfection, knew she was in her best looks. She always seemed to be these days, cheeks flushed with excitement, eyes sparkling in anticipation of the next time she would glimpse her lover. She was positively startled by the vision which greeted her these days whenever she looked into a mirror. And she noticed that nearly all the women of her acquaintance here in Vienna were blessed with those same heightened looks she perceived in herself.

She suspected that her senses had been sharpened by her body's unaccustomed state of awareness. Years ago, during her pregnancies, it had seemed that every other woman Jane saw was either increasing or had a babe in arms. Now every way she turned Jane saw a woman in love; or at least a woman mightily excited by the attentions of some man. There must be a thousand love affairs all going on at the same time in Vienna during these frantic weeks. What madness was the Congress bringing out in all its delegates and hangers-on?

The thought had struck Jane that what she had with MacGowan might be the result of some collective insanity, a notion which amused rather than distressed her. It didn't matter how they had found each other. They were meant to be together for these few precious weeks. And as for the future?

She could see it clearly. She would continue on her course as a fashionable widow and the mother of two daughters. She would see first Phyllida, then Chloe married to excellent young men. Phyllida would surely find her happiness in Vienna; hadn't her mother found hers?

And whenever the affair came to an end, Jane intended to be cool, collected, and willing to preserve a friendship with MacGowan. Most of the great ladies she knew in Vienna had ex-lovers in their circle of acquaintance.

Resolutely Jane concentrated on the matter at hand, dinner at the Kaunitz Palace. They were lucky to have been asked. Talleyrand's great chef, Carême, worked a peculiarly French magic almost nightly. The embassy was truly set off from the other delegations by virtue of this one asset.

"I say let that old fox Talleyrand try to impress us into thinking France should be included on the list of great powers," Averham murmured into Jane's ear as they waited in the entry to be announced. "I'm more than willing to reap the benefits of his table."

With an admonishing smile Jane shook her head at Robbie, then turned to shepherd Phyllida, Petra, and Lady Flora into the reception room, where their host awaited them.

"Ah, madame." Talleyrand clasped Jane's hand in

both of his. He was a small man, sixtyish, crippled in one foot since childhood, and unprepossessing physically. Yet he exuded a magnetism which could be ignored by no one. Bonaparte had bestowed upon this talented minister the title of Prince de Bénévent, and he was still accorded the style although its granter was in disgrace on Elba. No one would have known how to deny it to him. "I must thank you," Talleyrand went on. "You and your lovely charges make it an eternal spring."

"It is I who thank you, Prince, for the honor of the invitation." Jane warmly returned the pressure of his hands. Strange—this man had annoyed her on first acquaintance, even frightened her with his smoothness, his suave determination to be all things to all people and to use each soul he met for his own advancement. Now she was up to anything: even a lighter-than-air flirtation with one who had been Bonaparte's closest associate until he had prudently switched his loyalties to the Bourbons during the past eventful spring.

Jane's brother-in-law and the three girls next came in for their share of the great man's attention. Then Averham lingered by Talleyrand's sofa conferring with him, or at least exchanging subtle pleasantries, while Jane took the young ladies to make their curtsies to Talleyrand's niece, the Comtesse de Talleyrand-Périgord. Petra especially seemed to have much in common with Dorothea, Jane noticed. The beautiful young countess was barely past her twenty-first birthday, yet she was handling with an admirable, inborn ease the demands of her place as a political hostess. In her way, she was quite as pragmatic as little Miss Schmidt.

Petra would make no poor showing as a hostess, Jane suspected, seeing her goddaughter and Dorothea laugh together over some absurdity of the past night's ball. Dorothea was a princess of Courland, the sister of proud Wilhelmine, and had been brought up to run great households, while Petra .. yes, there was something to be said for chance as well as breeding. But Petra would likely never have the chance to let her talents shine despite her energetic plans to marry herself well. Poor Petra! And the girl would not appreciate one's pity, Jane thought, drawing her eyes from the sight of her vivacious goddaughter. She only hoped the girl was not getting herself into deep waters.

She turned to the other girls in her care. Flora and Phyllida, companions in coldness and languor, were standing by looking bored. Jane shot the fair, dissatisfied faces an exasperated glance and nearly said something very sharp. She had no control over Flora, of course, and though she wished the young woman would open her heart in private, would become more natural and easy in society, she really had nothing to say about it. She did have a chance of doing something with her daughter, however. How dared Phyllida look so sleepy, so languid, so pale and insipid!

Jane caught her breath. Suddenly she was back at the party in her own first Season as a young matron, hearing two ladies of her acquaintance refer to her in precisely those words which had just run through her mind. "Pale and insipid!" The insult had haunted her long after the pallor had given way to blooming cheeks, the shy awkward ways to social adeptness.

"My dear," Jane said softly, squeezing her daughter's waist, "I believe I might ask Dorothea to open the instrument. Would you be willing to perform, or would it bore you?"

"Oh, Mama!" Phyllida's shining eyes were all the answer Jane needed.

Dorothea, who had perhaps been a shy and awkward girl herself not so many years ago, was perfectly happy to open the pianoforte. "Indeed, Miss Bellfort, I would love some music, but I am afraid you might find yourself the only one playing tonight. My guests have many aspirations, but few of those take a musical turn. Unless you would oblige us also, dear Lady Flora?"

"I wouldn't think of it, ma'am," Lady Flora said, bowing in her frosty way. Then she let a little smile reach her eyes. "I'd never play on the same night as Miss Bellfort. I'm vain enough to wish compliments."

"Most generous, Lady Flora," Averham murmured quite near her ear.

Flora started badly, Jane noticed. Robbie did have an effect on the girl, if it wasn't precisely the one he wished. "Hardly generous," Flora said in a tone of dismissal. "You must have heard your niece play."

Phyllida hurried to the instrument in the wake of her hostess, leaving the rest of the party to find chairs in the elegant reception room. Soon the first movement of the *Fidelio* overture filled the air.

Jane cast a certain look in the direction of the pianoforte. For a wonder, Phyllida was not yet immersed in her art and caught her mother's eye. The playing softened appreciably.

"There!" Jane sat back in satisfaction. A little thrill of pride ran through her; a different sort of pride than any she had known. For once, she was being an admirable duenna. Phyllida was happy. Petra had moved across the room with Dorothea, and the two dark young beauties were talking to a trio of admiring Polish dignitaries. Flora might look displeased, but Robbie was making it impossible for the girl to escape his clutches. Her brother-in-law caught Jane looking at him and Flora. He winked in friendly conspiracy.

She smiled back, admitting to herself that, aside from her suggestion that Phyllida play the pianoforte, she had had nothing to do with the disposition of her charges. A real duenna would have directed the operations, perhaps to achieve the same results, but directed them nonetheless.

Alone for the moment, she watched her daughter at the instrument. Phyllida was so lovely with that expression of serene joy upon her face, varied now and again by a serious frown as she came to a place in the music which still dissatisfied her. Yet not one of the many young men here tonight seemed to notice. It was as if Phyllida were indeed stamped with the label she had given herself: "Not ready." That was nonsense, of course. Phyllida was precisely the proper age to have a grand time at this round of parties.

Or was she? Memories of her own early youth rushed in on Jane again, and she determined not to allow herself to wish that Phyllida were different. She must be satisfied that her daughter cared so deeply about her music, and trust to time—and a steady course of parties—to do the rest.

Her thoughts roved to the one of her girls who was absent tonight. Jane had put off for some time the engaging of another English governess for Chloe. The girl's last preceptress had left to go back to England a few months before. When a few efforts at replacing Miss Stoddard had come to naught—there were so many women of doubtful references and doubtful skill looking for jobs in Vienna just now!—Jane had decided to let the project wait.

Chloe was not altogether forsaken. She had a sort of half-nurse, half-lady's-maid, Anna, but that pleasant young Austrian was of no use in educating the girl. A drawing master came in once a week, for Chloe's chief talent was with her pencil. And though the music master still visited the house for Chloe as well as the more enthusiastic Phyllida, and though Jane herself was directing her younger daughter in a course of serious reading, Chloe's mama still felt a twinge of discomfort. She had allowed herself to be distracted from her maternal duties.

But this would change. She would be a model mother from this moment on. Yes, she had fallen under Mac-Gowan's spell, but a simple liaison was no reason to forget the rest of one's life. Sexual obsession was new to her; she was fascinated by the power of her attraction to Archie. But she must not let it rule her life.

"What are you thinking?"

Jane started at the familiar deep tones. Suddenly MacGowan himself was standing before her. She worked to steady herself. How glad she was that she was sitting down and in no danger, either of trembling knees or of another sort of unruliness of the limbs—such as casting herself into his arms for a passionate embrace. She noticed, through the sudden fog his nearness had induced in her, that his father stood beside him.

"Good evening, gentlemen." It was a struggle, but she managed to keep a cheerful, impersonal note in her voice. "I was thinking of something private, Mr. MacGowan." She let a hint of reproof work its way into the last words.

"Pardon my precipitate greeting, my lady." Mac-Gowan's tone was so casually friendly that Jane had to look deep into his eyes in order to be sure that their intimacy had not all been a dream.

There it was; that secret gleam which spoke so clearly. Assured for the moment, she relaxed and forced herself to smile at Lord Foxburgh.

"Lovely as ever, Jane," the earl said, bowing over her hand. "No, by George. Lovelier. You must indeed be enjoying this tedious round of parties."

Jane said nothing. The truth would be most imprudent, yet it was nearly on her lips: *The parties are nothing. I'm having a passionate affair with your son.* She bent her head to hide a smile.

Foxburgh was nodding sagely, quite as though she had spoken. "Now, I, my dear, have more and more wish to be at my own fireside as these days drag on. You ladies like to dress up, but do you realize I haven't spent an evening out of formal gear since I arrived in Vienna?"

"I trust you go home to rusticate after the Congress is over, sir?"

"Yes, and as fast as I can. I'll take that daughter of mine up on her wheedling and escort her back to Scotland as soon as I'm free. A few months of hunting and fishing in Perthshire, and I'll be much more fit to take up my next post."

MacGowan laughed at his father. "Don't you believe him, Lady Averham. He's reveling in all this activity. Father can catch only one salmon in our native burns before he's champing at the bit to be back on duty in some foreign capital."

"A fault you inherited, lad, so don't chide me for it," Foxburgh said, clapping his son on the back. "Now I'm off to pay my duty to our beautiful hostess. Let Lady Averham charm you for a while."

The earl made his way with a quick step toward the Comtesse de Talleyrand-Périgord. She and Miss Schmidt were still the center of a group of admiring Poles.

"Hmm." Archie's eyes narrowed as his sire moved out of earshot. "I know Father is interested in the Polish question. But your goddaughter is also an attraction, Jane."

"I've come to realize that," Jane said with a sigh. "I do hope Petra will be sensible."

"The young lady strikes me as the epitome of good sense." Archie smiled warmly down at Jane. "May I take this seat next to you, ma'am?"

She was sitting on a small sofa just wide enough for two. She inclined her head, trying to match his matter-of-factness.

Their thighs brushed as he settled himself next to her; rather than readjust his position as he might have done, he pressed his leg against hers. "Small consolation, my love, when I'm longing for so much more," he murmured.

Jane understood him and agreed, though silently. She let a happy little sigh escape her. The contact, slight though it was, was precisely what she needed to get her through another evening of being with her lover in a public setting. "I didn't expect to find you here," she said.

"Father insisted I join him. He wangled an invitation from the Périgord when he found your family—I mean to say Miss Schmidt—would be here. Young Phyllida looks more contented than I've ever seen her." MacGowan nodded in the direction of the pianoforte.

"Yes. I believe she would be happy to miss dinner and play for us without a break until the evening is over."

"Don't worry over your daughter, Jane. She'll find her own way," MacGowan said with a keen look.

"So she keeps telling me. But if that way doesn't involve the society of anything but black notes on a page?"

"Perhaps she'll meet a young violinist. Of good family, naturally. I know how you mothers are." MacGowan spoke in a tone of tender raillery.

Jane smiled in return, but she hated, somehow, to be reminded that in the area of parenthood she stood so far ahead of him.

"Come." Under a fold of her skirt, he pressed her hand, their fingers twining together for one brief exciting moment. "I didn't mean to make you melancholy. Let's laugh and chat like friendly strangers. By the way, are you ready for that trek I mentioned once, into the Vienna Woods?"

Their next rendezvous! Jane had been avidly awaiting news ever since he had suggested the meeting to her. "Why, yes," she said, managing an offhand voice, though she could not keep the eager sparkle from her eyes.

"I've mentioned it to Flora. I didn't tell her, though, that I'd asked Averham to come along. I suspect she'd refuse if she knew."

"I suspect the same thing. So we are to act as though we're trying to throw the two together. Who will be in the rest of the party? Flora will need a chaperon. I mean, she will have me, of course, but if you wish to make the opportunity to—'' Jane cut off her words abruptly and glanced about. She had so nearly said something most indiscreet. Their intimacy seemed much too normal and would lead her to betray them if she did not check her behavior.

"I've given that much thought," MacGowan said with an understanding grin. "What say you to the eminently respectable Countess von Rosselmeier, lady of that Prussian delegate who is always falling down drunk at parties? I have reason to believe she would be delighted to be of the party if we include a certain Russian prince."

Jane stared and spoke in a furious whisper. "You mean to leave your sister's chaperonage to not one, but two women who are bent upon dalliance? Do you care nothing for her safety?"

"You don't trust your brother-in-law?" Archie raised an eyebrow.

"Oh. Of course. I'd forgotten. Robbie is every inch the gentleman. And if I warn him besides, there will be no danger—but how will this happen, Mr. MacGowan?" Jane spoke softly, and though no one was near, she was careful to say nothing truly compromising. She had already gone much too far.

"I don't know. Perhaps we'll contrive to lose each other. Averham will surely not be behindhand in such a scheme, especially since he will think it for his own benefit. Never fear, my lady. I have some little experience in secret missions. I can make it look quite as it should."

Jane looked into his laughing blue eyes. "Do you know, I believe you can."

"Your confidence, ma'am, is most gratifying," MacGowan said with a wink.

Some German dignitaries approached them at that moment, and the conversation took a more typical turn as the new arrivals became quite passionate on the fate of Saxony, one of the most hotly debated issues of the present negotiations.

8

ANOTHER PERFECT DAY, a day of bright chestnuts and lindens and unseasonably soft air, greeted MacGowan's party of riders as they emerged from the walls of the city of Vienna and traversed the encircling meadows called the Glacis, heading for the Vienna Woods.

Jane was no great horsewoman. Though moderately skilled, she had no passion for the activity. Her joy was all in the company, in the blue sky and the light wind on her face. The weather was glorious. MacGowan had found her a marvelous horse, gentle yet not plodding. Even if the day was not to bring her another interlude with her lover, Jane would have taken great pleasure in the outing.

Archibald MacGowan cast many a surreptitious look at Jane as the party rode past ripe vineyards and under colorful trees. Though making every effort to converse with the dour Prince Sartov, surely the least forthcoming of all the czar's aides, he could think of no one but the lady who rode so near. She was loveliness itself in her form-fitting golden-brown habit styled *à la militaire,* but it was not only her looks that enchanted him. Jane was better than perfection: she was his. MacGowan spurred on his horse with a laugh, scarce able to believe in his good luck.

"I can see you are a fine horsewoman, Lady Flora," Averham was saying, over the pounding of hooves, as the three couples wound their way along. "Do you ride to hounds?"

"No," Flora said shortly, averting her face.

Averham frowned, then countered, "I admire your kind heart. The most sensitive ladies in the world are those who hate the kill."

"I didn't say I hated the kill," Flora said with a dark

glance. "In truth, sir, the notion of killing doesn't lack its attractions at the moment."

He laughed in appreciation, leaving Jane, who rode behind them, to rejoice in the way they were getting on. Robbie was evidently smitten. Tamping down her personal excitement about the day, Jane wondered if this outing would, indeed, serve to draw her brother-in-law and Flora closer.

Then she glanced at MacGowan, and all thoughts of others flew from her mind. The second time. Soon, if all went according to his mysterious plan, they would make love for the second time. Would their coupling be as exciting, as shattering, in the full light of day as it had been on that dark night in the Palm Palace? And how would MacGowan ever manage to make it possible?

Her lover soon proved himself to be a manipulator second only to Talleyrand. Jane had her first taste of his string-pulling when they arrived at the country inn where he had ordered a luncheon set out. The hostel was a charming wooden structure, its marked lean proving that it dated from medieval times, its window boxes brimming over with unseasonable flowers of every variety. The company ate lunch at a trestle table under the yew trees of the inn's garden.

"This is the season when the Viennese come out to drink the new wine at every little tavern," MacGowan informed the party. "I wanted something quieter for us, though. Something private. And so I hired this whole place."

"Is excellent," the Countess von Rosselmeier said with an approving nod. "One does not wish to mix with the rabble, not true?"

"My feeling exactly, ma'am," MacGowan said.

Jane's feeling, which she left unexpressed, was that somehow the privacy of the little inn was related to her lover's plans for their interlude.

Goose-liver pie, roast venison, and an array of exotic cheeses and dark, chewy breads kept the six equestrians busy for some time, along with the new white wine which seemed to be *de rigueur*. Jane was too excited to eat and spent most of the meal pushing food about her plate in an effort to make it disappear. Her only other pastime was watching Prince Sartov, who sat next to her, consume all of a private flask of some unspecified liquor as well as a quantity of local wine. He could apparently not rouse himself to social duties, though Jane would have enjoyed a conversation with one who had the czar's ear, and tried by all her arts to start him talking.

After one of these failed attempts, she stole a questioning look at the prince. Was he really the countess's lover?

He was as dark and gloomy as the Prussian lady was stiff and phlegmatic. The pair sat across the table from each other, exchanging not a glance, as though they were barely acquainted. Jane wouldn't have suspected, but for MacGowan's forewarning, that the two were intimately associated.

The countess was to all appearances the most proper of chaperons for the party. If Lady Flora MacGowan was under the joint protection of Lady Averham and Countess von Rosselmeier, there would never be a reason to doubt the respectability of the party, and so all Vienna would proclaim. Yet both duennas had dalliance on their minds. . . .

As Jane mused along these lines, the countess suddenly put a hand to her side. "Ach, I have an ache. Lady Averham, if you would accompany me to a bedroom? You and the child." The countess's light eyes swept over Flora, who was suddenly bristling with indignation at the Prussian's lady's slur on her maturity. "We cannot leave her with three men, *nicht wahr*?" Again the countess clutched her rib cage; a spasm of pain contorted her features.

"Oh, my dear, I hope you're not seriously ill." Jane sprang to her feet, truly dismayed. The lady's tones were so heartfelt that Jane couldn't suspect duplicity, and her spirits sank. If Countess von Rosselmeier were really ill, then all romantic meetings were off. Jane's glance met Archie's and found him looking back at her steadily, with no expression.

A maid of the hostel led the three ladies upstairs and into a charming, rustically appointed bedroom. The countess leaned hard upon Jane's arm and sighed sharply as she settled into the feather bed. "Ach, I dislike to spoil the party." She shook her head. "But I am subject to these little turns. If I lie here for an hour or two, then go directly to house, I should do.''

"But will you be able to ride, ma'am?" Flora asked in that peculiar loud tone of voice which she often used with people she knew not to be proficient in the English tongue—one of the girl's least endearing qualities, Jane thought with a wince.

"Ride? *Nie und nimmer.* Of course not. I shall have one of the gentlemen to bring me in a carriage. The Herr MacGowan, I think.''

Jane caught her breath at this new evidence that the countess's was an accidental illness, then cautioned herself sternly to stop thinking of her selfish pleasure. There would be other days for her and Archie.

"That Prince Sartov, he is not a comfortable man,'' the countess went on weakly.

Flora agreed with this, in tones so hearty that Countess von Rosselmeier looked curiously at her, and Jane admonished the girl to be more charitable.

"Well, he is a foreigner,'' Flora said, tossing her head. She had the grace to cover her mouth with her hand in embarrassment one second later, as she presumably recalled that the sick lady was also one of that suspect breed.

Jane sighed in vexation and cast another exasperated look at her charge. Turning to the countess, she said, "Dear ma'am, the maid is bringing some sort of restoratives—I didn't quite catch what she said. Is there anything else we can do for you? Let me loosen your stays.''

"Vielen Dank.'' The countess turned slightly to allow Lady Averham's ministrations. "It is so silly a thing, to spoil your outing over what is probably no more than the too-tight stays to begin with. But I like a waist. Forgive me.''

"Please don't worry over it.'' Jane was still chiding herself for her private feelings of ill-use that the day had taken such a turn.

The door soon opened, and the smiling young maid, bearing a laden tray, entered the room. She and the Countess von Rosselmeier exchanged some words in rapid-fire German. Jane was fairly proficient in the language, yet she had not heard many of the medical terms which seemed to refer to the things on the tray. She struggled to follow the conversation while Flora, who hadn't a word of German, stood by and stared into space.

The countess accepted a cordial of some kind, and some salts, waving away the rest of the strange-looking concoctions. The maid left the room.

"Now, my dears," the countess said in a weak voice, "I must ask for you to leave me. Quiet, it is the best thing for one in my condition. Forgive me, once again. We shall gather at my apartment for a party to make up for this day."

"You are very kind, ma'am," Jane said. "Come, Flora. We must leave the countess to sleep. She will be much better for an hour or so in bed."

"Ach, yes. Tell the Herr MacGowan that I am very obliged to him for his kindness in waiting for me," the countess whispered.

As she shepherded her charge out of the room, Jane thought she intercepted a strange look in the languid eyes of the sick woman. She soon shook off this impression, telling herself she must have been imagining a spark of something—was it conspiracy? glee?—in the cold blue eyes.

Out in the garden, Jane explained the situation quickly to the gentlemen. "She has asked especially for your escort, Mr. MacGowan, but she cannot manage to ride. Oh . . . I didn't think. How will we ever get a carriage?"

MacGowan frowned. "That is a problem. The stables here contain nothing but our own horses."

"Simple." Averham was ready with a solution. "The countess wishes to rest. While she's doing that, we'll be on our way back to Vienna. We can send back her very own carriage. By the time she has had a nap, her conveyance will be at the door. Dashed dull for you, of course, MacGowan, stuck here in the middle of nowhere."

Archie shrugged. "I saw some books in a little parlor. A small price for a gentleman to pay, a couple hours' boredom."

Prince Sartov, looking glummer than ever, offered to stay in MacGowan's place.

"Lady Rosselmeier asked for my brother specifically," Flora put in at this point, glaring at the Russian.

"Females can be a bit demanding," Averham said in a confidential tone to Sartov.

Flora glared harder, this time at Averham.

Jane chose to ignore this byplay. "You are absolutely right, Robbie. The four of us must hurry back to Vienna posthaste."

Averham nodded briskly and moved away to see to the horses.

"Mr. MacGowan, the countess will be most obliged to you for staying to escort her. She asked me to convey that message," Jane said once Robbie had gone on his way. She and Archie were virtually alone, Flora having strolled off to direct critical looks at a rosebush while Prince Sartov paced the perimeter of the garden with a distracted air. Jane knew that her eyes were no doubt conveying a wistful regret that her planned private meeting with MacGowan was not to be. She hoped, at least, that she was able to communicate this much.

He favored her with a devastating smile. "She is a charming woman, and so understanding."

"The countess?" Jane started in confusion.

MacGowan shook his head as though she had betrayed disbelief. 'You do her an injustice, ma'am. True, she is some relation of the King of Prussia's. One may see that by her countenance, and his has been called 'an arsenal of a face.' But the lady has a hidden softness, a sympathy, if you will."

Jane could think of nothing to say in return, but she wondered, thinking of that peculiar look in the Countess von Rosselmeier's eye when she and Flora left her room.

Their attention was distracted then by Averham and an apple-cheeked stableboy, who arrived with the horses at the garden gate. MacGowan called out across the garden, "Come, Flora, your steed is arrived. Don't cause Lady Averham any worries on the ride back to Vienna."

"Really!" Flora stalked up, frowning at her brother. "Archie, you say such foolish things. I never cause Lady Averham any worries; do I, ma'am?"

"I must tell you, Mr. MacGowan, that Lady Flora is all that is proper. A perfect guest." Jane smiled at the girl.

"Well, ladies, let me toss you up. Or should I allow Lord Averham to do the honors?" MacGowan gave his

sister an evil wink, then turned to assist her chaperon
first.

"You shouldn't tease the girl so," Jane whispered as
MacGowan's strong hands went round the waist of her
golden-brown habit. For a lingering moment he held
her; then he tossed her into the saddle with a practiced
grace.

"If you could only see how you look," he murmured,
kissing her gloved hand.

Jane would have made some reply, but at that moment
her brother-in-law rode up to her side.

"Jane, the stable lad told me your horse here showed
signs of a bruised fetlock." Averham scrutinized Jane's
bay mare. "Can't see it myself, but you'd better have a
care, my dear, on the ride back. Keep it to a walk."

"I shall," she answered with a worried look.

"Devilish situation," MacGowan put in. "I wonder . . .
No, Lady Averham shouldn't have to manage my great
devil of a horse, and there isn't another one to be had in
this hamlet." He scrutinized the limbs of Jane's mare.
"I think she does favor the right front. Do you care to
ride my Sulla, ma'am?"

Jane remembered with a shudder the massive black
MacGowan had been mounted on. "No, thank you, it
suits my limited skill much better to be careful on Gretel,
here."

"Very well, then." MacGowan gave a brisk nod.
Then, turning to Averham, he began to give directions
for the ride back to town. "I brought us out by a circu-
itous route, you know, thinking of the scenery. If I were
you I'd take the direct way back. You'll simply go out the
way we came, then turn left instead of right at the fork."

"Hadn't we better hurry?" Flora called from the back
of her horse, which she had mounted with the tight-lipped
aid of Prince Sartov while her brother dallied with the
Averhams. "Lady Rosselmeier can't wish to be stuck out
here all day."

"To be sure, Flora," MacGowan returned. To Averham he said, "Perhaps if you . . . I don't doubt the
countess will soon become quite vocal in her desire to
leave this place. If you and my sister could ride on ahead
to the Rosselmeiers'? I hesitate to abandon Flora to the
escort of Sartov. I don't know the man well."

"But what is to stop your charming sister from staying with her chaperon and the prince?" Averham's eyes had lit up at the notion of a ride *tête-à-tête* with Flora, but he was evidently determined to be realistic.

"Indeed. Why would she leave my protection?" Jane added.

"Impatience," MacGowan replied. "I know my sister. If forced to hang back to a walk, she will soon bolt and lose herself in the middle of the Austrian countryside. Wouldn't be very useful, would it, she not knowing a syllable of the local language?"

"Such a situation would be most unpleasant for Lady Flora," Averham agreed, looking quite happy.

"What's this about me?" Lady Flora rode up, eyes flashing. "Should we not be on our way?"

"Impatient. What did I tell you?" MacGowan remarked in an aside to Averham.

"I am *not* impatient," Flora snapped.

"Good." Jane nodded in approval. "Then you won't mind going back to Vienna at a walking pace."

"At a walk?" Flora gasped. "Why?"

"My horse has strained something."

"But we've found the solution to the problem of the Countess von Rosselmeier's comfort," Averham said with an air of great innocence. "I am to ride to Vienna as fast as the wind and send the lady's carriage back."

Flora looked unsatisfied. "Why can't Prince Sartov do that?" she asked in a peevish voice. "He can escort me, and I will make the arrangements at Lady Rosselmeier's house."

"My dear," Jane put in, "I hardly know Prince Sartov." At the moment, the dark Russian was sitting on his horse, maneuvering it around the garden hedge and looking more moody than ever. Mercifully, he was out of earshot. "I have heard no harm of him, but I couldn't trust you to the care of a stranger."

"But . . ." Flora hesitated, then tossed her head in Averham's direction. "I suppose you'd trust me to *him*."

The baron grinned widely. "She would have to, ma'am. I am the head of her family, am I not?"

"Flora, I will keep you by me if you don't wish to go with Lord Averham," Jane said with a frown at Robbie.

"But she does wish it. I can see that she does,"

MacGowan said. "You may have her brother's permission, Averham."

Flora cast a displeased look at Archie.

He intercepted it and said, "Oh, you *do* wish to stay by Lady Averham. It's your choice, sister."

"But . . ."

"Flora." Jane spoke again. "Don't let these gentlemen badger you into anything you have no mind to do. It is very bad of your brother—pardon me, Mr. MacGowan, but I must be honest—to put you into a situation where—"

"I'll go," Flora interrupted. Her normally pale cheeks had reddened, and a determined expression had appeared in her eyes. "I'll go with Lord Averham."

"Only if you're certain, dear." Jane faltered, recalling that these arrangements would place her in an uncomfortable coze with the dramatically scowling Prince Sartov, who was even now approaching her side on a horse which looked as stodgy and vile-tempered as he did.

"She will be safe with me." Averham touched his hat to Jane. Reaching down from the back of his horse, he shook hands with Flora's brother.

"Such a lot of fuss," Flora grumbled. "Well, Lord Averham? Shall we be off?"

The two riders, Flora stiff in the saddle, Averham looking quite jaunty, moved off down the forest road in the direction of Vienna.

"Don't forget to take the left fork," MacGowan shouted after them. Averham turned and waved in answer.

"Oh, dear. I hope they'll be all right," Jane fretted.

"Averham is a good sort of fellow," MacGowan said.

"I've always thought so." Jane had a pleased smile for this praise of one of her favorite people. She turned to Prince Sartov. "Well, sir, did you hear the talk of my horse's injury? I'm afraid I'll have to beg you to escort me back to Vienna at a walking pace."

"It is my pleasure," said the prince gruffly, his hand on his heart. "I take much pleasure in serving milady."

"Why, thank you," Jane replied, looking at him carefully. His last words had been almost enthusiastic. Ought she to worry that he would try to take liberties? But he was said to be in love with the countess . . . It was all most confusing.

Flora and Averham soon disappeared among the golden trees. The three others stood looking after them for a long time.

Finally Jane was moved to speak. "Well, gentlemen, I suppose we should get on with it."

"Ah. To be sure." Prince Sartov matter-of-factly swung himself down from his horse and proceeded to lead it in the direction of the stables.

Jane stared. "But, sir, shouldn't we start out too? It is such a long ride," she called after the Russian. He must have been hard of hearing, for he made no answer. He didn't even turn around.

"Your pardon, ma'am. I'll return in a nonce," MacGowan said with an intense look at Jane—a look she couldn't begin to interpret. He, too, disappeared in the direction of the stables, walking briskly.

Jane remained on her horse, not knowing what to make of either of the gentlemen. After a moment she began to walk the animal gently around the innyard. The ducks and chickens pecking about in the sun, the flowers spilling over the garden wall were the only signs of life. The inn's workers were all inside the little timbered structure for the moment. Jane looked up at the gabled window which she believed to be the countess's bedroom, wondering if the lady was having a comfortable rest.

As Jane watched, a familiar pair of brawny arms reached out to close the window, and a scowling face looked down. Her gaze met a pair of snapping dark eyes and she looked away, embarrassed.

Then, at last, light began to dawn. Jane turned her mare about and began walking the animal in the direction of the stable.

MacGowan met her when she was nearly there. He was mounted upon his black charger and smiling broadly. "You look astonished, but knowing," he greeted her.

"I saw Prince Sartov in the countess's chamber window. What is happening, Archie?"

"We're playing Cupid, of course." MacGowan reached out a hand to clasp Jane's. "Sartov and the countess are all gratitude that we were willing to help them find a way to be alone together. With Averham and

Flora out of the way, there will be no chance of tongues wagging about their little liaison. I've given them my word that our lips are sealed.''

Jane laughed. ''Not only that, you've managed to throw your sister into company with Robbie. And now you are to be the one to escort me back, I suppose. At a walk.''

He shrugged. ''If you wish, though I had hoped you might agree to a more scandalous interlude than that. I paid the stableboy to say your horse was lame. A little joke, I told him.''

Jane caught her breath. ''Then this *is* all your contrivance, and it explains those remarks of yours I was too dull to interpret, about the countess's understanding nature. And I was afraid the plan was not to come off.'' She smiled at him, delighted at his ingenuity. Then a thought struck her. ''We couldn't possibly stay here. The prince and Countess von Rosselmeier would certainly suspect—no, they would know. They might even hear.''

Archie laughed. ''Do you seriously think that my idea of a romantic rendezvous would be a room next to those two? Give me a little more credit, if you please.''

Eager and curious, Jane replied, ''I don't understand you in the least.''

''Well, why should you? Follow me now, please. Didn't we set out for a charming ride in the Vienna Woods?''

Jane followed where he led, under lindens and chestnuts and aged oaks, past little streams and yellowing vineyards and wayside shrines. The land was alive with birds and small creatures, and the early-afternoon sun slanted through fire-colored trees. Jane felt her excitement build with every beat of the horses' hooves.

Finally Archie turned into a thick stand of chestnuts. There, nestled in a little clearing, was a small cottage. A welcoming white cottage covered with vines, with a tiny front garden and ornately carved shutters.

Enchanted, Jane held out her arms for Archie to set her down from her horse. He couldn't manage to do so without clasping her to him for a long, most satisfying embrace.

''Oh, Jane. For hours now I've been longing to tell you how lovely you are. You're as golden as the day.''

No, it was he, a blond Norse god, she nearly answered, but she was not used to paying compliments to a lover and stopped before her tongue got away from her. She must hope that her admiring eyes would say what she could not.

He embraced her again, quite as though he had understood.

"This is delightful," she said when he allowed her a breath. "A fairy-tale cottage."

"Go in," he murmured. "There's a shed in back. I'll bait the horses and tether them in the grass."

Jane nodded and turned to the cottage door, her hands trembling very badly as she grappled with the latch.

Inside there were two rooms, front and back. A large feather-tufted bed dominated one. The furniture was all charmingly carved dark wood. A window had been left open to let in air and light, and Jane assumed this would be better closed now that they were here. She found candles and a tinderbox on the center table and set about lighting the room. Then, regretting the necessity, she pulled the shutters closed.

The room looked somehow even cozier than it had; and the painted decorations, the pretty patterned quilt on the bed, had impressed Jane already with their air of life and friendliness. She looked about. An attack of nerves threatened now that the moment was upon her. Ought she to disrobe and await Archie in the bed? That would be bold; yet hadn't she already shown him she was a very bold female indeed?

This point decided, she fumbled at the high neck of her habit.

The door opened, and Archie stood still for a moment, looking at her. "No, don't undress," he said. "Wait. Let me."

Jane's hand fell to her side, and she did wait.

He paused to bar the cottage door behind him, and then he was beside her, taking her into his arms to kiss her. Jane returned his caresses in a fever of excitement, running her hands over his thick hair, then down the muscles of his arms, then wrapping her own arms about his neck.

"Come." His voice was hoarse as he broke away. Taking her by the hand, he led her to the bed. "Let me undress you slowly, piece by piece. I've been doing it in my mind for days.''

"Oh, yes." Jane immediately settled herself on the quilt. "Please."

He laughed at her eagerness, then knelt to undo one of her riding boots, not sparing a number of strokes and kisses as he worked the boot free. "You must have the loveliest legs on the Continent. In the world."

And so it went, garment by garment. Jane looked on as though she were seeing the tableau from a great distance: this handsome man exclaiming with delight, caressing each part of her, as she was slowly, so slowly uncovered. Every inch of her, each feature, came in for its share of exclamation and worship.

Finally, after what was either a few moments or an eternity, she was naked. And not only naked, but burning with a fever she had never experienced. "Let me do the same for you," she whispered, stroking his face as she sought to contain her impatience. She had a feeling she would perform the task much quicker than he had.

"No, darling," he returned, smiling. "This time is all for you."

These words spoken, he quickly stripped off his own clothing and joined her in bed.

They came together quickly, even frantically, though he had taken such pains to see that their lovemaking was slow and languorous. Her own need, a near-frenzy, took care of that. The second time was more leisurely, as she paid his body the full attention he had earlier given hers.

And then Jane noticed there was no longer a shaft of sunlight gleaming across the bed from the crack in the nearest shutter. "Oh, dear." She sat up. "Why do I fancy that we have all the time in the world when we are together? We must go. What will people say?"

"Nothing." Archie pulled her back down. "You're riding back to Vienna at a walk, remember?"

"And what if your sister possessed the wit to send my own carriage out after me?" Jane demanded. In truth, the thought had not struck her before.

"Flora do something practical, something thoughtful? I doubt that very much."

Jane sighed, relaxing against his chest. "So do I. Now," and she looked at him hesitantly, "I suppose that

while we're alone we ought to discuss whether . . . when
. . . you know.''

He kissed her. ''You are the most delightful contradic-
tion, Lady Averham. You can spend hours doing it, but
you can't mention it even once. And what do you mean
by 'whether'?''

''I don't mean anything. I simply wish to know.''

''Then you aren't going to fling me aside now that
you've had your way with me,'' Archie said thoughtfully.
''Gratifying. Most gratifying.''

Jane punched his arm. ''You are impossible! You
know—or perhaps you don't know—I'm not a woman who
has affairs.''

''I'm afraid you can no longer claim that title,'' he
reminded her with another kiss.

''And I've never been so happy. This is truly an enchanted Season, an enchanted Congress. I'm so terribly
grateful to Bonaparte for arranging the whole thing, however inadvertently.''

''I must toast him soon. But not in front of any of the
delegates in Vienna.''

They lay in each other's arms a little while longer.
Then Archie sighed, looking around the little room. ''Not
much of a place, is it?''

''It's perfect,'' Jane said. ''Did you borrow this cottage from a friend?''

''I'm not so indiscreet. I bought it.''

''You bought it! For one interlude with me—for I suppose we'll have no excuse to come here again.''

''Don't worry over the matter. If we don't manage to
come here again, I imagine I can lend it to friends. Every
other person in Vienna is looking for a secret place to
conduct illicit *amours.*''

''Somehow I don't like the thought of others here,''
Jane said. ''Am I foolish?''

''No. Neither do I. This is our special place, our own
secret. I bought it for you and you alone.''

Contentment warmed Jane from deep within. Nobody
had ever paid her such a compliment. She looked around
the little dwelling with misty eyes. Her husband had had
several homes, of course, but she had been a tolerated
presence and no more in any of them until she had made
the Vienna house hers after his death. Now her lover had

actually bought her a house, however humble. A tear rolled down her cheek and landed on Archie's chest.

"Now, don't turn into a watering pot, Lady Averham," he cautioned her. "What's the matter?"

"I'm happy."

"Shall I make you happier, or did you mean it when you said we must go?"

Jane sat bolt upright, sentiment forgotten. "Heavens! I let the time slip my mind again. Yes, we must hurry back to Vienna. I'm taking the girls to the ballet tonight, and then there is a *soirée* at Wilhelmine's."

Archie shook his head. "Real life invades once again. If only . . ."

"If only what?" Jane asked as she slipped out of bed and began to gather up her clothes.

He got up too, a magnificent creature whom she couldn't help gazing at in pure appreciation. He stared back at her for a long moment, a considering stare. A thoughtful stare.

Jane drew back a pace from his intensity, clutching petticoat and stockings to her chest.

He put his hands on her shoulders and kissed her softly, his lips lingering on hers. "This is a fantasy, isn't it? That's what's wrong. It isn't worthy of you, my dearest. Not this house, not my complicated machinations to allow us time in bed. We can't meet again."

"Can't meet again?" Jane echoed, appalled. The clothing dropped to the floor.

"I don't like it. Sneaking around, fearful that your daughters or my sister will suspect something—not to mention the very alert Miss Schmidt."

"That would stop you?" Jane stared. "I don't like it either, yet I, with so much more to lose, am willing to . . . You want this, don't you? Only moments ago you said—"

"I want you," he interrupted with another kiss. Caressing her bare shoulders, he pulled her closer. "I doubt if I can stop wanting you. But you're not simply a toy to be played with. You deserve more than this, Jane. So much more."

"But there isn't any more!" Jane cried, astonished. "Can you imagine anything better than what we've been sharing?"

"Yes," he said sadly, "I can. And I fear you cannot."

"Archie." Jane's eyes pleaded with him, though her words did not. "I don't understand you."

"Don't you?" He looked at her and shrugged. "I think you will someday, Jane."

"I am being thrown over." Speaking half to herself, she picked up the clothes she had dropped and covered herself. Suddenly it seemed important to cover herself. "This is what it's like when an affair ends. Oh, much, much worse than any of my friends told me it would be."

"I am not throwing you over," Archie said.

Jane gave him an ironic look. "You're doing a fair imitation, sir. Yes, you've had your way, and I suppose you had a sudden revelation that this was enough. You know my body now and can move on to the next woman." She shook her head, still unbelieving. "Not two minutes ago, in bed, you were so very ardent. You actually made a joke about me throwing *you* over."

"What can I say?" Archie, still naked, walked about the room retrieving his own clothes. "I wanted you more than I've ever wanted anyone, and I knew you wanted me. Let that be my excuse for plunging us into this discreet liaison. But when all is said and done, I don't want a discreet liaison, Jane."

"Then what do you want?" Jane cried, repressing with difficulty a childish urge to stamp her bare foot.

"You." Again he shrugged his broad shoulders. "You have me."

"No, I do not." He paused in the act of putting a leg into his drawers. "But perhaps there's hope. What do you say, Lady Averham? Would you marry me?"

Jane gasped. "That's what you want?"

"The idea came to me not a moment ago. I've been a fool to be satisfied with less. Why should we have secret rendezvous? You're not married; I'm not. Yet if we were, and to each other, we might spend whole days in bed if we wished it. We might talk in front of others with no fear of discovery. We—"

"I'm a widow with growing . . . with grown daughters. I'm older than you," she interrupted, before he could say any more impossible, alluring things. Fascinated, she stared at the sight of a man in the act of dressing himself. He seemed so calm as he fastened the drawers and drew on stockings. This was a momentous event in her life, and he acted as though nothing was out of the ordinary. Had he really said he wished to marry her? "Much older," she added conscientiously.

"I can count, Jane, and I call five years a trifle and your scruples a nonsensical excuse."

"I don't wish to be married. I've been married," Jane said, a hint of desperation plain in her voice.

"What is it you really fear, dear Jane?" He smiled, reaching for his shirt. "Is it the physical contact?"

She was near hysteria, she suspected. And he was not helping, trying to make her laugh at such a serious moment. "The helplessness. The taking of orders. One does promise to obey, you know."

"And you know, Jane, that husbands and wives are allowed to disagree."

"*I* was not." Jane lifted her chin. "I soon found out that the best way to handle marriage was to agree to everything, then deviously work my way around whatever I couldn't stand for. I'm not proud of the person marriage made me. I've been climbing out of that . . . that pit for three years now. Would you have me fling myself back in?"

"But marriage is a contract between individuals. You won't be tying yourself to the late Lord Averham."

"Are you so different from other men, Archie, that you would never force a wife's inclinations?" Jane's voice shook. "I've not only been a wife, I've seen other marriages. I couldn't smile at your mistresses when I met them at parties, as Laure Metternich does at Wilhelmine. I can't be that sophisticated."

"You think I'd have mistresses?" he asked incredulously. "When you're all I want? You can say that after the afternoon we've spent together?"

Jane shrugged. "Passion cannot last forever. It simply can't. I've planned already that we'll always be friends, Archie, when our liaison is over."

"Oh, have you?"

She nodded. "I . . . we will go our separate ways eventually, but I couldn't bear to lose your friendship altogether."

"None of this makes sense," Archie murmured. He pulled on pantaloons and boots, wound his cravat around his neck, and donned his riding coat in a chilly silence. "Jane, Jane—why be stubborn?" At last he put on the final garment. "I want you so much."

She was still naked behind her shield of underclothes. As he looked at her, she felt very naked indeed.

"You must give me time." She was shuddering from the cold and other things. Excitement was part of it, for no woman could be unmoved by an offer coming from such a man, but there was something more. Fear, and another feeling. Was it really only the certainty that in time he would turn to other women, and that she wouldn't be able to bear it? Not this time, not when she loved him so much—

She caught her breath. So that was it. She had thrown her heart over this particular fence. She was his, she was vulnerable, she could be hurt.

"I'll give you time," Archie said. And, immediately true to his word, he left the cottage, muttering something about seeing to the horses.

Jane began to dress, struggling with buttons and strings, making a mull of the business she usually entrusted to Pauline. If her hands weren't shaking so badly, she told herself, she could do it.

She stared into the tiny mirror above the hearth. How had this happened? How had she let herself be caught? Her traitorous body had led her heart right into a trap.

Love. She had felt it swell inside her when she looked upon the tiny faces of her babies, still knew that she would give her life for either of her girls. She welcomed that sort of love.

Love, though, in combination with passion, with marriage—absurd to open oneself to that much hurt.

She looked sternly at the flushed, anxious face in the glass. Archie must not know that he had the ultimate weapon at his disposal. He was already aware of her desperate passion. Let that be enough.

9

"OH, MY DEAR, you are so very lucky!"

Jane winced. What a fine idea it had seemed to tell her friend Wilhelmine, in the strictest confidence, about MacGowan's proposal. The worldly Duchess of Sagan, who openly talked of her wish to take only lovers, never again a husband, would surely ridicule the young Scot and urge Jane to stand firm, to keep her independence.

How was Jane to have known that Wilhelmine had been cherishing the secret hope that her longtime lover Alfred de Windischgraetz would marry her? The Duchess of Sagan was ready, even after two divorces, to settle down.

As Jane sat and sipped her tea, Wilhelmine elaborated on her own situation. She was giving up Metternich. Time alone would tell if Alfred would really come to the point, but she meant to be prepared for the possibility. For years she and the young Austrian prince had been as good as husband and wife to each other, but there was a world of difference between ties of the heart and those of the state. He, the heir of an old and distinguished family, to take to wife a twice-divorced woman! It would cause a scandal, to be sure, and she doubted if she could give him children . . .

Windischgraetz, Jane knew, was six years Wilhelmine's junior. Jane was acquainted with him, and she somehow knew he would never marry the beautiful duchess whom he clearly adored. Somewhere behind Wilhelmine's excited talk, Jane suspected the duchess knew it too. The fact remained that, for the moment, Jane could expect no help from Wilhelmine in scoffing at either the age difference between her and MacGowan or the gentleman's odd demands.

"And so you are to marry, Jane! He is truly the most charming man. I couldn't be more pleased."

Something like panic rose up in Jane's breast. If everyone was against her, would she find herself married

whether she wished it or not? She much doubted her abil-
ity to stick to any ideals in the face of universal disapproval; all the world knew hers for a wavering character,
easy to convince. She had not changed that much in the
few years of her widowhood. She had not had time.

Desperately, while Wilhelmine eyed her over the tea
table, Jane considered another angle which might save
her. If Archie's offer became public knowledge, she
might count on any number of objections to the match.
Lord Foxburgh would surely call such a union obscene—
his son ought to marry a very young lady, not a young
lady's mother. As for Phyllida and Chloe, they would
never approve of their mother's marrying.

Marriage! What was it but a waste of time? Already
Jane missed her affair. In the two days since the trip to the
Vienna Woods, Archie had been avoiding her house, and
she hadn't even glimpsed him at any of the parties. His
father, in answer to Jane's delicately phrased query, had
told her Archie was busy about some project which, in
common with most other projects in Vienna, couldn't be
discussed; but Jane knew that MacGowan was also vexed
with her for needing time to consider his suit.

It had happened so fast, she thought in exasperation.
One minute she had been looking forward to exciting
interludes with her handsome lover, the next he had given
the whole idyll the disagreeable scent of reality.

"Why did he do it?" she asked with a sigh.

Wilhelmine evidently understood. "Men sometimes
want more," she said in a soothing tone. "For you it
was enough, not so? The passion, the excitement of secrecy. But sometimes men are not so easily satisfied."

"It was news to me that any man has ever had a reason
to offer for a woman who would take him to bed without," Jane said glumly.

"You are cynical, my dear, and it does not become you."

"I asked him to give me time," Jane said. "But I was
only looking for something to say. I don't really want time,
and I don't need it. I know that marriage is not for me."

"You say that only because you are so recent a
widow."

"Three years?" Jane laughed.

"What is that? A pitiful few days compared to the time
you spent with that wretched husband of yours."

Jane stiffened; her marriage was a thing she preferred not to discuss.

Wilhelmine saw the look and laughed. "You may as well face it, Jane, it is no great secret that your husband treated you as many men treat their wives. I do wish he had left you with more matter for pride. The late Lord Averham will never be remembered as a great lover, alas, and he had no other qualities to lift him up in the eyes of the world. He was not a bad diplomat, but he had no talent, no style. And he was not kind to his wife. That makes all the difference in the matters of the heart, and the heart directs the bargaining table, whether the men know it or not. Metternich, you know, always treats Laure with the greatest of respect."

A tear appeared in the corner of Jane's eye as Wilhelmine confirmed what she had long suspected. The world knew her story and sympathized with her. She didn't know whether to be shamed or relieved, and wiped the tear away in irritation. "I don't miss being married. It was miserable. But for my daughters, I wished every day that I had never been born, much less married. If I had loved him even a little, though—if I had grown to feel anything but a sort of chilly contempt—how much more miserable I would have been!"

Wilhelmine shook her head. "You are too sensitive, my dear. Men should be the only ones with hearts, for a woman cannot afford one in today's world. So we come, at last, to the reason you would not accept MacGowan."

Jane nodded, brushing ineffectually at more tears even while she managed to keep her expression composed. "How could I marry him, only to watch him dally with other women? I've allowed myself to care." Sensible of Wilhelmine's situation, she did not mention her belief that MacGowan would tire soon of a female older than he, no matter what he swore to the contrary. Even older husbands strayed. The late Lord Averham had been twenty years Jane's senior, yet his eye had always wandered—as well it might, for love and even physical attraction had played no part in their connection. By the time Jane had grown into someone her husband might have found desirable, they had known each other too well and had too much bad blood between them.

Jane had always resented the late Lord Averham's

clumsiness in the arena of dalliance. She had known about each of his liaisons almost before he had. And his cold authoritarian manner to her had not been easy to obey, for she had had no respect for him.

She respected Archie, even more deeply now that he was wishing to do the honorable thing by her. She loved him. Yet marriage was a tie of state and custom as well as—rarely—of love. At least Archie wasn't Foxburgh's heir; still, a young man ought to marry an innocent girl, someone who had years of childbearing ahead of her. Archie would make a delightful father. He might even be the kind of man who would get to know his children— Jane had always varied between sorrow and relief that her daughters had enjoyed barely a speaking acquaintance with their papa.

Wilhelmine patted her friend's trembling hand. "Let me ring for something much stronger than tea, dear Jane. And think hard before you cast your young man aside. Is he not worth a little risk?"

Jane looked up at this. "I don't mean to cast him aside. My plan is to get him back as I want him. As my lover."

"Ah! I see. I was going to suggest sherry, but now nothing but champagne will do." Wilhelmine had a maddeningly knowing twinkle in her dark eyes. "We will drink to the chase, *ma chère.*"

Jane nodded, swallowing hard. She was a sophisticated woman of the world now and must act as such. And she must ignore the pricklings of doubt at the back of her mind, that odd, nagging notion that the heart might overcome obstacles more serious than those which stood between her and MacGowan. Was Archie not worth a little risk?

This, she knew, was her soft side speaking, that part of herself which she had always disdained. No woman of firm principles would give in to such sentimental meanderings.

Archibald MacGowan, meanwhile, was still reeling from the shock. That he should make the unprecedented offer of marriage to a woman; that she should refuse! Either circumstance would have been enough to make him shake his head in disbelief; the combination of the two was overwhelming.

Luckily he was able to clear his mind in the days after the ill-fated riding expedition. Castlereagh had need of him in the Polish project, and he spent all his hours in chasing down one person or another, in mixing casually at gatherings where those he sought would be found.

The job was easy enough. Every event in Vienna these days was a multinational crush at which an Englishman would be no uncommon visitor, and MacGowan possessed a knowledge of Polish which no one save Castlereagh knew about. Not even his father was aware that MacGowan had received instruction in the Polish tongue before his trip to Vienna; and few people would expect one of the block-headed British to be able to pick up what was said even in the more common languages of French and German.

Before two days were out, MacGowan had the identity of a young adventurer who was working diligently among the Polish element in the city, whose efforts, while passing for those of a patriotic Pole, were in reality most useful to the Czar of Russia's plan to annex as much of former Poland as possible in the negotiations to come.

The British were not so foolish as to believe that Czar Alexander sincerely wished to guide Poland into a free constitutional monarchy; but the Poles, robbed of their country, were desperate for someone to fight for their cause. Most were ready to set up the czar as their new hero, and the czar's agent was talented at stirring these fires. But if Russia did gain control of the kingdom of Poland, the balance of power in Europe would be dangerously shifted. Castlereagh was alarmed and working as hard as he could to prevent such an occurrence; and MacGowan had unearthed the new Russian agent's name.

Bronsky. Anatole Bronsky. MacGowan was mildly amused to find that Alexander's instrument was his sister's most persistent suitor. Flora would not take the young man seriously, of course; she had never yet allowed a man near her and would be unlikely to make a fool of herself over a foreigner. She was much too prejudiced. Archie expected Flora to marry some dour, countrified Scottish laird someday.

Still, he felt he must put a word in his sister's ear lest he be proved wrong; lest she think more highly of Bronsky than anyone believed possible. Archie thought he knew Flora about as well as anyone did—not well at all, in fact—but women were full of surprises. His situation with Lady Averham was proof of that.

Warning Flora entailed seeing her; and this would mean either coming upon her at some party of pleasure or calling at Lady Averham's house. MacGowan chose the latter option. At Jane's house there was always the chance that Jane herself would receive him. There might be an opportunity for a private word with her. At any rate, he would be sure of seeing her, as he could not be at a party. Two days without that pleasure had been of no use at all in dampening his enthusiasm.

Shown into the reception room where Lady Averham usually received morning callers, Archie found himself most unexpectedly alone. He associated Jane's house with crowds, he realized. She must be enjoying a rare morning of solitude. Either that or—his spirits drooped at the thought—she was out.

"Oh," said a high voice, "you must be looking for Flora."

Archie turned, surprised—for he had been certain he was the only occupant of the vast chamber—and beheld Jane's younger daughter stepping from behind a set of velvet draperies.

"Are you contemplating a career in espionage, Miss Chloe?" he asked.

"Yes," the young miss answered with every appearance of satisfaction. "Among other things. Shall I fetch your sister for you, Mr. MacGowan?"

"Yes . . . no, stay a moment. The servant already knows I wish to see Flora, and I must suppose he is alerting her. Would you sit down with me, ma'am? I wish your opinion on a matter of the utmost importance."

Chloe's eyes widened, either at being addressed with the welcome and mature title of "ma'am" or at having her opinion solicited. She looked very pleased as she sat down in one of the large tapestried armchairs which dotted the room.

Archie placed himself across from her. "You are most kind, Miss Chloe. Now." He believed a direct approach would be most useful with a child, yet couldn't quite bring himself to state his wish to marry her mother. For one thing, the matter would be all over Vienna by nightfall if this young girl was anything like as gossipy as she looked, and Jane would be mortified. Subtlety, then, must carry the day. "Do you ever contemplate a change in your household circumstances, Miss Chloe?"

She became even more alert. "Is Flora going away, then, sir? Will your papa finally let her go back to Scotland? Or"—she paused and looked wise beyond her years—"is she being sent there in disgrace over the Bronsky affair?"

MacGowan was so astonished to hear that name pass the child's lips that he couldn't maintain his trained-on impassive air. The fact that he had been endeavoring to sound out Chloe on the subject of her mother's remarriage was forgotten. "What the devil . . . what the deuce are you talking about? A Bronsky fellow is Flora's admirer, I know that, but she isn't encouraging him." He paused. "Or is she?"

Chloe shrugged. "Oh, I thought you knew more than you do, because of being on Lord Castlereagh's staff and all of that."

"What do *you* know, Miss Chloe?" MacGowan asked in careful tones.

The young girl looked fit to burst with her news, whatever it was. MacGowan wondered, studying her excited face, if she had anyone in the house to listen to her. Chloe's older sister, he knew, was wrapped up in her music—one could hear the pianoforte quite clearly from an adjacent room right now. And Flora would not be one to waste words on a child. As for little Miss Schmidt, she must be embroiled in her matrimonial schemes to such a great degree that spending time with an infant would hold no appeal.

"As a loyal British subject, you would be under an obligation to disclose anything you might know which would affect the security of the present negotiations," MacGowan said, quite as he might address an adult.

Chloe's dark eyes sparkled in excitement. "Oh! That's true, isn't it? Well, I suppose I must tell you, then."

"Please do," her fascinated auditor said.

Leaning forward in an attitude which Petra often used but which lost something in its translation to Chloe, the girl said in a rush, "The Bronsky person is a spy, you know, for Russia. He is to stir up things somehow, so that the czar will have an excuse to annex the whole of Poland. I didn't even think Bronsky was Russian, mind you. People think he is a Pole, but he has really never said, and we all assumed he was merely one of the hangers-on who are looking for opportunities this Season. Nobody minds what countries they come from.''

MacGowan was unable to make any response other than an astonished stare. A child barely in her teens was favoring him with the information he had just spent days in collecting.

Evidently pleased by this reaction, Chloe continued, ''I do feel it my duty to tell you also, since you are Flora's brother, that she is quite serious about Bronsky.''

''Is she?''

''Yes. I assume she wouldn't have had him investigated otherwise.''

MacGowan gaped. ''My sister has had that young man investigated?''

Chloe giggled. ''She wouldn't wish me to know it, mind you, but her Jeannie is such a rattle! And I can understand most of what she says, though the Scottish words are sometimes funny. I still haven't figured out what 'hash' means when you call a person that.'' She looked expectantly at her Scottish visitor.

''Why, something like 'blockhead,' I believe.'' He satisfied her curiosity with a smile.

Chloe nodded. ''It's what she calls Johann when he flirts too hard. Well, to continue. Of course, once I found out Lady Flora was conducting an investigation, it was a simple matter to find out the results.''

''Was it?'' Archie was having the devil of a time making sense of this morning. ''May I ask your methods, Miss Chloe? I find your . . . er, hobby to be most fascinating.''

''I must keep some of my mystery, Mr. MacGowan,'' Chloe said demurely. ''My mama says a woman needs to preserve her mystery.''

That was the God's truth, MacGowan thought. He was nowhere near knowing what Jane would be at. She seemed to want him, yet marriage was out of the question. Most unusual. Now her schoolgirl daughter was revealed as an amateur spy. At least he hoped the chit was an amateur.

''You aren't working for anyone, are you, Miss Chloe?'' he asked. It occurred to him that a girl of

Chloe's age would be the perfect agent. Who would suspect such a baby? And she was most clever.

"Heavens, no," the young miss responded. "It would be fatal, would it not, to concentrate too much on these political things, amusing as they are. I would lose sight of my main purpose in life."

"Which is?"

Chloe giggled again. She had seemed unsettlingly older in the last few minutes, but now she was again a thirteen-year-old girl. "I've already said that I cannot tell you everything, sir. Some things are . . . personal."

"Aha! A beau." MacGowan was satisfied to see Chloe blush. At least he had guessed one thing correctly. "Nothing serious, I trust?" He would make sure to warn Jane if her very young daughter looked to be contemplating rash actions.

"No." Chloe sighed. "At least," she went on in an earnest tone, "I did mean to be quite as abandoned as a great lady must be in these times, but there are problems. Do you know, I met *him* in the street and he didn't even see me, much less stop and stare in admiration."

"The beast," MacGowan said with an uneasy laugh. He had never yet heard a young lady discuss intimate subjects so frankly.

"Oh, no, it was no fault of his. You see, he has never met me," Chloe confided, "and I am not yet a great beauty."

MacGowan fought to preserve his serious expression, though her last remark tried him sorely, and he guessed that the child had fixed her maiden interest on some one of the notables crowding Vienna. Harmless enough. "I'm glad you don't plan any elopements or secret rendezvous."

"No," said Chloe with a lift of muslin-clad shoulders, "that must wait."

MacGowan had the unsettling feeling that Chloe would indeed carve quite a career for herself as time made her more mature, both in looks and in judgment. Jane would have her hands full someday . . . as though she didn't already, what with Flora and her antics.

"Tell me," he said, "does my sister plan to go to the authorities with what she's discovered about Bronsky?"

"I don't think so,"Chloe replied after a moment's silent thought. "I believe she was more interested in the fact that he hasn't a *sou* than in any political feelings he might harbor. She was most happy to find that out, Jeannie said.''

''Flora was happy to find out her suitor is penniless?'' MacGowan was not too surprised, upon reflection. Someone of Flora's cold temperament would naturally be relieved that a young man wasn't eligible.

Chloe nodded. ''Singular, don't you think? But Lady Flora is sometimes most singular, I find.''

The lady's brother laughed. ''Well, I believe I'll have a talk with her on the matter, whatever the case. I did come to see her, you know, but I've been waiting a long time now. Do you think we should ring and have the message sent again?''

''Oh, no. I'll go.'' And with a pleasant nod, Chloe got up from her chair and bounced across the room and out at a door—not the one to the main hall. What must be Phyllida Bellfort's pianoforte playing, which had served as a background to MacGowan's strange conversation with her little sister, grew louder as the door opened, then diminished as Chloe closed it behind her.

Once alone, MacGowan let several chuckles escape him. What was the world coming to? A schoolroom chit was privy to the same secrets the British delegation had been at some pains to obtain. Should he tell this story to Castlereagh? The great man would find it most amusing . . .

''Well, Mr. MacGowan,'' said a delightfully familiar voice, ''am I interrupting something?''

He found himself looking into Jane's face. She had entered the room silently and was looking at him in frank curiosity. He supposed that for a lone gentleman to be found laughing in her drawing room was an unusual occurrence. He got to his feet and shook her hand quite formally. Though he longed to do more, at any moment someone might come in, and that someone would be the sharp-eyed Flora.

''I've been talking to your younger daughter, and she said something funny.'' He would not chance any more of an explanation than that. Miss Chloe could evidently keep secrets from her mother.

''Chloe is an amusing little creature,'' Jane said, sitting down in the chair her daughter had just vacated. ''Well Mr. MacGowan, I'm surprised to see you here.''

''Why so? As it happens, I've come to see my sister,

but you must know that I can't stay away from you," he responded in a low tone. All at once, he didn't care whether Flora or a hundred other people came into the room. He reached out to clasp Jane's hands.

She withdrew them gently. "Not here. If you've sent for your sister, she'll be here at any moment."

"I know. And she'll see only that I'm making every endeavor to court the woman I want for my own."

Jane shook her head. "I can't listen to you, Archie, for you won't listen to me."

"Won't I? What remains to be said, Jane? I thought I'd said it all." He paused. "And please don't feed me anything more about your grown daughters or the couple of years longer you've been in the world than I. That's all evasion, and you know it."

Jane was surprised at his insight and not a little pleased at the compression, in his mind, of five years into no more than "a couple." "I may know that or not, but how do you?"

"Jane, I've been your lover. Can't you give me some little credit for using my opportunity with you to know more than your beautiful body?"

Blushing to a fiery hue, Jane was about to return some comment when Flora entered the room and put an end to the unsettling exchange. "Well." Flora looked hard at the pair she had interrupted. "Chloe told me I should find you here, brother. What do you have to say to me?"

MacGowan knew that his former purpose in coming to see his sister, to hint delicately that there might be something not quite right with her friend Bronsky, was no longer necessary. According to Chloe Bellfort, Flora was privy to an entire dossier on the subject of Bronsky and was well aware of the young man's foibles. Still, he supposed he must do what he had come to do.

"I merely wished to tell you, sister, that I have reservations about one of your beaux," MacGowan said with a smile which he hoped was disarming. From Flora's glare, he deduced that it hadn't been.

"Must you lecture me before Lady Averham?" she said in icy tones.

"Yes," her brother answered. "Her ladyship has been saddled with the dubious pleasure of looking after you, Flora, and she must be kept current with your goings-on."

"Do forgive me, Mr. MacGowan, but I think your sister is right and that I ought to leave the room," Jane interrupted with a smile. "If Flora wishes to confide in me, she knows my door is always open." And Jane got up in a swirl of muslin draperies, favoring MacGowan with an elusive whiff of her intoxicating scent as she held out her hand in an affable manner to bid him farewell.

"Thank you, ma'am," Flora muttered with another sidelong glance at Archie. She had the grace to look a little ashamed of herself.

MacGowan was surprised at how bereft he felt once Jane had left them. He had been counting on being with her for a much longer time.

Shoving a hand into his pocket, he realized that he had been holding on to something. Jane had passed him a note when she shook his hand in parting.

"Well, Archie?" Flora snapped. "I suppose you want to warn me off Bronsky. Why don't you mind your own business?"

"I merely wished to tell you that the young man might not be all he seems," MacGowan said, looking at his watch to calculate the probable length of time of this discussion. Let Flora take care of herself; he had a note from Jane.

"I know all about him," Flora said with a toss of her head.

Yes, she did. He consoled himself that his sister had seen to her own safety quite without his aid. "I don't wish to choose your friends for you, but be wary. And that's all I have to say on the matter." He bent to kiss his sister's cool cheek.

Flora looked surprised that what had promised to be a lengthy harangue had resolved itself in a sentence or two.

MacGowan didn't care what his sister thought. In two minutes he was out in the Johannesgasse, unfolding a piece of paper while a member of the Emperor Franz's secret police watched him, as he usually watched, from behind a convenient corner. Archie devoured the few words; wished he could keep the paper forever.

Then practicality reasserted itself. With a little wave of his hand in the direction of the hovering agent, he proceeded to light a cheroot with the precious note.

10

JANE RECLINED on the couch in her boudoir, the picture of fashionable languor. Though her attitude was by no means active, her mind darted here and there as she thought over what she had done. It would work; it must work.

She had been bold as any courtesan, but anyone who knew the situation—and understood it—would admit she had her reasons. Archie did want her, she had sensed that in their short interview of the morning. *I must see you tonight in my bedroom. Enter at the back at one,* she had written on a slip of foolscap, then tightly folded and concealed it in her sleeve before going down to the drawing room, where she knew her lover was awaiting Flora. The message could hardly be termed a hint. Would he take her up on it?

A knock came at the door. *"Herein,"* Jane said absently.

Petra entered the room.

Immediately Jane came out of her torpor. Petra was always so calm and practical, the only one of the girls who could be counted on to remain serene in any situation. Why, then, was she committing the singularly useless action of twisting a handkerchief in her hands, and, more important, why did she look to have been weeping?

"Dear girl, what's wrong?"

Petra came to sit on the carpet at Jane's feet. She was still crying, Jane noticed; those were tears sparkling at the corners of the deep dark eyes.

"Oh, madame," said the girl with a sigh.

"You must tell me if something is troubling you." Jane sat upright and patted Petra's shoulder. "Now, then. Do you know, I am probably guilty of an injustice where you are concerned, my dear. You are always so collected, so in command of yourself that I might not pay you as much attention as I do someone like Lady Flora, who is always out-of-sorts.''

''Ah, most gracious lady, how could I ever expect you to look after me as you do an English milady? Do not bring yourself to task on the subject.''

Jane smiled at the earnest words. ''You are too modest, Petra. You're my goddaughter and my honored guest, as I hope you know. Now, do tell me what's troubling you. I've never known you to cry.''

''I never have,'' Petra said with a sniff. ''It is a most useless pastime.''

Jane knew enough about the girl's upbringing to believe that she might indeed have blocked up the tears under a wall of bravado. ''You may find it does you good to cry when the spirit moves you, though I know it doesn't seem so at the time.''

Petra nodded, as though studiously digesting this information. ''I will consider what you say. And now, madame, may I make my confession?''

''Your confession! Don't tell me it's that serious.'' Jane had an inkling of what was going on, and she decided not to draw out the difficult moment. ''Besides, I believe I can guess.''

''You can?'' Petra's face registered disbelief.

Taking a deep breath, Jane looked her goddaughter in the eye. ''Petra, there is no easy way to ask this. Are you in the pay of the French?''

Petra gasped, and her eyes grew wide and scared. ''*Mein Gott*, is it that obvious?''

Jane shook her head. ''Not at all. But I know you, my dear, and I know how you long for security. I merely happened to notice, at the Kaunitz that night we had dinner with Talleyrand, how very well you and Dorothea got on.''

''We are friends, no? But I will not hide that what I say to her is sometimes of practical use to her uncle.''

''And only one such as I, who know something of your circumstances, would suspect that you came to Vienna with any other view than that of establishing yourself creditably by marriage.'' Jane gave the girl a reassuring look. ''Don't worry, dear. Your activities can't be common knowledge. Now, what shall we do about this? You have been picking up information at my salons, I expect." She spoke calmly, for when she had first suspected the situation, she had not let it worry her overmuch. After all, Vienna was a hotbed of intrigue. If people were unwary when they spoke at parties, it could not be said to be the hostess's fault. Yet if the hostess provided a spy . . .

"I must believe that no blame would ever attach to you and your house, madame." Petra lifted her chin. "I am prepared to say that I tricked you, for so I did."

"That ought not be necessary, dear. You won't be doing any more spying, I believe, or you wouldn't be speaking to me now."

"True," Petra said. "But I must make a confession to one other than you, and it is killing me. There is someone special—I have been using him shamefully. And you have guessed right: I can no longer do this, and so I have told Dorothea. I have stopped taking her uncle's money."

"Have you indeed?" Jane was much encouraged; if this episode was in the past, then there need be nothing said about it in the future. Petra seemed to have the project in hand, as she always did. "Now, may I guess the identity of this person you feel you must confess to?"

Petra flushed. "You may." There was an ominous rip as her handkerchief again twisted in her hands.

"Lord Foxburgh?" Jane brought forward the name with every appearance of casualness.

A convulsive little sob escaped Petra's throat, and then she nodded furiously while burying her face in the maltreated wisp of embroidered linen.

Jane was silent, stroking the girl's shoulder. She simply waited.

Finally Petra looked up. "I am ashamed of myself, madame. For a long time now I have been flirting with him, making up to him, and using the little tidbits he lets slip; turning right round and telling them to the French. But now I find that I have another motive than espionage."

Jane had never been able to imagine Foxburgh as a romantic hero, but she knew that Petra's taste for older men was genuine. She made what was not too wild a guess. "You are fond of him?"

Again the girl nodded, dashing another tear from her

eye. "You comprehend, madame, I do not feel that he can give me the establishment I crave. These English— your pardon, madame, but they always maintain the respectability, even in second connections. It is only on the Continent that I might find someone older, someone who has satisfied his duties to lineage already and wishes to please himself. But now," and she heaved a deep sigh, "those days are over. I have decided, madame, to offer myself to Lord Foxburgh as his mistress."

Jane caught her breath. "Petra, surely you're joking."

"You do not think he would have me?" Petra squared her shoulders proudly. "I flatter myself that I have every qualification for such a post."

"But what about your plans? Your very sensible plans? I have never thoroughly approved of such a cold-blooded approach to marriage as yours, but it is the way of the world, and so eminently practical that I've never felt it my place to counsel you. I understand you too well, my dear. But this new start I can't comprehend in the least."

"To become his mistress, it is the only way I may have him," Petra said in her ordinary matter-of-fact voice. "No English milord of his stature would marry a bastard."

"I wish you wouldn't call yourself that, dear Petra. Such a label in no way expresses who you are."

"But it does, madame." Petra shook her head sadly. "I have grown to . . . to care, and because of my birth I have no hope of more than a discreet arrangement. Oh, why did no one tell me about love? That is, I knew it to be a danger, and so I have handled myself. But why did no one tell me that this stupid love could not be avoided by the prudent mind?"

Jane had the unreasonable desire to laugh, but she held it back, knowing how levity at such a moment would hurt poor Petra. The logical little thing was in a sad state. "Don't do anything rash, Petra," she urged. "You have said you've stopped accepting money from the French; let that be enough for now. You may always tell Lord Foxburgh later about your activities—if you decide to— and meanwhile you can be thinking over your wishes. I would hate to see you make a choice you would come to regret—a choice that would close other doors to you later on. You are very young."

"Not really, madame," the girl said in that peculiar honest fashion which Jane had seen before in children who had grown up too early.

She clasped Petra's cold hands and warmed them between her own, wishing that she could see an answer to her goddaughter's problems. It was to be hoped that Lord Foxburgh, whether he harbored tender feelings for Miss Schmidt or not, would intercede for Jane's sake if Petra's spying should have some consequences—if Talleyrand's people should be so angered that they did something rash, for instance. Meanwhile, they would surely wish to know that she was not playing them false, spying for some other faction . . .

"I suppose we can expect a new would-be servant knocking on our door soon," Jane said smiling. "Or do you think Talleyrand will be more clever than that?"

Petra shrugged. "One other idea I meant to put to you today, madame, was that I might suddenly find myself in need of a waiting maid. That way, their agent could be close enough to me to see that I have given up all such activities."

"You are practical as ever, my good girl," Jane said. "The very thing."

"But it shames me to ask you to pay for such a servant—"

"Don't give it another thought. The price is cheap to set Monsieur Talleyrand's mind at rest. I sometimes quite like that man."

Petra nodded. "Dorothea says the same. Indeed, despite the young men gathered round her, I have come to feel that she is almost besotted with her old uncle. Take care he casts no spell on you, madame."

Jane laughed. "Why, Petra, you are the one who is fond of older men."

Despite the interesting revelations from her goddaughter, Jane found the day passed slowly. Yet again the household went to hear *Fidelio* in the evening—it was still all the rage. They joined Lord Castlereagh's party. Phyllida was thus assured of a fine evening, wrapped in the spell of her favorite Beethoven, and Jane had the pleasure of hearing the opera to the end. She had missed it on the night of her first tryst with MacGowan.

Would tonight see another such encounter? It would; it must.

This evening she did not allow her anticipation to blind her. She kept a sharp eye on her charges and was encouraged to observe Petra's maidenly and retiring manners with Lord Foxburgh. Good. At least the child hadn't decided definitely to cast her reputation to the winds.

MacGowan was nowhere in sight this evening. Jane's logical side excused him. This was the regular night for the Princess Bagration's *soirée,* not to mention any number of other politically inclined social offerings, and his duties—or his pleasures—might take him almost anywhere.

So much for logic. Jane spent the evening wondering whether her lover was avoiding her. By the time the chorus was hailing the faithfulness of the opera's heroine, to loud acclaim from the audience, Jane was in a fever over whether or not Archie would respond to her request for a meeting.

She tried by all her arts to still the many tongues which wished to speak to her, to deflect the requests for her company and the girls' at little midnight suppers, and finally succeeding in directing her party's footsteps homeward.

The hour of one found her just returned to her bedroom. Pauline, who had been taken into her lady's confidence perforce, was downstairs on the watch to let MacGowan in and was thus not available to array Jane in her most seductive nightrail or to brush her auburn hair into loose curls on her neck. Short of time as she was, Jane satisfied herself with removing her opera cloak and gloves and taking a quick glance into a mirror. Her gown was a low-cut silk in a rich gold shade which became her to a nicety. Her cheeks had a hectic flush, her eyes a strange sparkle.

A small sound at the door made Jane jump and put a hand to her heart. When MacGowan entered the room, having turned the handle carefully so as to make the minimum of noise, he took one look and laughed.

"No, I'm not here to murder you." He started forward, looking splendid and somehow larger than ever in his dark evening clothes.

Jane supposed she had this impression because he had

never been in her bedroom before; nor had any man. He seemed to dwarf the delicate furnishings. She eyed him uneasily.

"My dearest! Such a look! Have you been worried?"

"I thought you wouldn't keep the engagement," she said, and her odd discomfort disappeared all at once. He was here; he had come to her after all. She reached out her arms.

To her surprise, he stopped a few steps short of her. "I can't let you seduce me, Jane. That's all you're trying to do, isn't it?"

"It should come as no real shock," Jane said. "A woman doesn't often ask a man to her room in the small hours of the morning without having such a thing in her mind." She looked at him sorrowfully. "So you don't want to. You might simply have failed to show yourself here tonight. Now I suppose we must quarrel."

'I don't want to be enticed into your bed, Jane. That's what I don't want."

She sighed deeply. "Is it because you don't believe in a woman being so bold?"

"What a ridiculous thing to say! You know what stands between us. I want more from you than you want from me."

"I want you in my bed," she whispered.

She could not know how enticing she looked and sounded, he thought in a confusion of irritation and desire. So she wanted him, did she, and was bold enough to say it: her white arms stretched out to him, her lovely face pleading with him even as her body did. Did she think he was an animal, to be done in so easily by female charms? Did she think he had no rational side, no logic to guide him? He knew very well that the only way to win Jane would be to hold out for what he really wanted: all of her.

These thoughts lasted only seconds, and then others were crowding in to take their place. Two strides, and he was beside her. She was trembling as he took her in his arms. "I don't like it. You must know I don't agree," he had time to mutter before his lips descended to her neck. As hungry for her as she seemed to be for him, he brushed a wisp of sleeve off her shoulder.

Jane laughed low in her throat as she heard the fabric give. She had won.

An hour later, she wasn't so sure. They had come together furiously, as though it had been months instead of only a few days since they had last touched. She had no reason to be dissatisfied. He had been tender as well as wild; that had not changed. Yet something had.

"You're still angry with me," she said, speaking into his chest as they lay together.

He heard the soft words and kissed her hair. "Yes, my love, I am. You know why. Shall we discuss it?"

"I can't." Jane was a coward and knew it; but any talk of his wish to marry her would lead to a confession of her love. Worse, in any discussion of marriage Archie would probably show himself to be a man like any other, eager to bind and subdue a woman—and Jane was not ready to give up the perfect lover of her fantasies.

"Is it still time you need? This couple of days hasn't changed your mind, then. I had hopes that you had called me here to celebrate our betrothal." His words were satirical.

Jane could not miss his anger, his disappointment, as she felt his muscles tense under her hand. She didn't blame him a bit.

Some moments more passed in silence; on Jane's part, in a state of near-panic as she wondered what she could possibly say. She simply could not promise to marry him.

"No one wishes to be treated like a whore," Archie said into the uneasy quiet.

She had never realized those words could be spoken by a man, but she knew all at once that he had cause. She felt herself flush deeply and was glad the night would hide the physical signs of her mortification. "What a beast I am, what a selfish, horrid beast. How could I? I'm so very, very sorry." Pressing closer, she kissed all of him she could reach.

"You should be sorry." He disengaged himself from her arms, rose from the bed, and looked down at her. Even in the candlelight she could see the disillusionment in his eyes. "Jane, I am sorry too. I started this thing between us. I set the tone. But when it turned into so much more than what I expected, I imagined you would follow me. I was foolish enough to think that you must feel what I felt—what I feel.''

And what was that, precisely? He had spoken no word of love. Jane didn't know what his saying it would have done to her; perhaps she would have blurted out her own sentiments in the next moment. But what seemed to her his careful avoidance of that simple word gave her strength.

''If we must part, we must,'' she said, willing herself not to cry. There would be time for that later. ''Once again, I'm so very sorry for . . . for wanting you so much tonight. I hope you can forgive me for that. For all of it.''

He leaned down and kissed her lightly on the forehead. ''Jane, you've given me more happiness than I ever looked for in a woman's arms. I can't regret any of it.''

''Good. I certainly cannot.''

He dressed in silence and turned to look at her again only when he was at the door, his hand on it. In his eyes was a strange dullness, a sort of resignation.

From her bed Jane reached out for the bell rope. ''There. That ring will bring my maid to the door you entered by. She'll let you out.''

He gave a stiff nod, then left the room.

Jane lay back as stiffly on her pillows, and wasn't surprised to find hot tears running down her face. What did astonish her was the dead, finished feeling in her limbs— as though the fevered lovemaking of the night had never been.

MacGowan gave the maid a vail on his way out. Then, cursing his foolishness, Jane's lust, his own lust—cursing everything he could think of, in fact—he stalked down the alleyway and into the Johannesgasse.

He was staring at the shadowy cobbles, scowling, when he bumped straight into a dark-cloaked figure.

Even in his distracted state he automatically caught the person by the shoulders and took a look under a voluminous hood. ''Good Lord! It's Miss Schmidt. What the devil are you doing out here, my dear? It must be nearly dawn.''

Petra's dark, fearstruck eyes were visible in the light

of a nearby torch. "Winter is coming. It is not light so soon."

"A prudent change of subject, you think, to get my mind off the reason one of Lady Averham's charges is prowling about in the dead of night? In the dangerous night, I might add." MacGowan waited for the clever Miss Schmidt to allude to the fact that *he* had been prowling at their very doorstep. But she said nothing.

She looked too overset for slyness. "It is quite pleasant to see you, Mr. MacGowan, but I must be going now. As you observe, it is dark in these streets; though I think you mistake about the other. In Vienna, one is safe as in one's garden."

"No young woman is safe in the night. If nothing else, one of the spies skulking about could haul you off to Baron Hager's office."

She winced at his words, and Archie decided to be stern and fatherly. "I insist that you go back inside, my dear. What is it? Have you had words with her ladyship?"

"Never," Petra declared passionately. "She is the most gracious lady—an angel."

"Then why are you leaving her house? I am correct, am I not? You are running away?"

"I am certainly not running away," Petra said in haughty tones. "I am a guest, not a prisoner. And I must go from here for my own reasons. Private reasons, sir."

Archie glanced around at the dark walls of houses and saw several shadows that had no business to be there. "You are right about one thing, young woman. We can't discuss anything here. Come with me. Is this your portmanteau?" He picked up a small case she had been endeavoring to hide in the folds of her cloak. Briskly he offered the young lady his arm.

A few streets away was a small café which was open all the time; so Archie had noticed before on his wanderings through the neighborhood. It was a favorite resort of the young equerries of several delegations. Naturally a certain female element had made the place their haunt as well, the junior members of the various embassies having, almost to a man, the reputation for preferring dalliance to every other activity.

MacGowan ushered Petra quickly to a table in a dark cor-

ner, knowing that all who glanced up from their own in-
trigues and saw the pair would conclude that Miss Schmidt
was not a respectable woman. Thank God she was wearing
that hooded cloak which covered her almost entirely.

"Leave it on," MacGowan said when Miss Schmidt
moved to push back the hood once they were seated.

Nervously she nodded, glancing about. She was a sharp
young woman; he could tell that she had understood instantly the reasoning behind such discretion.

He ordered coffee for two and waited silently until it
had been set before them. "Now, Miss Schmidt." He
raised his cup, eager for the strong Viennese brew to work
its customary magic: to clear the head, to make everything
seem simple all at once. "Tell me what's amiss with you."
He paused and spoke the next words carefully. "You can
tell me if it's Lady Averham. I have reason to know she
can sometimes be a little unreasonable."

"You are a monster to say such things!" Petra looked
shocked by his lack of gallantry. "I can never repay the
debt I owe madame."

"A debt? It isn't like Jane to be motivated by avarice,"
MacGowan said, frowning at this new idea of his love as
a usurer.

"Fool!" Petra uttered the word in a tone of deep disgust. "It is not that kind of debt. I leave her in order to
repay her for all she's done for me."

MacGowan thought it most prudent to nod and say
nothing. He was amazed at his own words. Where had
those ungenerous remarks come from? He had told himself, as he walked down the back stairs of her house, that
he bore Jane no ill will for what amounted to a rejection
of everything about him except his body. Yet in the last
moments he had accused her of squeezing money from
her goddaughter; of being hard to live with.

Petra was looking at him carefully, as though gauging
his trustworthiness or his honesty. For the moment
MacGowan forgot to be insulted that a young woman
would doubt either one. He merely waited to see where
her examination would lead her.

"Yes, I will trust you," she said at last. "Who better
than you? You are his son."

"What has all this to do with my father?" MacGowan
asked sharply.

Petra cast down her eyes, then looked up again, directly into MacGowan's. "I have been a spy, sir," she said in the soft voice proper to such a confession. "I have been profiting by my acquaintance at Lady Averham's. Your father is among the people I have tricked into thinking I'm nothing more than a frivolous girl. He has let things slip—nothing important, from what I can judge, but I have given the information to the French. For pay." She stopped speaking and shuddered eloquently.

MacGowan was suddenly alert, and it wasn't the effect of the coffee. "Tell me more," he urged.

"I have said to them, those who paid me, that I can't do it any longer. I have told Lady Averham too, and she was gracious as ever, wishing me to continue in her house as though nothing has happened. But I am afraid they may be angered, those I worked for. I am afraid the whole story may come out, and that blame might attach to Lady Averham for sheltering me. I go away to prevent this. It is really quite simple."

"And my father?" Archie gave the girl his most penetrating stare.

"I go from him too. But if you would agree, sir, to choose the proper time and tell him why I go—that I stopped doing what I was being paid to do for his sake— I would be most grateful."

"I see." Now Archie's head was whirling. He gulped coffee and signaled a waiter for more. This young woman was evidently infatuated with Father. Most confusing. And Jane had been harboring a spy, however unintentionally. Petra was right; if the story came out—and all stories seemed to come out in Vienna, sooner or later— Jane might be looked at askance by all of society. And she would be devastated to be ostracized by the *beau monde* she thrived upon.

"And I will tell you something else," Petra said. Her small fist came down upon the flimsy table. Coffee sloshed over the edge of her cup, which she hadn't touched. Several nearby patrons looked askance at such an emotional display.

"Quietly, ma'am, if you please," MacGowan said, glancing eloquently about.

"To be sure." Petra leaned forward, speaking in no more than a whisper. It fitted in perfectly with the buzzing from nearby tables. Only an occasional shriek as a girl took exception to some liberty broke into the low tones all around them. "I belong to the Averham household in a way you would not guess, and it is all due to Lady Averham that I take my place there. It is due to Lady Averham that I live, sir. This I will tell you to prove how much I owe her, how much I would dislike to hurt her in any way."

MacGowan nodded at her to go on, wondering idly where all this was leading. He wasn't of a mind to listen to girlish confidences. The revelation that this particular young lady had been a spy was much more interesting.

"Years ago, my mother met the late Lord Averham in Dresden," Petra said, averting her eyes. "My mother was pretty, not educated, not of noble family. You may guess what happened. When she found she was with child, she followed him to England."

"Oh." Suddenly MacGowan saw a great deal he hadn't seen before.

Petra sighed. "She tracked him down somehow, I will never know how, for Mutti has not a word of English. She has told me of the shock she felt when she found he was newly married. And he rejected her, called her claim a lie, and left her, penniless, in that strange city of London, heavy with child."

"A sad story, ma'am, and it doesn't better my opinion of the last Lord Averham."

"It could have been sadder," Petra said. "My mother has talked of the way she wished to kill herself. There are many bridges in London. But luckily a young lady came to see her one day."

"Lady Averham?"

Petra nodded. "She had found out from her husband's own lips the story of my mother; and instead of laughing, as a society lady might have done, she sought Mutti out, she helped her. She sold some jewels to buy my mother and me passage home, and before that, when I was born in London, she became my godmother. And so she has been for all my life; a true godmother. She visited us when she could; she made sure we had all we needed, for my mother has continued to make foolish choices about . . . about men. Once or twice she even brought her own little girl to play with me. Phyllida has no idea we've met before," Petra said with a smile.

"Jane is an angel."

The statement was plain, matter-of-fact. Petra looked keenly at the man opposite her. "So I have been telling you. And she has been most gracious to me, buying me gowns, letting me share in this wondrous world of Vienna. I came here, sir, but to find a husband. The spying, it was only in the nature of a little pastime, to allow me to send some money home. But marriage has been my main object. I was not to be deceived as my mother has been time and again. Now"—Petra's eyes took on a special glow—"that wish is changed. Blood will out, as they say. But Lady Averham was so kind as to let me wish for a good marriage in peace and to work my wiles on anyone I cared to."

MacGowan did not stop to wonder over Petra's cryptic words about her wish for marriage having changed. He was marveling at the generosity of a woman who would seek out her husband's mistress and see that his bastard child was cared for. His heart went out to Jane, a girl in her teens, newly married, making what would have been to her kind heart a shocking discovery about her husband's habits.

An uncomfortable thought struck him. Had Jane helped Petra out of love for the late Lord Averham? He didn't sound like a model husband, yet women weren't noted for loving wisely.

Did her reluctance to marry again mean that she would let no other man take her late husband's place in her life? She had had no qualms about sharing a bed with another, but she was a woman of strong desires, vibrant with life.

And she had waited long enough. MacGowan knew that she was not a woman who commonly had affairs. He had been the only one with her since her marriage.

He had overwhelmed her, hadn't given her much chance to say no to him. But she never made illicit love before. That augured a strong attachment to her husband's memory, for Jane moved in a fast international set where ladies did not hesitate to take lovers. Where it was nearly *de rigueur,* to hear some of them tell it. The Duchess of Sagan had praised Archie for his conquest, saying that it would do her stodgy friend Jane the world of good to experience life at last.

"What are you thinking, sir?" Petra asked curiously.

He came out of his reverie with a snap. Jane's present problems must be his concern for the moment; and those problems included not only himself but also this girl. "I was thinking that you ought to go back to Lady Averham's soon, before you are missed. I'll work on finding a solution to your problem; but you needn't deprive her ladyship of your company. You are a valuable part of her household, Miss Schmidt."

"Oh, do you really think so?" Petra's eyes sparkled at this flattering comment.

"I know so. Jane . . . Lady Averham has told me that you are true to your name. The rock of her household."

"Ah, is that so? I am most happy. I do not wish to make her worry and fret."

"Then you couldn't do better than to let me take you back. I assume you can get into the house the way you got out?"

Petra nodded. "It was most simple."

"I'll wager, then, that Miss Chloe showed you how." MacGowan remembered his earlier conversation with the talented youngest lady of the Averham household.

"How did you know, sir? I might have been an actual spy for a time, but Chloe is the one whose skills lie in that direction. I am convinced she could work her way out of a steel box and leave no trace."

"Let us say that I'm coming to know all of the ladies of your house extremely well," MacGowan said. His tone was ironic; he hoped that Miss Schmidt didn't stop to interpret it.

Luckily, it was very late at night, and Miss Schmidt's normal powers of observation, though keen, were not infallible. She accepted his escort back to Jane's, where he left her at a certain small door.

Then he went on his way home, thinking over all he had heard of Jane's marriage. Once, her brother-in-law Averham had sworn that hers had been no love match. He had hinted strongly that Jane had not been happy. Then Miss Schmidt had come out with her shocking tale.

It *was* very late. MacGowan went to his bed undecided about any of Jane's motives, past or present.

He was newly determined, though, to overcome them and to have his way in the end.

11

PHYLLIDA'S FINGERS roamed over the keys of the old schoolroom pianoforte in an abstracted manner most unlike her usual careful style. For once she wasn't concentrating on the technique of the Beethoven, deploring her lack of this or that perfection, cursing the length of her fingers or her lack of true genius. She was simply letting the music overcome her.

The notes swelled and seemed to soar, overflowing the low-ceilinged room. Phyllida was trembling when she finished.

"I like that," Chloe said. The younger girl was sitting at a scarred table, making random numbers and letters on a piece of foolscap. "Was it one of the ones by Herr van Beethoven? It was different."

"I've played it ten thousand times," returned Phyllida. "My mood was different." She had difficulty in speaking normally, and she clasped her hands to stop their shaking. Something wonderful had happened, and it seemed absurd that it should have taken place in this shabby, neglected schoolroom, with the uncaring Chloe in attendance. *I have the secret*, Phyllida told herself silently, in a kind of awe. *At last I have the secret. Such a small thing, really, to let oneself go . . .*

"I will never have genius," she said aloud, "but I'm coming along."

Chloe shrugged. To her the mysteries of music began and ended with her losing battle to translate the annoying black dots and lines onto the keys. So much more mysterious than writing in code. Chloe was able to make up ciphers as easily as she liked, and was at present working on another message to drive Johann, the footman, into the fidgets. "I think it was mainly Herr van Beethoven," she said. "He wrote it, didn't he? How I should love to meet him."

"I'm the one who wants to meet him," Phyllida said with a scathing look.

"Well, I can want to too, can't I?" Chloe countered. "Do you remember the time the Countess Zlotska said it would be difficult to be mistress to a genius?"

Phyllida colored at the mere thought of that morning. How dreadfully embarrassing it had been for the countess to so misconstrue one's admiration for the composer. "I do indeed remember that occasion," she said, eyeing her sister in suspicion, "and you were not present."

There was a short silence. Chloe busied herself with her paper. Then, "Well, are you coming to breakfast?" she asked briskly.

Phyllida took one last penetrating look at Chloe and gave up trying to understand her. The child was getting altogether too good at spying. "I thought I'd play some more." Phyllida never failed to wake at dawn eager for her music, no matter how late the party had been the night before. She had been playing for an hour already.

"Suit yourself." Chloe shrugged, got up, and tucked the cipher away into the bosom of her gown. "Uncle Robbie is coming to breakfast. I teased him into it, for it's such fun to see him spar with Flora."

"Chloe! You know Flora doesn't like Uncle!"

"I know she *says* she doesn't like Uncle. Do come, Phyllida. I've already been to Petra's room, and she tells me she won't be rising before noon today. Odd, don't you think? Petra is always so energetic."

"Not so energetic as you," Phyllida said, strumming some chords. "Go along, now, or stop talking. I want to get on with it. Please." The last word had no hint of supplication, but rather brooked no argument.

Chloe understood the inflection well enough. "Beast!" she was muttering as she swept from the room in imitation of the Countess Zlotska. Much though she hated to give Phyllida credit for anything, she had to stop and listen in admiration outside the schoolroom door for just a moment. Her sister was really very talented. And as for Beethoven . . . !

He was magnificent. How splendid indeed it would be to have it over Phyllida; to announce that she, Chloe, had succeeded in meeting the great master while Phyllida only mooned about over his music.

Chloe went humming along down the corridor, thinking over all her plans.

In the breakfast room she found Uncle Robbie. He rose to his feet and grinned at her. "The first one down, Chloe? I am charmed to see you looking so pretty and bright."

Chloe was fond of her uncle for a number of reasons, but his way with a compliment figured highly in her list of his virtues. "Thank you, Uncle," she said, feeling immeasurably more grown-up. She had scrutinized herself in the mirror this very morning, and she agreed with his estimation. Matters were definitely mending, though more slowly than one would like.

Averham grinned wider. "Now, where are the other young ladies this morning?"

"Where is Flora, you mean. She will be down directly. She is very prompt. But Petra and Phyllida aren't coming to breakfast. At least, Phyllida may, but when it suits her." Chloe seated herself with her uncle's aid, then watched admiringly as he placed himself opposite her.

"Mama says that the test of a true gentleman is whether he is as polite to little girls as he is to grown-up ladies," Chloe said. "You are her model."

"You'll turn my head with your flattering talk." Averham tossed off the compliment, but he did look pleased. He turned the subject at once, though. "Let me ask you something. You appear to have noticed that I have a marked preference for Lady Flora. You are sharp, Chloe, and you see more than most people. Tell me, do you think I have a chance?"

"No," Chloe said without hesitation.

"Oh." To his surprise, Averham was a bit disconcerted by this diagnosis. Lady Flora was deliciously antagonistic, of course; he was enjoying that aspect of their relationship. And it was not that he had any serious desire to jump into parson's mousetrap with any young woman, however desirable she might be. As a handsome and eligible bachelor, though, he didn't expect any young lady to be unmoved by his attentions.

"Flora is not really very sensible, you know, Uncle Robbie," Chloe said with a shake of her head. "Do you suppose we could ring for breakfast now? Perhaps she's heard you are here and means not to come down."

"By all means, ring." Averham sat back, folding his

arms, and mulled over his niece's news. At least Chloe put Lady Flora's reluctance down to a lack of sense! His masculine pride needn't be completely deflated.

Chloe made a show of giving instructions to the footman who answered the bell. "And never mind Lady Flora's porridge. She may want it in her room this morning."

"Oh, is that so?" a feminine voice inquired crisply in a slight Scots burr. To Averham's delight, Lady Flora entered the room, cool and enticing in a plain white morning gown and a plaid shawl. "Max, please bring the porridge," she ordered, gliding to her accustomed chair. It happened to be next to that of Lord Averham. She gave him a frosty nod.

"Lady Flora, how delighted I am to see you," Averham said. Winking at Chloe, he added, "My niece had some idea that you might take breakfast in your room this morning."

"I? I am not so indolent." Flora directed a glare at Chloe, who giggled.

"It was not indolence she suspected you of, ma'am, but . . . shall we say avoidance?" Averham looked innocently over Flora's shoulder while delivering this remark.

"Lord Averham! Are you calling me ill-mannered?"

"I am sure it would be more than my life is worth to do so, ma'am."

Flora appeared to turn this over in her mind very carefully. Then, without warning, she smiled.

Chloe stared. Flora hardly ever smiled even at Bronsky, and she had never, to Chloe's knowledge, accorded Uncle Robbie such an honor.

Averham managed to resist a sudden desire to take Flora into his arms, or at least kiss her hand, and returned a bow in acknowledgment of the favor of Lady Flora's great condescension.

Jane walked in just in time to see Flora smiling and seemingly in great charity with Averham. Her eyebrows shot up at sight of the pair. Chloe, naturally, was watching most intently from her place across from them, and Jane understood her daughter's evident puzzlement. How extraordinarily natural Flora looked!

"Well." Jane disliked to break the mood, but she couldn't stand in the doorway forever. "I'm glad to see you, Robbie. I'm sorry Miss Schmidt won't be joining us, but she sent me word that she is extremely fagged from her late night.''

The trio at the table had to pause in their games to greet Jane. Averham sprang to his feet to help her to her chair.

Phyllida came in on her mother's heels, causing a fresh distraction. Jane was just as glad that everyone was pre-occupied: Phyllida with her music; Averham and Flora— for a wonder!—with each other; and Chloe, as usual, with the breakfast that soon came in. It was well that Petra, with her sharp eyes, had stayed in bed. Jane wouldn't wish to think that anyone was looking too hard at her this morning. Pauline had done her best with powder and paint, but there was still a telltale pinkness about Jane's eyes, a certain droop to her shoulders that she couldn't seem to disguise.

Her affair with MacGowan was over. She was abso-lutely certain that it was over. She had treated the man she loved as a man would treat a streetwalker. At least well-paid courtesans were sought after for their conver-sation as well as their bodies. Last night, she had not given MacGowan even that dignity. A deep sense of shame threatened to overwhelm her and send her into tears whenever she thought of how she had blatantly sum-moned him for no other reason than to satisfy her desires. How could she have been so stupid, so selfish?

''Mama?'' Phyllida's voice broke into these gloomy thoughts.

Jane snapped to attention. ''Yes, my dear?''

''I wish to stay home from that dreary ball, if you please. I do so wish to work on my music. I have dis-covered the most wonderful—''

''My dear, I accepted the Zichys' invitation for all of us. You know how I feel about your burying yourself at home,'' Jane interrupted, speaking firmly.

Phyllida subsided at once, without even one more plea. Jane knew she should rejoice that her motherly authority had not diminished overnight. It seemed that every other quality of hers had.

She had looked old to herself in the mirror this morn-ing; old and somehow used up. She had had to drag her-self out of bed; not that she had slept.

''Jane?''

Again she came out of a heavy mist to answer her

brother-in-law. "Yes, Robbie? Do forgive me, all of you. I'm feeling a bit vague this morning."

"I suppose that's why you filled your coffee cup with tea." Looking sympathetic, Robbie signaled a footman to replace her ladyship's cup.

Jane stared down at the noxious mixture of half-coffee, half-tea. She had drunk several sips without noticing. "Oh, dear. I *am* vague."

"Perhaps you'd better return to bed, Mama," Phyllida suggested with a rare daughterly concern.

"Perhaps I had." Jane rose to her feet and found her knees shaking. She willed them to steady before she took a step.

"I hope you're not sickening for something," Phyllida continued. "Would you like me to write to the Zichys, Mama, and tell them we aren't able to come tonight?"

"No. A little rest will put me in fine fettle." Jane directed a sharp look at her daughter. "You are going to that ball," she added with a little edge of satire.

Phyllida's hazel eyes took on a hurt expression.

"I'm sorry," Jane said, and was annoyed to hear her voice break. She escaped the room and the speculative eyes without another word.

A day spent regarding the ceiling above her bed sufficed to restore her tranquillity, if not her spirits. By the evening she was sick enough of plasterwork angels to risk a foray into the great world beyond her room. She dressed for the ball in a trancelike state.

Pauline, seeing, though she did not ask, that something had gone wrong with madame's love affair, brought up all reinforcements. With a determined set to her chin, the maid arrayed Jane in the finest ball gown, the most stunning jewels, and did her hair in a new way: slightly tumbled, to give the impression that her lady might have just arisen from a bed of love.

If something had gone awry with the handsome lover, Pauline reflected, Lady Averham would have no trouble in attracting another.

On this particular evening Jane wouldn't have noticed if she were wearing a sack or if her hair were still in a boudoir cap. She never did really focus on her reflection except to observe to Pauline that the great Leroy's gown, a fawn-colored gauze shot with silver, might be all that was Parisian and up-to-date, but someone had forgotten to attach the bodice.

"It is necessary to the look, madame," Pauline said, her face expressionless. "And this is nothing to the Princess Bagration's usual necklines."

"I suppose you're right," Jane said with a sigh. As Pauline had shrewdly known she would, she straightened her shoulders, which had that annoying new tendency to droop. Perfect posture was vital to the fit of this particular gown.

As her mistress left the room, Pauline emitted a worried sigh of her own. Fatal, these affairs of the heart. Perhaps madame had been wise to avoid them up to now. Pauline had effected repairs to a nicety this evening, but much more unhappiness would end by being seriously detrimental to her lady's looks.

Phyllida, dressed in a ball gown of peach-colored silk, was just leaving her room to go downstairs when she had a sudden urge to show Chloe her costume. Her sister was always teasing for such a treat, and though Chloe had found another outlet for her vicarious dressing in Petra, Phyllida still sometimes felt guilty that she was leaving her little sister out of the only thing she could share of these silly festivities.

She walked into Chloe's room without knocking and surprised the girl putting on a dark cloak over her simple white dinner gown.

"Really, Phyl, you might knock," Chloe said, whipping the cloak back off.

"You're going out? Mama made no mention." Phyllida scrutinized her sister. Chloe wore her best dress and a new sash, and there was something different about her face—she had been using that old rouge pot she had filched from Mama, no doubt.

"I was pretending to go out, if you must know," Chloe said with an injured look. "And now I suppose you'll laugh at me."

"Pretending to go out? And here I've been pretending I could stay in. I came to show you my gown, since you're always asking." Phyllida, preoccupied as usual with thoughts of Herr van Beethoven, accepted her sister's words easily. Chloe was forever making believe about something or other.

"It's a pretty gown," said Chloe.

Phyllida turned about so that the ankle-length flounced hem would show the clocks on her stockings, but Chloe made no exclamations of admiration or envy. Phyllida put the odd reaction down to the way she had been snubbing her little sister of late. "If you wish to play pretend with some of my other gowns, please do feel free," she said, coming to a stop.

Chloe's eyes flashed, and Phyllida was immediately chagrined. "I know. You're not a child," she said by way of apology. "And I do so wish you could go to all these affairs in my place. But your turn is coming."

"You sound like Mama. My turn will come when we're living somewhere else, somewhere dull. I just know it. Well, run along, Phyl, I know you're probably late."

Since this was indeed the case, Phyllida allowed herself to be pushed out of Chloe's room with very little trouble. As she opened the door, she happened to glimpse a framed sketch that stood on a small table. The picture had one candle burning before it.

"You have a drawing of Herr van Beethoven? Did you do it?" Phyllida recognized at once the beetling brows, the wild hair, as those of her hero. She had seen his picture many times; and of course she had seen him in the flesh, from a great distance, usually across a crowded theater.

"Why should I not?" Chloe countered. "You know I'm collecting pictures of all the Congress notables, and he is certainly one of those."

"I should say so. The greatest musical genius of this or any other age," Phyllida said with a faraway look.

"As you say. Herr van Beethoven is more than qualified to take his place in my gallery," Chloe said grandly.

"Your gallery. Oh, yes." Phyllida went away feeling a little confused. She really ought to pay more attention to her family. She hadn't even known that Chloe was making such a collection.

Down in the small saloon, the ladies were all awaiting Phyllida. "Where are the gentlemen?" she asked in surprise as she entered the room. There were usually at least a half-dozen, including Uncle Robbie and, more often than not, Flora's brother, to surround the ladies on their way to any social event.

"I decided we would go independently to this night's

ball,'' Jane said. Even Phyllida noticed how beautiful her mama was looking this evening in a gown that would make heads turn. ''I thought we would cut more of a dash that way for once.''

''Most sensible, ma'am, I assure you. All those men are quite unnecessary,'' Flora put in.

Phyllida was quick to agree. Only Petra looked askance at the suggestion that the absence of gentlemen could be preferred to their presence.

''Is always best to have a male escort,'' Petra pronounced with a hint of severity which made the other girls smile, ''but madame has her point in this case. We will cut the dash.''

In the coach, Phyllida found her thoughts returning to Chloe. At first she didn't quite know why, and felt she might be sorrier for her little sister than she had believed. Then she realized that her musing was tempered by a good bit of uneasiness. She kept fixing on the image of Chloe, dressed to go out for the evening. Pretending, was she? Upon reflection, that excuse didn't quite ring true. But she couldn't be going anywhere; she was just a child. Who would invite her?

Then the drawing of Herr van Beethoven would simply not leave Phyllida's consciousness. It was a remarkably fine likeness; perhaps she could persuade Chloe, who was really quite an artist, to make a copy for her. How odd the picture had looked on that table with the candle. Almost a shrine. How could Chloe, who was so careless about music, think so much of the great man? But apparently she did. Phyllida could understand her sister's taste, but she mistrusted her motives.

She sat bolt upright as a memory came to her. For the merest moment she was in the schoolroom that morning, and Chloe was running on about a desire to meet Beethoven. And fancy her having heard that remark of the Countess Zlotska's, about being the mistress of a genius! Chloe was indeed becoming altogether too skillful at ferreting out other people's business. Had she been up to her trick of hiding behind the draperies on that occasion? Phyllida took a deep, shuddering breath. Exactly how skillful *was* Chloe?

''What can be the matter, dear?'' her mother asked in concern.

"Nothing." Phyllida squeezed herself into her corner of the carriage and willed it to arrive at the Zichys'. Chloe couldn't be so foolish as to go, in the evening, to the house of a man she had never met. Not even her sense of adventure would permit such ruinous bold behavior . . . would it? Phyllida remembered, with growing uneasiness, Chloe's frequent wild chattering about becoming a woman of the world, a woman who experienced grand passions.

At thirteen she could not be expecting to experience anything of the sort. The idea was ridiculous.

Yet Phyllida wondered, in a sisterly way, if the idea was any more ridiculous than Chloe herself.

Once the party arrived at the ball, Phyllida whispered an excuse to her mother and made unseemly haste to be off to the ladies' cloakroom. Jane was plainly concerned, but she couldn't ask her daughter anything, so swift and so demanding was the crowd of men that swarmed about her as soon as her cloak was removed from her shoulders.

Phyllida didn't go to the ladies' room. She ran instantly back out to the carriage, which had not yet moved away. "The Schottenbastei, and hurry," she told the fatherly coachman. She could trust Bergen. He had been with the family for years.

So trustworthy was he that he eyed her in suspicion and asked whether her mother had approved this odd plan.

"I must hurry, Bergen. This concerns Miss Chloe. She could be in danger," Phyllida exclaimed, climbing into the coach. "I know you will protect me." She cast a look of appeal at Bergen, then at the startled footman, whom she had not given time to assist her into the vehicle. He was still perched up behind. "As will you, Peter."

Her call to their protective instincts must have worked. The coach moved away; slowly, as the streets around the Zichys' house were still crowded with carriages conveying people to the ball.

The Averham vehicle picked up but little speed as it went on its way to the north side of the city. Vienna's streets were all so narrow and winding, not to mention crowded every evening with carriages full of partygoers. A striking number of these coaches were the green ones, emblazoned with white crests, that the Emperor Franz had had made for his royal guests. Phyllida looked anxiously out the window, absently counting green coaches by the flaring light of torches and carriage lamps—a favorite game of hers. If only she had guessed wrong and Chloe was in bed at home—or, at the very worst, trying on all of Phyllida's new dresses.

When the carriage pulled up across the street from a certain number in the shadow of the city walls, Phyllida hesitated on the steps of the carriage. Peter, who was assisting her down, looked at her in query.

Phyllida scrutinized the house. She had walked past it herself, with her maid, on one memorable occasion. But she had seen nothing, heard nothing, though she had hoped at least for a snatch of immortal music to drift down from a window.

Now all seemed quiet. A friendly lamp was burning in a window. No; not even Chloe could be so daft as to invade such a great man's privacy.

"Let us wait," Phyllida said after a few moments' reflection. "For only five minutes, but let us wait."

Peter nodded. Phyllida saw him exchange a certain glance with Bergen. She felt her cheeks grow hot.

She was standing very still, for she had never been this close to a genius. Those times when she had seen him from a distance, she had been clear across the theater—and once, the Ballhausplatz. Even in her romantic haze, Phyllida had to smile at herself. How close to a genius did she think she was? Though she imagined him sitting right next to that yellow lamp, she didn't even know if Herr van Beethoven were at home this evening or if that window belonged to his flat. Indeed, if Chloe's plan was what Phyllida suspected, she must hope that the poor man was far, far away.

Luck was with Phyllida. She had not been standing there on the coach steps for more than the allotted five minutes when two females, a tall one and a short one, turned into the shadowy street.

"Chloe!" Phyllida called when the two were opposite the coach. She had nothing to lose; if one was not her sister, the women would only think she was mistaken and go on about their business—and an odd business it must be. Females had nothing respectable to do alone in the streets at night.

The smaller figure stopped, and even in the darkness Phyllida could tell that a piercing look was being directed at her. A piercing and disgusted look.

"Blast." It was Chloe's clear, high voice. "Of all times for you to become clairvoyant, Phyl!"

"Chloe," Phyllida whispered furiously, "come over here at once! I can't believe you would be so foolish."

Chloe, followed by the taller female, who turned out to be her faithful Anna, crossed the cobbles to Phyllida's station. Phyllida hoped that the servants couldn't understand English, but spoke softly anyhow. "Now, tell me what you are doing here at the very steps of Herr van Beethoven's house."

Lifting her chin, Chloe spoke proudly. "I was simply going to throw myself at his feet, Phyllida, as you say you want to do. You tell me he is the greatest man in Vienna; well, I wished to see him."

"What about your crackbrained statements this morning, about being a genius' mistress?" Phyllida demanded. "You surely weren't going to offer . . . no, I can't even speak the word. You're thirteen, you silly girl."

"I wasn't going to do anything of the sort," Chloe said with a sigh. "Truthfully, the thought had crossed my mind. But I'm afraid I'm not quite ready yet." Another, deeper sigh escaped her. "I knew Herr van Beethoven would be at home this evening; Johann is acquainted with his servant. But I truly wish only to cast myself at his feet and thank him for the music. I'll be able to tell my children about that, you see. As for being a mistress, I believe I should start out with balls and parties, like other girls, before I go on to bigger things."

"Well, that's some small comfort," Phyllida said. "Now, climb in, you and Anna, and I'll have Bergen drive you home. He must drop me at the Zichys' first."

With a shrug, Chloe translated some portion of the foregoing to Anna. Just as she was about to make her resigned way into the carriage, the front door of Herr van Beethoven's house opened and a dark, sturdy shape emerged.

Phyllida trembled. "It's he!" she whispered, for she knew well enough the craggy profile, sharply outlined against the lighted corridor behind.

"Oh!" This was too much for Chloe. She tore across the street and curtsied deeply at the feet of the man.

Phyllida hurried after. Her idol was said to have lost nearly all his hearing. She would not be able to make any apology for her sister's behavior. The most she could hope to do was to drag the chit away before she did something worse, and to resign herself to the fact that Herr van Beethoven would remember them as encroaching and witless girls. At least he didn't know who they were.

She caught Chloe's arm and gazed up into the man's face with a pleading expression. A stormy pair of eyes softened as they looked back into hers. She could see the face quite clearly in the light still streaming from his doorway. It was indeed Herr van Beethoven.

Phyllida found herself curtsying as deeply as her younger sister had done.

To her shock, Herr van Beethoven's hand raised her up. "You wished to see me, did you? I am always proud to meet pretty young ladies."

Phyllida stammered out some words of excuse and admiration. She knew she was making a fool of herself.

He nodded as though he had heard, and Phyllida wondered frantically if perhaps he could understand a little.

"Herr van Beethoven," she said, enunciating clearly in case this was so, "I am so proud to live in the world with you."

He smiled, pressed her hand, and reached forward to kiss her cheek. Then, shaking his head at both girls, he went on his way down the street. Someone finally closed the door after him.

"Really, Phyl," Chloe snapped, "this was my adventure. Do you have to spoil everything?"

Phyllida didn't seem to hear. She drifted back to the carriage, where Anna had sensibly settled herself inside, and gave Bergen instructions for the Zichy house. Chloe followed, still muttering darkly about her sister's meddling ways.

"He smiled at me," Phyllida said. "He kissed my cheek." She touched her own face carefully, reverently, in the spot he had saluted. "I thought he'd growl at us. But I should have known he would not. I've heard he can be quite kind. The Countess Zlotska told me that a ten-year-old German girl wrote to him, and he answered her most cordially. He *is* kind. I know it."

"He didn't even notice me," Chloe mourned.

"Well, never mind, my child." Phyllida patted her sister's hand. "You got to see him up close. Didn't he seem quite grand, quite magnificent?"

"No," Chloe said flatly. "He was quite an ordinary-looking man."

Phyllida shook her head. "You could see it in his eyes," she insisted. "I'm so glad you had this mad start, my dear. Now my sojourn in Vienna is all I could wish."

"Simply seeing him makes you feel that?" Chloe scoffed. "Well, I suppose he did kiss you and touch your hand; that is something." She was silent for a moment, then added, "Now what shall *I* do?"

"About what?" Phyllida asked with her customary vagueness.

"About excitement; about romance; about anything," Chloe exclaimed, flinging her arms out at her sides. Luckily she was sitting across from the placid Anna and her sister and didn't hit either one of them in her exuberance. "Plotting how to meet Herr van Beethoven has been quite a time-consuming project."

"I'm sure you'll think of something," Phyllida murmured. She stared out at the dark streets. This morning she had found out the secret to the pianoforte; this evening she had met the man whose music she lived through. Such perfection was nearly too much. The ball would be a definite anticlimax.

"Oh." Phyllida straightened her back in sudden apprehension. "I do hope Mama hasn't noticed I'm missing. Anna, would you mind calling out the window to Bergen? Ask him to hurry, please."

The maid rolled her eyes; traffic was much too heavy for words to have any effect. But she did the young lady's bidding. It was common knowledge in the servants' hall that the Bellfort girls were strange ones; and Anna, who was Miss Chloe's personal servant, must know this better than anyone else.

"Oh." Phyllida thought of something else. "Be sure, Anna, to tell Bergen and Peter that this night's adventure is to remain a profound secret among the five of us."

"Phyl, Anna never tells on me," Chloe protested.

"I'm sorry, Anna," Phyllida said, noticing with a twinge the maid's injured expression. "I know how trustworthy you are, of course. I'm simply a little distracted this evening."

12

To THE DISGUST of at least a dozen other ladies, Jane was finding herself the belle of the Zichy ball. The situation rather bewildered her, but she put it all down to her shocking gown. She even caught the Princess Bagration looking murderously at her from another part of the room. That lady, as usual, was adrift in transparent gauze and roses, her décolletage so deep as to be embarrassing. Jane squared her shoulders. She couldn't help it if she was almost as naked as Vienna's famed "naked angel." She would not be cowardly and send for a shawl.

Her success was of the type the French call *éclatant* but which Jane herself was inclined to regard as *fou*. She waltzed with Czar Alexander, who hinted strongly for a rendezvous. She did the same with a handsome Polish prince, who did not hint, but demanded a tryst. She sat out a dance on a sofa with Talleyrand, who flirted with her in a refined and courtly manner. Then she accorded the same honor to her old friend the Prince de Ligne, who was nearly speechless—but not quite—on the subject of her appearance.

"You are divine, madame," the old nobleman exclaimed, his hand on his heart. "I shall have to make sure tomorrow morning that I am indeed among the living. You make me believe I must have been transported to paradise."

"I thank you, Prince," Jane said, laughing. "I have need of all your gallantry this evening."

"But, madame! You are the toast of Vienna tonight."

Jane shook her head. "It's merely a fluke, sir. I don't regard it." Despite her fondness for her old friend's company, she found her mind drifting. Out of one corner of her eye she noticed Phyllida was at last in sight. That was a relief. A young officer was asking the girl to dance.

Phyllida looked so elated, so radiant! Was she at last to fall in love? Who was that officer?

"How sad for a beautiful woman to doubt the honesty of the world's homage," the prince was exclaiming. This brought Jane's wandering thoughts back to her own concerns. "Do you not think so, young man?" He gestured to someone standing behind their sofa.

"Sad indeed."

Somehow Jane was not as surprised as she had thought she would be to hear Archie's voice. So he was here, watching her. Did he mean to taunt her with the end of their affair? Or did he feel as sad as she? Only by a great effort of will was she able to look into his eyes and try to find out.

His expression was unfathomable. He had put on a facade of politeness and gallantry; anything, or nothing, could be beneath it.

"Your sister is dancing with Monsieur Bronsky, Mr. MacGowan," Jane said, speaking brightly, trying for the tone of a careful chaperon. "If I were you I would go and intercept them when the music stops. I don't mean to suggest the young man would monopolize her, but . . ."

"You are wishing me away. I go to do your bidding," Archie said with a stiff bow. He moved off.

"You were harsh with the young man," the Prince de Ligne informed Jane. "He wished only to stay by you and admire your beauty."

"Oh, sir, you exaggerate."

"Not at all," the prince said in such an intimate wise tone that Jane wondered uneasily how much he had seen in the past.

She changed the subject. "Tell me, Prince, since you introduced my family to Monsieur Bronsky, do you know that young man well? He is most persistent in his attentions to Lady Flora."

"He drinks at the fountain of beauty," the prince said.

"Too poetic by half, sir." Jane laughed. "Every other word you say tonight is 'beauty.' "

"But how can it be otherwise in such angelic company? Let us be serious, then. You are a wise woman and will be on your guard for Lady Flora's sake. No, I do not know Bronsky well. No one does. I have seen that he is a most practical young man, out to better himself in any way he can. There are many who watch him for various reasons. Do take care of Lady Flora. I teased you about her brother, but you were good to send him off to her side.''

Jane nodded. This was quite a lot of information to digest all at once, and it confirmed all her own guesses about Bronsky.

''Let me tell you something else, and with frankness,'' the prince continued.

''Please do, sir.''

He leaned closer. ''You have preoccupied yourself, dear lady. Now, don't deny it! This is a magical time for all of us. But if you wish to know what Bronsky would be at, it is best you find out at last for yourself. I will handle this matter *moi-même*. Here he comes, trailing Lady Flora and her brother. Ah, he is like the dog with the bone, that one; he does not give up.''

Jane started; the words could apply as easily to MacGowan as to Bronsky, or could have before last night. She watched as Flora, looking like a blond snowflake in a white-and-silver gown, approached on her brother's arm. *He* was magnificent as always. The light hair, which Jane had smoothed with her own hands so recently, the strong arms . . . No, she wouldn't think of it. She couldn't think of it and retain her composure.

Behind the MacGowans walked Bronsky, who appeared to be quite put out.

The Prince de Ligne hailed them all. ''Now, Monsieur Bronsky, I have arranged for you to be the envy of every man here tonight. Lady Averham consents to have the next waltz with you,'' he announced, a shrewd eye on Jane.

She hid her surprise.

Flora did not do likewise. She frankly stared. Her chaperon had never sought out Bronsky's company.

Bronsky, to do him justice, was polite about the forced dance and gallantly offered his arm. Jane took it, determined to do her duenna's duty and interrogate the young man about his feelings for Flora since the good Prince de Ligne had arranged this opportunity. MacGowan she managed to ignore but for a slight nod.

''Is Lady Averham vexed with you, brother?'' came

Flora's too-loud voice as Jane and Bronsky moved away to the dance floor.

Jane tried her best not to hear what MacGowan said in answer; and since he was always unfailingly courteous, his voice was soft enough that she could not do so. She returned her mind to the task at hand, giving Bronsky her most charming smile. "I thought we should get to know one another better than we do," she said pleasantly. "We are both so fond of Lady Flora." In her case, she exaggerated slightly. Though Flora had been resident in Jane's house for weeks now, the girl had not let her guard slip. Jane sympathized with her charge, for she could sense her unhappiness, but she had tried in vain to get to know her.

Bronsky, she suspected, didn't care if he knew Flora or not; he was simply out for her fortune. She watched his reaction to her words. He seemed to mull them over carefully.

"I honor milady Flora," he said finally, bowing to Jane. The music started, and he placed his arm about her waist for the waltz.

Close proximity to Bronsky didn't incline Jane more in his favor. She supposed he could be considered handsome, and that the calculating expression in his dark eyes would be muted when he gazed at Flora. Still, she did not know what the girl could be at by encouraging the attentions of this . . . And who exactly was he? No one seemed to know.

"You do not trust me, madame," he said with disarming honesty.

"Why, no." Jane was surprised into something like tolerance. She gave him a smile to soften her words. "I don't."

"You think that milady Flora is not safe with one such as I. You are wrong, madame. I do nothing to compromise her, as you cold English would say."

"I am most relieved to hear it," Jane said.

With a sudden flashing grin which showed more of his charm than any of his actions had hitherto, he swept her about the room in a spirited set of turns.

He really was a superb dancer. To Jane's surprise, some other couples even stopped to watch their steps, and when the music came to an end, a burst of applause was directed at them.

Jane's first thoughts were cynical: Bronsky certainly knew how to put himself forward. If he had to dance with her, and if she was the belle of the evening, he would not let the honor escape anyone's notice. Jane was left breathless by the performance, but when she had time to reflect, after the young man returned her to the sofa where he'd found her, she wondered if Bronsky had perhaps danced so vigorously so that she would be unable to question him further. She hadn't found out a thing.

Then, quite suddenly, MacGowan was back beside her. He sat down on the sofa. The Prince de Ligne, who had previously occupied that place, had wandered away sometime during the waltz and was now bowing over the hand of a most seductive-looking lady.

"Well," MacGowan said, "I've managed to foist Flora off on Higgenbottom, an old school friend who is now a publisher. I even gave him a strong hint to present her to some of his cronies to keep Bronsky at bay."

"One of your school friends is in business? And you sent Flora off with him?" Jane asked in astonishment.

"Don't play the high-and-mighty aristocrat with me, Jane."

She looked at him in injured surprise. His words had been cold—he was disappointed in her again, though she truly hadn't meant to be snobbish. She felt again her mortification of the night before, on quite another issue, and couldn't think of a thing to say in her own defense.

MacGowan studied her carefully. Then his smile appeared, and Jane was as glad to see it as she would have been to glimpse an old friend after years apart. "Higgenbottom's father is one of the few gentlemen in the business of books—he and Murray have that honor—and the young man himself is in Vienna to put some concerns of international copyright law before the Congress. There are quite a few publishers here, in fact."

"Yes, I'd heard that." Jane recovered her social manner with ease. "And no one is paying them the slightest attention. I do hope they managed to accomplish something among themselves this autumn."

MacGowan smiled. "So do I. Do you know, you are a charming hand at small talk. We haven't had time for much of that, you and I, but it is not for nothing that the world sings your praises, Lady Averham.''

Suddenly Jane was near tears; she couldn't bear this polite stranger sitting where her lover had so lately been. ''Are you tormenting me for some special reason, Mr. MacGowan? No one could regret more deeply than I what happened when . . . when last we met.''

He looked at her for a long, long moment. ''I believe that. You were thoughtless, nothing more.''

Jane flushed. A part of her wanted to lash out. How dared this man, younger than she, pass judgment on her behavior? Yet he was right; she had been thoughtless.

He picked up her hand and kissed it.

She drew back in shock. She had never expected him to touch her again.

''Now, Lady Averham, may I have the next dance? Your charges are well taken care of. Miss Bellfort has been passing for some time from one juvenile military man to another. She appears to be most reluctant, but there are really not enough young misses of her age to go around, and so she has no more say in the matter than any conscript. Miss Schmidt is talking to my father; and Flora, as I told you, is in the clutches of Mr. Higgenbottom. A good sort of fellow, and just the man to set her down if she plays ice princess with him.''

''Do you mind that Lord Foxburgh enjoys my goddaughter's company?'' Jane asked, ignoring the question about the dance. His sudden return to friendliness made her wary, though to be sure his moods were shifting no more rapidly than her own. She must endeavor to cast out no lures to him. That had led only to embarrassment and the worst night of regret she had ever spent in her life. What was his game now?

MacGowan shrugged. ''Let's leave them to sort it out themselves. Think of yourself, Jane.''

''Too much of that has got me into trouble,'' she said in a low, sad voice.

''How can you say so? The girls are all perfectly capable of directing their own destinies. You have nothing of the matchmaking mama about you. Why shouldn't you enjoy this ball for yourself?''

''I've been doing that.''

''And I've been watching. Have you really?'' Mac-

Gowan's words teased at her. "Now may I claim that dance?"

"Very well." Jane told herself that she could not in common politeness refuse.

The waltz that followed was nothing like her last dance with Bronsky. She was in the very arms where she so desperately wished to be, and the man she wanted was smiling down at her tenderly. He was not being discreet; he was looking at her so intensely that anyone who wished to would be able to see his admiration. So it was still there, that admiration! Jane's heart surged with relief, and she almost felt herself begin to sparkle with the old light that had been missing all day.

"Oh, Jane," MacGowan murmured, kissing her ear, "this is what we both want."

She drew back in alarm. He might as well have fondled her bosom! That kiss was much too intimate for a public place. A nervous glance around told her that several people had noticed the salute and were looking at them curiously.

"Please, Archie," she whispered, "not here."

"Discretion," he said with a wise nod. "Secrecy. So kind of you to remind me, Lady Averham."

With that Jane had to be satisfied. The music ended at this point, and he escorted her back to the sofa. A bevy of men was waiting: mostly middle-aged gentlemen with honors on their chests, but also a sprinkling of younger souls in dapper, unadorned evening dress or flamboyant regimentals. As Jane sank down upon the sofa, she heard the flattering clamor of many voices begging for a dance, a turn about the room, her company at supper.

She sighed in momentary contentment. How surprising, how gratifying to shine in society; to be sought-after at her age. She was grateful to the modiste's magic, or to Pauline's skill, whichever had worked this miracle of turning her out in good looks on a day when she had arisen feeling she had one foot in the grave.

The man who embodied her reasons for having felt so depressed was still standing before her. "The next dance too, Lady Averham? I am most grateful. First let me procure you a glass of champagne. I'll return in a moment. Gentlemen, you may guard her ladyship for me. I would not have her stolen away, I warn you."

Jane stared after him. There was a jaunty set to Archie's shoulders that she knew well. He was pleased at having pulled off a joke. They had said nothing about the next dance; and it had been years since she had given any gentleman two dances. She thought hard. Had she ever done so?

"We cannot let that young man monopolize you, most gracious lady," cried a Prussian prince. "I insist upon the next dance."

MacGowan, who had retreated a good distance, evidently heard the remark, which had been uttered in booming tones. He turned back to smile slyly at the group. "We'll have none of that. Lady Averham, you are promised to me." He gave her a caressing look and continued on his way.

Some of the more astute among Jane's flock of admirers gave her inquiring glances.

She smiled and shrugged, which had the unlucky effect of riveting about a half-dozen pairs of eyes upon her neckline.

When MacGowan returned with the champagne, the gentlemen were still milling about Jane's sofa. Significantly, no one had dared take the place beside her, though Jane wouldn't have said no to any man who asked for the favored seat. She was too uneasy about what MacGowan would do next to wish for more of his company—especially in close proximity.

But he did sit next to her with a proprietary air, handed her the champagne, and leaned back to watch her drink it, which she accomplished by nervous sips while trying to respond with wit and charm to the various light questions posed to her by the court of gentlemen.

"Now, Lady Averham, let us dance." MacGowan rose the moment Jane's glass was empty. "The music has started, and I hate to miss an instant of our interlude together."

This speech caused a stir among the listeners. Jane was halfway tempted to refuse to go with MacGowan. Then she looked into his eyes.

"As you please, sir," Inclining her head, she rose and gave him her hand.

During this waltz he held her tighter than he ever had in public. Her nerves in a highly wrought state, Jane was

nearly undone by his nearness. She whispered sharply to
him to be more circumspect.

"Never," he responded, fondling her waist.

"Then, sir, I must refuse to dance with you more."
And she stopped immediately, meaning to leave him
standing on the dance floor.

"Would you have the room witness a lovers' quarrel?"
he said into her ear.

"I suppose not," Jane agreed. She let him guide her
about the floor once more. He was gazing down at her
with an unmistakable gleam in his eyes. He was being
impossible.

She was not too shocked to find her body leaning
nearer to his than her mind would have allowed. "What
is this game?" she asked softly as the music came to an
end. He showed no sign of releasing her.

With evident reluctance he removed his hands from
her. "No game, dear Jane. Merely the truth."

The truth! Jane saw at once where he was leading. He
meant to make their attachment public. Did he still hope
to marry her, or was he now only bent upon a small sort
of revenge for her ill treatment of him? She couldn't believe that he would be so petty, and yet . . . what else
could he be at?

When the girls gathered round her at evening's end,
Jane saw that the damage had been done. Lady Flora was
directing suspicious and hostile looks her way; Petra appeared speculative and pleased; and even Phyllida, who
still had that strange glow which Jane put down to an
infatuation, took her mother aside to whisper, "Mr.
MacGowan certainly likes you, Mama."

Jane did not know what to respond, and settled on
silence. MacGowan escorted them to their coach, hand-
ing her in almost reverently, as a very young man might
treat the maiden he was infatuated with. Then he spoiled
this impression by placing a kiss upon her cheek.

"I'll be with you tomorrow," he said. "I know it's
one of your mornings to receive. The only thing I'll regret is the crowd."

Jane settled herself in the coach under the earnest gaze
of three pairs of eyes.

Clearing her throat, she decided to deflect attention
from herself at this critical moment. "Phyllida, did you

meet someone special this evening? I'm sorry we were
apart much of the time, but you were so busy in your
crowd of young officers that I didn't have the heart to
interrupt.''

Phyllida managed to look both guilty and astonished.
''I didn't . . . I did . . . that is, they were only officers,
Mama. I couldn't like any of them. Whatever can you
mean?''

''Only that you appear to be excited, or something very
like it,'' Jane said. ''And I have never seen you so at a
ball before. I'm so glad your little indisposition cleared
up,'' she added, referring to Phyllida's instant dash to
the cloakroom on their arrival.

''Oh, that. It was nothing.''

''Good. If it should come on again, do have Liesl ask
Pauline for some of her special remedy. She has some
sure cures for these female difficulties,'' Jane said with
a smile.

''You are right, madame.'' Petra spoke up. She had
been scrutinizing Phyllida in the wavering light of the
coach lamps. ''Phyllida, you look different. As though
something has happened to you.''

''What a strange thing to say.'' Phyllida gave a nervous little laugh.

''Strange indeed,'' Flora added. ''She looks the same
to me.''

Jane looked across the coach at Flora. Naturally such
a young beauty wouldn't believe that mood could affect
one's looks. Flora was always herself; always frozen perfection. Next to her, Petra looked lively and interesting
and very foreign. But her goddaughter also appeared to
be tired.

''You stayed in bed late this morning, Petra, and you don't
look well-rested now,'' Jane said. ''Perhaps you ought to
miss a few engagements. I'd hate to have you jeopardize your
health.''

''Oh, never, madame,'' Petra cried.

It was her eyes, Jane realized; they had a special sadness. She was probably worrying over Lord Foxburgh
and the spying. Likely she hadn't told him yet about her
activities.

''Take care of yourself, dear.'' Jane reached across to
pat Petra's hand.

When the party arrived home, Pauline was waiting in her lady's chambers as usual to prepare her for the night. "The good God be thanked," she exclaimed when Jane came into the dressing room.

"What?" Jane was beginning to be very sleepy and couldn't imagine what the maid meant.

"A new lover? Or is it the same young man who cannot resist madame after all? Ah, I knew how it would be." Pauline bustled about, removing Jane's cloak, gloves, and jewelry.

"Pauline! You take a good deal too much freedom," Jane said, blushing.

"Madame must forgive any irregularities. It is my *métier* of which I think."

"What?" Jane was completely puzzled by this line of talk.

"Madame must go to sleep instantly. It is the surest aid to beauty." Pauline ignored her lady's question, evidently preferring to keep her mystery on some things. Guiding Lady Averham firmly to the dressing table, she began to undo her hair.

"Pauline, I fear you've been staying up too late to wait for me. You aren't making a particle of sense." Jane gazed into her own eyes. How odd. They seemed so much brighter than they had only a few hours before.

"As madame pleases," the maid replied with a shrug.

13

PETRA SQUARED HER SHOULDERS and knocked at the door of the tall ornate house in the Herrengasse. The porter let her in, looked suspicious in the peculiar manner of a Viennese porter—they were all spies for one faction or another—but allowed her to proceed to the floor where Lord Foxburgh had his residence.

There a very proper English butler also peered down his nose at the spectacle of a pretty unaccompanied young lady wishing to see a gentleman. Not only was she alone, but the hour was much too early for morning callers. Nevertheless, he let the young person in, perhaps judging that Lord Foxburgh would be the man to show her out— or not. The correct and supercilious servant had to be aware that his master was not immune to female powers, Petra considered in her practical way. She had not heard that Lord Foxburgh engaged in the frantic dalliances which were the vogue in Vienna; but neither did anyone say he was a monk.

Left alone in a fussily decorated salon, Petra chose a highly carved and uncomfortable chair and waited, worrying. How the fastidious and very British Lord Foxburgh must hate the rococo monstrosities of his residence, she mused as she sat folding and unfolding her gloved hands.

She had arrayed herself in her best walking things: a deep rose-colored pelisse with swansdown trim and a matching bonnet ornamented with a curling pale pink plume. She knew the ensemble became her highly; knew further that embarrassment must have tinted her cheeks to a matching shade of rose.

In the several days she had spent thinking over what she meant to do, her mind had become settled, even serene. She had done her plotting well and had found out

when Lord Foxburgh was sure to be in so as to time her
visit for this precise hour.

When a door opened, she jumped nervously. Turning
toward the sound, she stiffened, then drooped as she saw
not Lord Foxburgh, but his son.

"Oh, Mr. MacGowan." She nodded as calmly as she
could, remembering their strange conversation at the
café. "You come, then, to tell me your father will not
see me. You have given him my story, I must suppose."

"Miss Schmidt, you do me wrong." MacGowan came
to stand before Petra and take her hand. "As it happens,
my father is in an unexpected meeting, and he delegated
to me the pleasant task of keeping you company until he
should be free." He smiled. "I'm afraid he said 'the
ladies.' He was under the impression that you could not
have come alone."

"He thinks me most proper," Petra said with a sigh.

"And he is about to find out otherwise, I take it."
MacGowan gave Petra a keen look. "You've come to
make your confession. May I dissuade you from that
course, Miss Schmidt? It would serve no useful purpose
for you to tell my father about your little activities. I've
fixed it up, you see, with Castlereagh. I told him that a
certain nameless young lady had been playing at espionage, selling rather common secrets to the French. I gave
my word that the young lady wouldn't do so again. His
lordship was more amused than not, though I fear he
took my involvement as sign of an affair of the heart."

"This you did for me, sir?" Petra started in astonishment.

He bowed. "I will always do whatever I can for any
member of Lady Averham's family who requires my
help."

The delicate allusion to her place in the Averham
household touched Petra. She gazed up at him. "You are
so gallant, sir. I do hope you win her."

MacGowan looked pleased. "Do you refer to any particular person?"

"As you must know, I mean my godmother. I saw . . .
last night at the ball, naturally, but I have seen before . . . I
believe you would suit admirably."

Looking even more pleased, MacGowan sat down
across from Petra. "You have always struck me as a most

sensible young woman. Do you think Lady Averham will fight very hard against such a connection?''

"Yes,'' Petra said after a moment's reflection.

"Why?''

Petra was gratified by the gentleman's look of displeasure. Her dear godmother had indeed touched his heart.

She shrugged. "It is only a feeling, sir, it has nothing to do with reason. You speak of marriage, not so?''

"Naturally I speak of marriage,'' MacGowan retorted in some heat.

"Then tell me this: if madame has it in her mind to marry, why has she not done so? She is three years a widow.''

"Because of the love she bore her husband, perhaps. She has taken a while to get over his loss,'' suggested MacGowan.

Petra tried to stifle a nervous laugh but was only half-successful.

MacGowan looked at her narrowly. "I know, Miss Schmidt, that you told me the story of your birth and that it did not reflect well on the late Lord Averham. But many women love rakes.''

Petra considered this carefully. "Yes, you see the truth there. Some women do love rakes. I have always thought such a course was folly, but so it was always with my mother, and I have seen it happen with many others. I do not think thus of Lady Averham, though. She has an excellent understanding.''

He laughed. "Let us hope you are right. There would be nothing worse than trying to compete with a dead man. They're impossible rivals.''

"Is so,'' Petra said with a wise nod of her head.

They were unable to expound further on the theme, for at this point Lord Foxburgh entered the room. His naturally ruddy face took on a beetlike hue on seeing that Petra had indeed decided to visit him alone.

"Oh, Father.'' Archie stood up. "Miss Schmidt has something very particular to say to you, I understand. Or do you, ma'am? You mentioned a little problem—but I hope I solved it to your satisfaction.''

Petra gave him a grateful look, but she was firm in her resolution. "I do have a particular thing to say, sir. You are very good.''

"Well, what's this?" Lord Foxburgh asked as soon as the door clicked shut. "I don't mind telling you, Miss Schmidt, that I am most honored by this visit. Is it possible that Lady Averham knows of it, though? She would certainly have sent someone with you."

"You are correct, of course." Petra gave him a tremulous smile. "She does not know I'm here."

"Then, my dear, let us hope no one hears of your visit. I am a good bit older than you, of course, but there are still some unkind souls who might whisper that you'd been compromised." Foxburgh gave a genial laugh and sat down in the place his son had just vacated.

Again Petra smiled, more steadily than before. "How clever of you, sir, to bring up the very subject I wished to open. I have something to say to you of the most personal. Two things, actually. The first is a difficult thing, a confession of sorts."

"A confession?"

Petra was nearly undone by the kindness in his voice. He was such a gentleman, so good and chivalrous. She would be so sorry to have him angry with her, as he must be once she told him she had served the French, had used the occasional tidbit gleaned from him to ease Talleyrand's reading of the political winds.

She frowned in indecision. Which should she bring up first? The fact of her duplicity, or the more interesting, and, she hoped, more welcome news that she was willing to become Lord Foxburgh's mistress?

She was not a vain young woman, but she was knowing enough to have gauged her attractions and assigned them a market value. As a wife, she would have been worth much to a middle-aged or elderly gentleman who could afford to be a fool. As a mistress, she would be more than acceptable to any man with an eye.

But would Foxburgh balk at taking a mistress who had betrayed him?

"Lassie, what is this confession?" Lord Foxburgh's concerned voice broke into Petra's ruminations.

She took a deep breath and decided that honesty was her only course. Strange that she, of all people, should choose such a path, but there it was. "I have been a spy," Petra said without preamble. "I no longer am, but the truth must come out: I was in the past a despicable

character. Without Lady Averham's knowledge, I played
the listener at her British salons, taking what information
I could glean and selling it to the French.''

"Good God!" Foxburgh exclaimed. "Miss Schmidt,
I am astonished."

Her eyes filled with tears. There was the anger she had
feared. "I, too, am horrified that I could have done such
a thing. Your good son has made all right with your government, but since I used you, milord, used your kindness to me for my own benefit, I had to come to you and
tell you what a monster I have been."

Foxburgh's expression changed, became understanding
again, condescending. "My dear girl, you amaze me. Do
you think I say anything important in front of any pretty
girl? Vienna is too full of agents for an unguarded word
to slip past my lips. Don't worry, you could have done
no harm by repeating what you've heard from me."

Petra looked into his eyes and found them still friendly,
still admiring. Nearly unable to believe her good luck,
she said, "Truly, sir? You are not trying to make me feel
better?"

"I hope you do feel easier, for I can see the matter has
overset you. But rest assured you've done nothing that
could work to my discredit or harm the British cause."

Petra was not so sure. A gentleman might not think
his guard would slip, but there were times when it did.
She would be ready to swear to that, and also to swear
that she had indeed taken advantage of such comments,
carelessly made by Lord Foxburgh himself, and passed
them on to the French.

But he did not think she could have done harm—he
was a man, *enfin*, and had his pride—and her zeal for
confession went only so far and no further.

"You relieve my mind, dear sir," said the practical
Petra with a winning smile.

He gazed at her in evident approval.

Petra swallowed. Now was the time for the second
confession—or "offer" might be a better word. She had
never expected to be in this situation. Indecent propositions
were one thing, and she was expert at deflecting them. She
did wish she had paid more attention to how they were made,
though. She had never thought to do the thing herself.

"Lord Foxburgh," she said, her accent growing thicker

as her nervousness increased, "now is time for me to say the thing I came to say. The other thing." She took several deep, cleansing breaths and looked him in the eye. "I have noticed, sir, that you admire me."

Foxburgh looked suddenly wary.

Petra laughed her most charming laugh. "Oh, sir, you think I come to compromise myself. I come here without a chaperon, and *voilà*, the scandal. And I perhaps extort payment from you for keeping it quiet? No, sir, is nothing like that."

"Miss Schmidt, I assure you, the farthest thing from my mind was any such—"

"Yes." Petra tossed off his words with a wave of her hand. "You cannot be blamed for thinking me such a beast. What I have to put to you, sir, is another kind of thing. Scandal, true, but of a most pleasant kind. I was correct in my earlier statement, not so? You do find me attractive?"

"I find you an angel, Miss Schmidt," Foxburgh said, blustering a bit. He got up and began to pace the room. "Though where this could be leading—"

"I offer you myself," Petra said.

He stopped and stared at her. "You do what?"

"I offer myself as your mistress," Petra explained. "I ought to say 'lover,' for I wish not to squeeze money from you. Those days are over for me. I wish . . . I find I admire you too, my lord."

"You do." Foxburgh continued to look at her as though she had run mad, but he approached and sat beside her. "You, a beautiful young girl in her first Season, find me pleasing? Is this some sort of trick, my lass? I warn you, I wouldn't take it kindly."

Petra shook her head. Tears were trembling on her lashes. She imagined that she looked very pretty: she cried well. It was a newly discovered talent of hers. Desperately, she hoped this would help.

"Please," she said softly, "may I be your mistress? I do so wish to be with you, sir, for a little while."

"My dearest girl, you can have no idea what you're offering."

"I most certainly can," Petra said with a touch of indignation. She caught herself quickly. "I do not mean in a vulgar sense, sir. You will find yourself the first, make no mistake.''

Foxburgh's expression was absolutely disbelieving. Petra supposed that he was as shocked as he had ever been in his life to be having such a conversation with a person he had, up to this moment, considered a most proper young lady. Any respect he might have for her would be slipping fast, and from there it would be but a short step to . . .

He jumped up from his chair, pulled her from hers, and caught her by the shoulders, gazing into her eyes. ''My dear Miss Schmidt, take my advice and go home at once to Lady Averham. Forget this nonsense. I promise to forget it too.''

''You don't want me,'' Petra whispered, even as she thrilled to the touch of his hands and noticed how very blue his eyes were.

''Don't want you?'' The eyes bulged. ''My dearie, what maggot do you have in your brain? How should I not want you? You are everything . . . that is, you are a most pleasing young woman. But you must forget this mad start. Go home, I tell you. Go home.''

''You cannot want me,'' Petra murmured, more to herself than to him, looking down. ''No man who did would turn down such an opportunity.''

To her surprise, a twinkle had appeared in Lord Foxburgh's eye when she sneaked a look up at him again. ''I'm glad you have no unbecoming modesty,'' he said with a shake of his head. ''If it will ease your mind, Miss Schmidt, know that I think too highly of you to ruin you. Good Lord! Take as my mistress one of Lady Averham's charges! Ridiculous. I've known Jane for years.''

''You don't understand,'' Petra said. ''I am a bastard. It may come as a shock to you, sir, that such a young person as I have been living cheek by . . . jowl, I think you say? . . . with your highborn daughter. That I am in society at all is entirely due to Lady Averham's kindness.''

Foxburgh gave her a searching look. ''So you know. I was wondering if you did.''

''What?'' Petra cried. ''You cannot mean *you* know?''

''That you are some blood connection of the Averhams'? I'd have to be blind not to. You are the image of the late Lord Averham's mother, whom I saw many times when I was a young boy. You resemble little what's-her-name, Jane's younger daughter, to a great degree. Don't fret over it, my dear. There are too many love children wandering about for you to make a piece of work over your birth. It's different in England, I'll warrant you, but here on the Continent you need not let it concern you overmuch.''

Petra was in awe over this flood of information. She had realized she resembled Chloe, but trusted that it would go unremarked. And though it meant she could not go unrecognized in English society, it was gratifying to think that she looked like her grandmother. ''But you are English,'' she said sadly.

''Scottish,'' Foxburgh corrected her with a sharp look. ''And I don't know how it is with the English, but we Scottish, on finding out the circumstances of a young woman's birth are a bit irregular, don't offer her a slip on the shoulder. We stick to our morals. Miss Schmidt, will you marry me?''

Petra stood very still. Then, contrary to all her principles of control, and unaided by her robust health, she toppled over in a faint.

Lady Flora MacGowan was spending the morning going over the report on Bronsky, given her by Johann the enterprising footman and painstakingly translated by herself with the aid of a few battered grammar books she had found in the schoolroom.

She paced up and down her bedroom carpet. Bronsky was in every way suitable to the plans she had long held sacred. Penniless, of inferior birth, he would be unable to dominate her in a marriage in which she would be certain that the settlements favored her and secured her property to her descendants.

Descendants! They would be her brothers' children. Since Bronsky would be under her thumb, he would agree to a marriage in name only and never be a trouble to her in the physical sense.

She even had the unexpected power of blackmail in case he did not prove tractable on any of these issues: one word from her would bring the emperor's secret po-

lice down on him, as well as the agents of three of the
great powers, for Bronsky's work for the Russians.

Why, then, did she feel so halfhearted about the project? Flora sighed, stood still, and tapped her foot. If she
married Bronsky, she could be home in Scotland by the
end of the month, before winter set in. The winter was
so heavenly on the coast, so bitter and harsh. Even the
autumn was glorious, nothing like these disturbing mild
Vienna days. Flora longed to be in Scotland, walking the
hills with her dogs by her side, feeling the wind from the
North Sea whip back her hair. Her scruffy sheepdogs had
been unable to come with her to Vienna; not that anyone
had forbidden it, Flora simply hadn't had the heart to
force the animals on a frightening trip.

She shook her head. Somehow Bronsky did not fit into
the picture at all. She supposed she couldn't keep him in
the dungeons, but would have to let him out to roam the
hills as she did. Would he insist on walking with her and
the dogs? That would be intolerable.

"There you are, my dear."

Flora whirled around. Lady Averham was standing at
the bedroom door, looking extremely beautiful in a
charming morning toilette. Flora remembered that Archie had seemed quite smitten with Lady Averham the
night before, at the ball. There had been much more in
his manner than the usual gallantry, and the sight of his
silliness had disgusted his sister.

"Shall we go down together, dear? I was concerned
that you might not be feeling the thing, since you didn't
come down to breakfast."

The words were reasonable and indicated true concern. Flora scowled more darkly as she realized that these
very qualities of kindness and thoughtfulness which en-
deared Lady Averham to the world, not excepting even
herself, were the traits that had captivated Archie.

"You are old!" she burst out, more in irritation over
her confused feelings about Bronsky than out of real disdain for Jane. "He will never be caught by you."

Jane's face became devoid of all expression. "My dear
Lady Flora," she said after an ominous silence, "I will
not pretend to misunderstand you. You need have no fears
on that score. If your brother chooses to single me out,
I can hardly stop him. But you will see that, if anything,

his attentions are only a momentary madness on his part." Another pause ensued while Jane looked evenly at a suddenly uncomfortable Flora. "Shall we go down?" she repeated her earlier suggestion.

Flora nearly quailed under the firm stare of those large hazel eyes. Instantly ashamed of herself, for more reasons than one, and as determined not to admit it, she lifted her chin and proceeded out of the room, carrying herself like a queen. Jane followed her.

In the saloon which served Jane as a drawing room, the first of the morning callers were milling about, helping themselves to tea and other libations from the tray placed in a discreet corner, talking over politics or scandals. Jane cast an odd glance at Flora and immediately crossed the room to the Countess Zlotska, nodding and smiling at all the male admirers who sang her praises as she walked by. Not least among these was MacGowan, who swept a charming bow and gave her a look full of meaning.

Flora made a path to her brother, Jane noticed as she began to answer Masha's questions about the Zichy ball, which the countess had had the ill fortune to miss.

"You do not pay the attention," the countess complained after only a few minutes. "My dear Jane, your gallant is most attentive this morning. His little sister may try to keep him from you—young girls, they understand not at all the attractions of women of our age—but he thinks of no one but you. A dozen times he has glanced this way and nearly toppled *me*. But all this is no reason for you to gather the wool. That is the English expression, is it not?"

"Yes, it is," Jane said, smiling. "I'm sorry, Masha. You are quite right. Mr. MacGowan's attentions are most unsettling to me this morning, even from across a room. But I was thinking for the moment about my goddaughter, Miss Schmidt. One of the servants told me that she went out early this morning, and she hasn't yet returned."

"Do not worry. That one is a most sensible little thing. Most sensible. She is likely gone out to order fancy dress. All of us will have need of new costumes for the next Hofburg ridotto, and you may be sure Miss Schmidt will be wanting to steal the march on us all. She is clever."

"Oh, I do hope she is doing something of that sort."
Jane consoled herself with the thought that Petra, for all
her wild talk about becoming Lord Foxburgh's mistress,
had never yet done anything which might be construed
as improper—at least in the social arena, Jane amended
her thoughts, remembering the espionage.

Before she could rake herself more painfully over the
coals for not keeping a closer watch on Petra, and before
the Countess Zlotska could interrogate her further on the
past night's goings-on, Jane found MacGowan standing
beside her chair.

"Good morning, Lady Averham," he said with what
Jane considered much too smoldering a look. He sat
down between her and the countess. "Countess Zlotska,
I thank you for hinting me over here in your inimitable
way."

"Is that why you were smirking and winking so,
Masha?" Jane, torn between embarrassment and pleasure, turned on her friend.

"But of course." The countess was not one to be intimidated by a false show of displeasure. "You wished
to speak with this young man, did you not?"

"Ah!" MacGowan seized upon this. "You have something particular to say to me, ma'am?"

"Nothing particular," Jane answered, beginning to be
vexed. He as well as Masha was baiting her, trying to
get a reaction. "I do feel I should tell you, sir, that your
sister has noticed your ridiculous attentions to me and
has registered her disapproval."

"Unlike the several humble fishermen who belong to
her estate, not to mention her old nurse, I see no need
to tremble before the displeasure of the great Lady Flora
MacGowan," the lady's brother said in a flippant tone.
"Are you frightened of her, Lady Averham?"

Jane smiled and shook her head in an attempt to ad-
monish him for his lack of gallantry to his sister.

"I take it you're not. Good, for Flora wouldn't like
this. I came over here on purpose to tell you how lovely
you look this morning. You have a special glow."

Jane proved this statement to be fact by turning the
fiery shade of red common to those of her coloring. "Sir,
you mustn't tease me so. Are you perhaps trying to be-
devil your poor sister? I assure you, she's looking dag-

gers at me even without hearing your extravagant compliments.''

"Ah, but she couldn't possibly hear me. You see, I have no ulterior motives in complimenting you." Archie leaned back in his chair and eyed Jane in a certain way.

If she had been capable of blushing more, she would have done so. He had directed that very expression at her when her clothes were off. Was he mad to expose himself—to expose her—in such a public way, with Masha lapping up every glance and inflection for later use and the rest of the guests in the room beginning to cast curious looks their way?

"You must know, Countess," Archie said, turning from Jane to address his other listener, "I find myself in a romantic quandary. I am an ardent admirer of Lady Averham's, but she'll have none of me. I must assume it's because I'm a younger son. Untitled. Perhaps she thinks to make a more brilliant match *en second noces*. She deserves it, mind you—"

"Why, how dare you?" Jane interrupted in a furious whisper. "Do you want this to be all over Vienna by this evening? Oh! Your pardon, Masha."

"Do not ask pardon. You and I both know that I am the incurable gossip," the countess said, waving her hand at Jane as she concentrated on MacGowan. "Tell me more, sir. You spoke of a second marriage for Jane?"

"No, ma'am, I believe Lady Averham thinks I've told you quite enough, and I am her slave in these matters."

The Countess Zlotska nodded, scrutinizing Mac-Gowan. "Do you know, Jane, for you I would keep this quiet. But your young man, he doesn't want it quiet."

"I realize that." Jane sighed deeply. "And I have no idea what he would be at."

"Will you walk about the room with me, Lady Averham?" MacGowan asked. "I have the sudden urge to be alone with you. I have every hope that the Countess Zlotska will forgive us."

"Hardly alone, in a roomful of people," Jane said, but she got up at once. She suspected there would be no stopping him; that a refusal to walk with him would bring loud recriminations down upon her head and the attention of the whole room to their little corner.

She placed her hand upon his arm. All was most formal. The salon was large, and at this very moment other pairs were promenading. Among these were Flora and Bronsky, who had managed somehow to sneak his way in, though Jane had left standing instructions with the servants not to admit him.

"What on earth are you doing?" Mindful of the watchers and listeners, she gave MacGowan a brilliant smile that did not match her remark.

He kept walking, acknowledging her words with a nod. "Dear Jane, it should be evident. I don't want you to be mine in secret. I'm taking a gamble that you will one day be mine honestly, in front of the cacklers whose opinion you care so much for."

"You make me sound like a hopeless ninny," Jane said with a sigh, still maintaining the socially correct expression which more than half-proved his accusation that she cared for the world's opinion. "But you can see already where this will lead. Flora is seriously alarmed that you would think of me. She called me . . ." Jane hesitated, unable, somehow, to utter the dread word "old."

"What? If Flora has been causing you trouble, if Flora feels herself compelled to meddle in my affairs, I assure you that she need not remain under your roof an instant longer. Do you really mean to say she called you some name? I'll speak to Father at once and have her locked up in a convent. The girl's rag-mannered and quite impossible." Archie's brows came together in a scowl remarkably like the one Flora had favored Jane with earlier in the morning.

This resemblance served to remind Jane that Archie's family, no matter how he might disdain their opinion, was part of him. She had no wish to cause strife in the Foxburgh clan. Flora's youth played a large part in her disgust over the attachment, of course, but might not Lord Foxburgh have better reasons for going against a connection between Jane and his son?

"Please. Flora is young and thoughtless, but she means no harm," Jane said.

"How like you to think nothing of your own situation, but to plead for others." Archie lifted her hand to his lips and gave it a lingering kiss. "I'm certain she said something unforgivable, and I'll see to it that she apologizes to you.''

"Oh, I beg you not to mention it to her. I wouldn't have her think I go running to her brother every time she and I cross swords.''

"Every time? Flora has been less than the perfect guest, then. I knew how it would be.'' Archie still retained his hold on Jane's hand, and he pressed it warmly between both his own. His ardor and concern were evident to all who cared to look.

These numbered quiet a few. Jane noticed sundry pairs of eyes observing his maneuver and did her best to seem unmoved, no matter how his touch might dazzle her, playing havoc as it did with her memory as well as with her present desires.

"It won't be long,'' Archie prophesied.

Jane knew what he meant. The resulting surge of indignation worked to dispel her physical longings. Was she then so transparent? And was he only another coxcomb? How dared he assume he was irresistible?

Easily, she suspected. If he were the most modest man in the world, he could not doubt that he was indeed irresistible to her. Jane looked at him out of the corner of her eye as they reached the tile stove, their nominal goal, and stood to warm their hands before it.

The strong lines of his face, which Jane had so often admired, were set in determination.

"Mr. MacGowan,'' she said in quiet desperation, "I believe you know I can't stand against you forever. But I wish you would respect my feelings in this matter. I don't like this public display, I tell you.''

"You don't like my admiration? You seemed to melt a little bit last night.''

"That's not what I mean, and you know it,'' Jane said. "If it were up to me, we would still be . . . Oh, you know very well what we would be. Why have you this idiotic urge to tell the world? The next thing you know, somebody will guess what we've been to each other.''

"Oh, is that what has you skittish?'' Archie smiled in that tender way which never failed to make Jane catch her breath. "I don't think to give information on our past. It's only our future which concerns me, ma'am.''

"What future can we have? We were already having

the very best of the present, and you gave it up.'' Jane
knew that she betrayed her resentment, even speaking as
softly as she did. She didn't care.

His blue eyes were sad as he listened to the words.
''Ah, Jane, I can't help trying for more. But you may be
sure I won't trouble you forever, if such is truly your
desire.''

Jane was stricken, unable to say a word. Somehow the
thought that he would obey her and give her up was more
troubling than the notion that he would plague her forever
with these unsettling public attentions.

She was standing still, feeling oddly bereaved, as
though he had already left her instead of being close beside her, when the door opened and Johann announced
Lord Foxburgh.

Jane turned automatically toward the earl with her usual
welcoming smile. Foxburgh's face, she noted in concern,
was a hectic shade of purple. He approached his hostess
with a quick step.

''Sir, are you feeling well enough to be out this morning?''

Foxburgh laughed. ''Never better, Jane. I've come to
tell you that your little ward, Miss Schmidt, has just
agreed to make me the happiest of men. Brought her
back home and sent her straight to bed, by the way. She
wasn't feeling quite the thing. I believe the notion surprised her.''

Jane put out a hand to steady herself. MacGowan
quickly placed his arm about her waist.

''Singular,'' Lord Foxburgh went on, eyeing his hostess. ''Miss Schmidt had the same reaction. It's that odd,
is it, to think of me being married? Makes the ladies
topple over like a line of dominoes, eh?''

Jane managed to laugh and shake her head politely
through the double excitement of the news and Archie's
comforting arm. Lord Foxburgh to marry Petra! However
had it happened? This piece of news would indeed be the
talk of Vienna.

''I wish you will do me one favor, Father,'' Archie
said with a wicked grin. ''Let me be the one to tell
Flora.''

14

"Oh, Petra," Chloe said, "I knew how it would be. You are no fun anymore."

Petra smiled serenely. "I simply said, my dear, that I would not be able to continue harassing poor Johann. If I am really to marry—and I must believe I am, for Lord Foxburgh was most insistent—then it isn't quite proper for me to engage in such children's games."

"See?" Chloe frowned. "You have grown up in the worst way. Proper! I can hardly believe it's you talking." She bounced off Petra's bed, where she had been sitting, and moved to the window seat. Once there, she dropped down and began to drum her fingers against the sill. "We have Johann in a fine fever of confusion," she threw back over her shoulder. "He is beginning to jump every time he sees anyone, of whatever nationality, and you tell me we have to quit. The fun is only beginning. Unfair, Petra!"

Petra shrugged and repositioned herself on the snowy pillows propped behind her head. Lord Foxburgh had told her to rest, and she felt honor-bound to do precisely that. "We only set out to make mischief, my child, and we have done it, if I do say so myself. Johann is indeed confused, and I don't think he's been bothering to glean information about the household. He's too busy trying to discover who's been giving false information about him." She laughed. "In the past weeks we've written ciphers which accuse him of trafficking with English, French, Prussians, and Russians. He must be having a difficult time explaining his position to Baron Hager! So we have attained our objective."

Chloe turned an exasperated face to Petra. "We have? Then why must it be so dull? I expected something great to come of our baiting Johann."

"What?" Petra asked in surprise.

"Oh, I don't know. Perhaps for the emperor's men to drag him out of the house in the middle of the night. Something, at any rate, to keep me from being bored to death." Chloe lifted her chin. "Well, I shall simply have to make my own fun, without your help."

Petra looked up alertly at this. Chloe's ideas of fun were bound to be exactly what her mother would not like. And Petra could sense that Lady Averham had problems aplenty without saving Chloe from some extravagant scheme. "Don't do anything rash," Petra warned. "Think of your mother."

"How can I do anything rash?" Chloe asked with an eloquent shrug. "Even when I try, I never fail to make a mull of it. I've told you what happened when I merely wished to meet Herr van Beethoven and fall at his feet."

"Yes, Phyllida stole your thunder, so to speak."

Chloe sighed at the memory. "What I had planned as the most exciting experience of my life turned into another bore. And you ought to hear Phyllida go on about that night, simply because he gave her a little kiss! It's quite sickening. And now I have nothing to concentrate on, especially if you're determined to stop baiting Johann."

Petra hid a smile which she felt Chloe would censure as unbearably grown-up. Chloe simply would not see how rich her immediate environment was. Even though not out in society, a girl of Chloe's spirit might find much to observe and learn from this Season. Her own mother was desperately in love with the handsome Mr. MacGowan. Petra herself had succeeded in becoming engaged.

She lay back and shook her head at the wonder of it all. How surprised Mutti would be that her illegitimate daughter was to marry an English milord—was to marry at all. When Petra had left their little village in Switzerland, her mother had given her dire warnings about the cruel fate which surely must await a young girl of doubtful birth in the whirl of sophistication that was Vienna.

And so it had nearly been. Petra could hardly believe her good fortune. When she had risen from this very bed this morning, she had prayed that Lord Foxburgh would do her the honor—it had seemed a very great honor—of allowing her to become his mistress. She had been more than ready to tread her mother's path, even knowing that someday, when he was finished with her, she would likely have no kind Jane Averham to save her from misery as Mutti had once been saved.

And now! "He is to marry me," she told Chloe, exulted beyond her customary reticence.

"Yes, I'm quite aware of it," the younger girl replied. "You've told me so at least five times since I've been in the room. But think a little more, I beg you. You are marrying an old man! Really, Petra, I never thought you would carry your mercenary schemes this far."

"He is not old. He married young before. He is scarcely more than fifty."

"If my father were alive," Chloe said, "he would be that age. How can you, Petra?"

For some reason, talk of the father they shared made Petra acutely uncomfortable. How she wished that she could tell her half-sisters of their relationship! But she had settled in her own mind that they had better not know. "I find Lord Foxburgh most attractive." Petra hesitated, then took the plunge. This was, after all, her sister, though Petra would never be the one to let Chloe know it, and Petra wished to be as candid as she could with those she considered her family. "I love him."

"Oh, heavens." Chloe's dark eyes widened. "This puts another face on the matter. You poor creature."

"It isn't that bad," Petra said with a laugh.

"I suppose you'll let him touch you, then. And you'll have a baby and die. Flora says that's what happens to married women."

Petra narrowed her eyes. That remark did much to explain Lady Flora's attitude toward the married state, but it was unfortunate that she was contributing to Chloe's education by such talk. "Tragedy isn't the lot of everyone," she said. "Look at your mother, or mine, or any dozen ladies you know, all of whom lived through childbirth."

"Well, I suppose that's true enough," Chloe said, frowning. "But Flora was most insistent. It hurts, her old nurse told her, and then later you have a baby and you die. Flora's mama—"

Petra let out a peal of laughter. "You, the future mistress of I don't know how many great men, are listening to Flora's tales of the marriage bed? I thought you were wiser, my girl.''

''Well, I suppose it must not always hurt.'' Chloe was thoughtful, looking off into the distance and pursing her lips. ''The great courtesans would never—''

''Of course it doesn't. No woman would stand for something so objectionable. The race would have died out long ago. And as for children—that hurts, of course, but it is not always fatal. Me, I look forward to having a child of my own if I am so blessed. Lord Foxburgh has said . . . He has been most kind.'' Petra blushed, thinking over the conversation. He had said he would be delighted to father her children, but that she must not feel herself obliged to procreate. He was marrying to please himself, not beget more heirs. ''And only think, it makes no matter whether or not I have a baby. He has his heir and Mr. MacGowan. I shall have no reason to worry.''

''That's true too.'' Chloe nodded vigorously, as though determined to accept these sordid facts of married life. Returning to her former theme, she went on, ''And you really won't mind such an old man touching you?''

''No,'' Petra said. She could hardly confess to a thirteen-year-old her wish that Foxburgh do that very thing, and soon. He was a perfect gentleman, alas, and their wedding was to be in Scotland, after the Congress. ''Now, on to the next problem,'' she went on briskly. ''Lady Flora will not be at all pleased when she hears this news, which she will. Her father is set on announcing it at once. He is down in the drawing room even now telling Lady Averham.''

''Only fancy! He must really mean it.'' This mischievous hit served to put Chloe into a better mood. Laughing with her customary spirit, she neatly dodged the pillow Petra aimed at her head. She grabbed up one of the tapestried cushions on the window seat to retaliate in kind.

''I cannot believe Flora will be pleased,'' Petra said when their hilarity had wound down. ''If only she would fall in love with your uncle! That would take her mind off my affairs.''

''You can't be certain her mind will even be on your affairs, Petra. Flora might be pleased as anything to have her father marry again.''

"To me?" Petra let the question hang in the air.

There was really no response to this. After a few moments of thoughtful silence, Chloe said, "Have I your permission to tell Phyllida about your engagement? She's hiding out in the schoolroom, going over some of her new Beethoven pieces instead of seeing the callers. This should surprise her."

"Of course you may tell her."

Chloe went off on this errand to one sister, leaving her unacknowledged sister to lie back and contemplate a future life much rosier than that she had planned for herself so lately.

Petra even managed to smile sunnily when her new maid came in with a tisane Lady Averham had ordered. A pleasant little Austrian girl whom Petra couldn't quite like, the servant appeared to have no inkling that Petra knew she was Talleyrand's spy. Petra judged this to be Maria's first foray into the world of espionage. Having so recently been in that situation herself, she believed she knew the signs.

"It makes no matter, you know," Petra said to the maid.

"Fräulein?" Maria turned curiously from the window seat, where she had been rearranging the pillows Chloe had dislodged during her visit.

Petra was quite astonished at her own need to keep repeating the exciting news. "It makes no matter what I have done or not done, or what you tell your true masters," she said serenely. "I am to be an English milady!"

Maria looked impressed, but noticeably indignant that Fräulein Schmidt had guessed her to be other than an ordinary serving girl.

"Don't worry about it," Petra advised the girl, seeing the frown which crossed the pleasant rounded features, and guessing its cause. "It takes time to become a good spy."

In the drawing room, Flora was reacting predictably to her brother's news. "How dare you tell such lies, Archie? And get that silly smirk off your face!"

"No lie, sister dear, merely a simple statement of fact. Our father has announced his intention of taking a countess; your good friend Petra Schmidt. Miss Schmidt ought to make an admirable political hostess. She is sensible, discreet, and knowing about all the little nuances which make up polite life. Add to this her knowledge of languages and her beauty, and it's no wonder Father was smitten. He couldn't have found a better helpmeet had he advertised in the *Times*.''

Flora glared. ''That insignificant little nobody will never marry the Earl of Foxburgh. Are you mad, Archie? Father looks quite as usual.'' And she indicated her sire, who was cheerfully talking to Lady Averham. ''He appears to be appreciating Lady Averham's charms,'' she added, not quite ingenuously, with a sly look at her brother.

The flash of jealousy which quickly crossed Archie's cheerful face served to demonstrate to Flora her brother's feelings for Jane. Her heart sank; but more important at the moment than Archie's silly infatuation was their father's insane plan. ''Petra Schmidt is a scheming little fortune-hunter,'' she said bitterly. ''I never trusted her; never liked her. Why, she said right out that she was in Vienna to marry herself well! But how could I have guessed that she'd hit on my own father for her victim?''

''I know you'll think better of Miss Schmidt when you come to know her well,'' Archie said. ''And you will soon be much better acquainted. Naturally she will chaperon you next Season in town.''

''Impossible!'' Flora's sharp intake of breath was eloquent.

''Who better than your stepmama?'' Archie continued, his expression bland.

''Beast!'' Flora dashed something from her eye, turned on her heel, and walked quickly away. She brushed right past Lord Averham, who had just been announced. Jane turned from her conversation with Foxburgh and stretched out a hand to Lady Flora, but the girl said not a word to anyone. The door of the salon slammed behind her.

Averham had apparently noted the source of Flora's flight, and he approached MacGowan at once. ''Your sister seems out-of-sorts this morning,'' he said on a note of query.

Archie sighed. ''I did it, to my shame. I was not fair, Averham. I poked fun at her and baited her. But, devil take it, Flora can try a man sometimes, and I'd just found out that she had been particularly rude to . . . to a certain lady.''

Averham nodded sagely, his dark eyes sparkling. ''I can vouch for the fact that Lady Flora can be a trial. As her brother, you haven't the compensating factors of . . .'' His voice trailed away.

''Of what?'' MacGowan asked curiously.

''I was trying to think how to put it into words.'' Averham shrugged. ''I find it hard to explain how a quarter-hour's exchange of insults with that young lady is worth days of the fawning and simpering I usually get from young misses.''

Archie smiled. ''So you're in love with her. Best of luck to you, man. Flora badly needs love.''

''But perhaps not from me,'' Averham said. ''She hasn't warmed to me, despite the attention I've shown her. I never fail to cozen her into a dance; I send flowers which she doesn't bother to wear or to thank me for; and despite my evident admiration, she is still capable of walking right past me when I greet her. I had hoped that some intimacy would develop during our ride back to Vienna that day of our excursion into the woods, but I caught cold at that. She was dumb as a post the entire way.''

Archie felt a stirring of emotion at even the most casual mention of that fateful excursion, the enchanted afternoon when he had made love to Jane, the day he had discovered he wished to marry her. He could not but warm even more to a man who would mention that occasion, however innocently. ''Did I say Flora needed love? It's discipline I meant. That and a sense of humor. Flora lacks the saving grace of laughter—even to the smallest degree. I feel sorry for the lass.''

''What was the news you told her that so upset her? I don't ask you to relate it to me if it was spoken in confidence, you understand.''

''It concerns Lady Averham's goddaughter, Miss Schmidt.''

Archie wondered if he only imagined the knowing look which the mention of Petra's name brought to Averham's face. Yet why should Averham not know who Petra really was? His late brother might possibly even have bragged

on the situation. And Averham must have noticed the
resemblance Petra bore to the females of the Averham
line. Archie's father had informed him of that interesting
tidbit.

"What is this news about Miss Schmidt?" Averham
asked in an easy tone.

Once again Archie couldn't be sure if Averham knew
or didn't know that he was speaking of his niece. Well,
no matter, the news was the same. "My father has swept
her off her feet," Archie said with a grin. "They have
decided to marry."

"You don't say!" Averham looked amazed. "Since you
tell me so, I won't disbelieve it, but what news! And
Lady Flora is overset, I'd wager, because she doesn't
fancy a new stepmother."

"You state the case lightly, but yes, that's it."

"Poor girl," Averham muttered. "I dearly hope she
does nothing rash."

"I rely upon you, sir, to join with me in seeing she
does not," Archie said. He felt another twinge of guilt
that he had been so hard on Flora. Her rudeness to Jane
he could only imagine, since Jane wouldn't comment on
the details and had been sorry she had let the matter slip.
But he had punished Flora for it.

"Delighted to help you, sir," Averham said with a
sunny smile. "We will keep Lady Flora too occupied to
dwell on her father's plans."

At this moment Jane walked up to the pair, her expression eloquent with concern. She had left Lord Foxburgh with the Countess Zlotska. "What happened to
Lady Flora?" she asked MacGowan. "I know you were
about to tell her a particular thing, but I'd hate to think
it distressed her so."

"It did," MacGowan said with a bow. "And you
needn't be reticent in front of your brother-in-law, Lady
Averham. I've told him my father's news."

"I'm astonished Miss Schmidt could bring off such a
coup," Averham put in.

"If you only knew." Jane shook her head, thinking of
the details which Foxburgh had just imparted to her. Petra had indeed offered her virtue, only to be saved by the
earl's notions of chivalry. How amazing, and how lucky.
Her eyes happened to meet MacGowan's just then, and

she started at the look in his. He was longing for her, even now while they were speaking of other things. She understood, for so it was with her. No matter what the subject of conversation, no matter where her thoughts, she wanted him. Extraordinary that he should feel the same. . . .

Her brother-in-law cleared his throat. "Perhaps the two of you will excuse me. I see young Thompson is here. Must speak to him about a certain matter."

Jane looked after Robbie. "Do you know," she said to MacGowan, "I believe he thought we would be glad to be left alone."

"An astute man," Archie said. "I wish above all else to be alone with you."

"And I with you," Jane returned. "If only you weren't so stubborn. It's by your desire that we are no longer . . ." She hesitated, a fatal hesitation, for he laughed aloud.

"Jane, you must really try to develop some bold language to match your behavior." He was indeed laughing at her, but though his lips were smiling, his eyes betrayed a certain sadness. "I wonder if you'll ever understand what I feel?" he said in a near-whisper. "Is there nothing for you and me but passion?"

Jane glanced away. She understood how *she* felt, and that was bad enough. Love, helpless and hobbling, was not an experience she would wish on any intelligent woman. If only she were an innocent, like Petra, who must be looking forward to her coming marriage with a joy only a little alloyed with pragmatism. If only she didn't know already how painfully she chafed under the bonds of matrimony; how little faith she had in the sacrament itself.

If only she could have her lover back.

Suddenly, standing beside him was torture. "I must leave you." She turned to walk away.

He caught at her arm. "It isn't so easy as that, Lady Averham. I've begun bringing my feelings for you into public, and you're vexed with me. There, I've said it. After last night, all Vienna must know what I think of you. And should someone still be ignorant, I'm not above helping the slow of wit." Pulling her to him, he kissed her as only he knew how. Starved for him, Jane clung eagerly despite everything.

The effect of this embrace on a crowded drawing room was electric. Jane felt her face turn scarlet as every eye in the room riveted on her and MacGowan. Furious, she stared into his eyes and read there the triumph of one who has succeeded in a clever scheme.

"This is not fair," she whispered.

"Precisely my point, dear lady," he returned, not releasing her. "You have declared war. So be it. Let us see who shall win this skirmish." And he kissed her again, more roughly than before.

Jane pushed him back, and he was at least gentleman enough not to hold her imprisoned in his arms. "That will be quite enough, sir."

"That's where you're wrong." And Archie tightened his arms for a third kiss, a gentle one this time, a sweet memory of their shared passion. "Three dances would shock London society," he murmured as he released her. "What will three kisses do to Vienna?"

Jane had nothing to say. A timid look around revealed all her friends avidly watching for the next move, quite as though they were engrossed in a theatrical performance. Lord Foxburgh looked as though he would soon be picking his jaw up off the floor. The Countess Zlotska rested her hand on her cheek as she stared at the tableau; Jane knew for a fact that Masha had never paid half so much attention to a play or opera.

A very proper English matron, who had brought her young niece to Lady Averham's for the first time, was apparently scandalized, while the white-gowned miss she shepherded betrayed awe and pleasure. As for the young English equerries and the sprinkling of foreign gentlemen, they looked embarrassed or mischievous, according to their nationalities and temperaments.

Jane was only glad that neither of her daughters happened to be present, that Petra was in her bed, and that Flora had left the room. The girls would find out about this soon enough. All Vienna would, as MacGowan had so kindly pointed out.

She spared one last menacing stare for him and took a deep breath. Not for nothing had she trained herself in drawing-room manners.

Nodding pleasantly to MacGowan, she moved away from him. She struck up a conversation with the nearest person, who happened to be the Prince de Ligne. The old man's twinkling eyes and twitching smile nearly undid her, but not quite.

She determined to act as though MacGowan had committed some gaucherie at a dinner table and ignored the situation with all her energy, as any good hostess would do.

If she sensed the mood in the room change again and thought that a tinge of admiration for her poise was present, she was probably not altogether wrong.

Lady Flora MacGowan hadn't yet done with slamming doors. "Blast and double blast!" she cried, bursting into her bedroom and letting the heavy door crash against the wall. A delicate piece of Meissen toppled over onto the carpet from its place on a small table.

Jeannie the maid was in the room picking up discarded clothing. She let fly her mistress's nightrail and rushed for the figurine. Tenderly she restored it to its place. "Didna break. Dinna ye worry, my leddy," she said in a soothing tone, noticing that Flora was looking murderously at the scrap of china.

"I wish it had." Flora restrained herself from snatching the insipid piece from Jeannie's hand and throwing it against the tile stove. How she hated the fussiness of this chamber, and most especially that disgusting pink-and-white rendition of embracing shepherd and shepherdess. "And close that window, if you please," she added, crossing to the bed. She flung herself down upon the counterpane and placed a pillow over her head.

"A wee bit out-of-sorts today, my leddy?" Jeannie did as she was told, letting the window down with a snap that was most satisfying to Flora in her disordered state.

One of the undeniable features of her bedroom was that when the windows were open, any pianoforte music from the schoolroom could be clearly heard. Often she had no objection to hearing Phyllida play, and she knew Jeannie liked it. Yet any noise from a member of Jane's family was excruciating today.

"Jeannie, I must do something rash," Flora said.

"Beg pardon?"

Flora sat up, tossing the pillow aside. She had forgotten that her words would be completely muffled. "I need to act, and act soon," she said, glaring at her maid as though that innocent had caused all her troubles.

"Act how? Not the plan with the Sassenach, is it?" Jeannie quailed beneath her mistress's stern gaze.

"I think it must be," Flora said, half to herself. "He is indeed a stupid foreigner, but at least he hasn't betrayed me."

"Who has betrayed you, my leddy?" Curiosity and sympathy were clear in Jeannie's voice.

"Only my brother and my father. Not to mention Lady Averham and that sneaking, sly Petra Schmidt." Flora looked as though she would happily strangle any one of them.

"Fancy that! Poor lass." Jeannie came forward to stroke her mistress's hair.

"Stop that!" When she was feeling low, Flora could not bear to be touched. "Now, bring me my desk, Jeannie, and be ready to carry another note to that Bronsky creature. I can't wait any longer."

These ominous words made Jeannie cluck and murmur, but she did as she was told.

15

JANE WENT TO HER ROOMS as soon as her last caller had
disappeared—and her dratted friends took a long time in
leavetaking this morning. Once safe in her boudoir, she
took a seat and thought long and hard.

Archie, his outrageous scheme complete, had left her
house quite tamely with only one formal bow to Jane and
a sheepish grin in the direction of his startled father.
MacGowan was evidently pleased that he and Jane would
perforce become the talk of Vienna.

Jane pressed her hands to her hot cheeks at the memory of those public kisses. She supposed it would be only
a matter of time until the girls heard of them. What could
she possibly say by way of explanation?

When the door opened she turned guiltily, expecting
to meet the first accuser.

"Oh, Phyllida." She stretched out a tentative hand to
her daughter, feeling suddenly shy. The child didn't look
disgusted or even overly distressed, she noted in surprise.

"I must talk to you, Mama." Phyllida came forward
to perch on a hard chair opposite Jane's couch.

"I can explain," Jane said, though she doubted very
much if she could.

"What do you mean?" Phyllida looked puzzled. "I
know you believe you can tell everything I'm thinking and
feeling, but I haven't even begun to say what I came to."

"Go on, dear," Jane said in relief. "Tell me."

Phyllida took a deep breath. "I've been so happy this
morning, working at my music, though I knew you would
scold me for not appearing before your guests. Mama, I
must have it out with you over this business of a Season
in Vienna. You must let me beg off the chore of any more
parties. I don't like them. I find the young men silly,
braying idiots. You must let me stay at home for the rest

of the Congress. I . . . I hate to waste my time any longer.''

Jane was silent. Phyllida's rash statements were not altogether unpredicted. The old arguments rose to her lips about Phyllida's need to know the world, to know young men so that she might one day make a wise selection. But somehow she could not utter them.

''Mama, stop trying to live your life through me,'' Phyllida added, her color rushing up to her face quite as Jane's was wont to do. ''Please. Go to the parties for yourself, not for me. You're beautiful and glamorous and you enjoy them. Perhaps that will come later for me. But the social whirl is torture to me now.'' She paused. ''I've settled with myself that as long as I have the good fortune to be in Vienna, Herr van Beethoven's home, I will study and work all day, every day, at his music. That is Vienna for me, Mama. His music.''

''Oh, my dear girl,'' Jane said. ''You are missing so much.''

''Am I?'' Phyllida's face was glowing. ''What would I think of myself years from now, Mama, if I looked back on Vienna as a round of parties when the greatest man on earth was working right here? I must work too. I cannot become Herr van Beethoven's friend, I know that, but I can certainly see him whenever he appears at a concert, and hear all his music whenever it is performed, and, most important, perform it myself. Don't you see, Mama, by playing his music I may come to know *him.*''

Jane frowned, puzzled. ''If I didn't know better, Phyllida, I'd say you were in love with the man. But I know you can't have met.''

Phyllida's flush deepened. ''This isn't a personal sort of love,'' she said. ''If I could do anything, I would be a . . . a monk of some kind, sitting at his feet. I can't do that, for I'm certain he would not like it, but I can still take pleasure in being in his town playing his music. I've only recently found the secret which will make all the difference in my playing, and it's all due to his music. Oh, Mama, it is the most wondrous music the world has ever known.''

''There are many who agree with you, child,'' Jane said. ''I might be among them if I didn't have a bone to pick with Herr van Beethoven. How dare he turn my daughter away from her social duties at such a time as this?''

Phyllida saw her mother's smile and wasn't offended. "Oh, Mama, I knew you'd understand," she cried, throwing her arms around Jane. "Then I may stay home from the balls? You'll save no end of money. I'm sure you were about to ruin yourself in gowns for me."

"You have a very poor idea of your father's provision for you if you can think so," Jane said severely. "Don't think motives of economy will turn the trick with me, child. Since you come to me and plead so eloquently, I have no choice but to grant your request. Yes, you may stay home from at least a ball or two. We'll see. You might regret the parties once you're stuck at home every night with Chloe."

From the stubborn set of Phyllida's jaw, Jane rather doubted this, but one could always hope.

"Phyllida," she added hesitantly, "I must tell you something that happened to me this morning. I only mention it because I don't want you to hear gossip on the matter and wonder about the true story. Though, come to think of it," and here Jane frowned, wondering if she was being too hasty, "you will hardly be in a position to hear gossip if you intend to immure yourself at the pianoforte."

"Is it that Petra is to marry Lord Foxburgh?" Phyllida asked. "Chloe told me that. Did it upset you, Mama? I was so certain you'd be pleased."

Jane met the eyes so like her own and smiled a reassuring smile. "No, it is not Petra's news. That does please me. It's something about me. Our friend Mr. MacGowan had some mischievous impulse this morning and kissed me in front of the company. The story will be all over Vienna, and I wished you to know that there is nothing to worry about."

"Kissed you!" Phyllida's mouth gaped open. "Good heavens, Mama. What can he have been thinking?"

Somewhat less than flattered, Jane answered, "I told you, my love. He was feeling mischievous. Nothing more. He wishes to cause a nine days' wonder." She paused, considering a new idea that might possibly serve as an explanation. "You know he's been working for some cause or other, for the British office. Perhaps he thinks to deflect interest from whatever his real project is by raking up a scandal which involves me." A little smile played about her lips as she spun this air-dream.

"Perhaps Lord Castlereagh may someday thank me for my patriotism. What do you think?"

"I don't know what to think, Mama," Phyllida stated, looking at her mother with a new penetration. She rose and kissed Jane's forehead. "I ought to leave you now, so *you* can think."

Jane looked sharply at her daughter. "Think? What should I have to think about?"

Phyllida only shrugged, gave a lopsided grin, and went away.

Jane leaned back on the sofa. Did everyone in the world know her heart? This was deeply embarrassing.

It was also the saddest situation she had ever been in.

Archie, so ardent and loving, so incredibly innocent in his assumption that . . . that what? Perhaps he thought that love would conquer all problems that might arise from their union. He had spoken no word of love to her, however.

She was grateful for that small blessing. If he loved her, and she believed he must, since he was going to so much trouble over the matter, then he would penetrate one of the last chinks in her already patchy armor. At least she wasn't certain of his love. At least he had not spoken the words.

Jane believed this to be a simple accident of vocabulary. Surely his speech and his actions had made the situation clear enough. He wished to marry her; he, who had no need to be fettered by matrimony at all, wished to marry her. By kissing her in public, he was obviously trying to force the issue.

Here Jane's panic sprang up and mixed with irritation. He was indeed trying to force her; he didn't trust to her wisdom in handling the situation.

Why should he? a voice whispered. In his eyes Jane had shown herself to be recalcitrant, had refused to act in what he considered to be both their best interests.

But that shouldn't matter. Jane brought a fist down on the arm of the couch. He ought to respect her feelings, for they were valid. Even if they were silly to him, he ought not to brush them aside as of no account.

That he had done so with no inkling that he had acted in a less-than-honorable manner augured poorly for their future together. Jane knew she would have no patience

with herself, would hate herself forever if she let her
disreputable love for that young man coerce and prod her
into another unequal match.

She ended her morning's contemplation on that note,
but she was somehow disappointed over her conclusion.
Abandon all to love, her romantic side insisted. But Jane
could not.

That night at the ballet, Jane made sure her shoulders
were straight and her expression serene as she faced down
curious Vienna. Pauline, who had naturally heard of Mr.
MacGowan's scandalous behavior, had employed all her
arts to make certain her mistress was gowned and coiffed
to admiration, since every eye would be upon her.

The Czar of Russia leered at Jane from the imperial
box. Emperor Franz looked immensely amused, his frail
empress bright and interested.

Rows of royal and noble personages eyed Jane with the
speculation she had once thought she would fear more
than anything.

Strangely enough, she was almost amused by the sensation she was causing. As though from a long way off,
she watched herself attending the ballet, sitting calmly
among the giggles and whispers and sly looks, and
couldn't make herself mind it.

She almost felt herself float with the freedom. She really didn't care what society thought of her. She need not
care! It was an intoxicating notion.

When she saw MacGowan she came down from the
clouds. Of course he would be here, would enter her box
with that eager air. Who did he think he was?

Her declared lover, of course. The onlookers' stares
became understanding, indulgent. Jane felt like throwing
her fan at everyone; but as she had only one fan, this
would not have done much to relieve her indignation.

On either side of her, Flora and Petra sat in blissful
ignorance of the morning's events. Petra had spent the
entire day in her room; Flora had done the same after
her dramatic exit from the salon that morning. Luck had
seen to it that neither of their servants had informed them
of Lady Averham's odd conduct with Mr. MacGowan.

Flora, Jane knew, would be snappish or freezing if she
had an inkling of her brother's odd start. Petra would not

care, but she would at least look conscious. No, neither of them knew a thing. Trust Phyllida not to spread gossip; though in this case Phyllida's mother would have been glad if she had. Jane dreaded making such a communication to the girls under her care, yet she must do so, and soon. She would have to say something about the strange looks everyone in society had given her this evening.

"My dearest Lady Averham." MacGowan nodded briefly at his sister and Miss Schmidt, then grasped Jane's gloved hand and carried it to his lips.

"Sir, we are glad to see you," Jane said in a remarkably even tone, considering her galloping emotions. "Won't you sit down?"

"No, thank you. I only stopped in to inform my sister and Miss Schmidt of our situation."

"What situation?" Jane set her jaw. She had been wishing the girls already knew about the three kisses but surely he would not be so mad as to . . .

"So that you may not hear it from some other source, Flora, Miss Schmidt, I come to tell you that I kissed Lady Averham this morning, three times in fact, in full view of the visitors gathered in her drawing room." MacGowan paused, looked at Jane significantly, and continued. "I did this to proclaim to the world in the easiest way possible my love for Lady Averham and my wish to marry her."

Jane's mouth dropped open, and her thoughts flashed back to the infuriating way he had made his original marriage proposal—one leg into his drawers as he dressed himself in the woodland cottage, in the middle of another thought. Now here was the declaration of love, phrased, not to her, but to his sister and Petra! He was impossible.

Yet her body tingled with the new security that he loved her; did not merely desire her or wish to cause a sensation by marrying an older woman, but loved her.

"Brother, you're being very silly," Flora said with severity. "Lady Averham is old enough to be your mother."

"Ah, Flora, there may be some five-year-old mothers somewhere, but if there are, I find the situation too sad to comment upon. And so should you."

Flora glared.

Petra, meanwhile, was squeezing Jane's hand in excitement. "Oh, how beautiful, madame," she whispered into Jane's ear. "I will be your mama."

Jane was astonished by this thought. Indeed, such would be the case were it not for one small fact: she wasn't going to marry MacGowan.

He was eyeing her warily, as though they were indeed at war, as he had told her earlier, and he had pulled off a daring skirmish. "There, ma'am, our secret is out," he said in satisfaction. "Do what you will now, but you need not worry over keeping our situation from your young ladies."

"I suppose you've already told Chloe and Phyllida?" Flora inquired. Her voice sounded scratchy as Highland wool.

"I thought I'd leave that to you," Archie said. "Or perhaps Miss Schmidt would like to tell them. Their mother should be the one, of course, but I happen to know that Lady Averham is remarkably reticent on this subject."

"Mr. MacGowan," Jane said evenly, "please leave the box. You've overset my charges sufficiently for one evening. And I must protest the way you continually tease your sister."

"Ah, my lady, who else is there to bring her out of herself? She will hardly allow your charming brother-in-law near her."

Flora emitted a little sound of frustrated rage. Jane looked eloquently at MacGowan and made a telling motion with her head.

"I live but to obey your commands," he said, lifting her hand once more.

She halfway expected him to strip off the glove so that he might kiss her bare skin; nothing he did would surprise her. But he only saluted her quite tamely, then followed suit with Petra. Flora snatched her hand out of her brother's reach, or he would have kissed it too.

"Until later," he said with a significant look at Jane. Then he was gone.

Jane was left with two more pairs of eyes on her in addition to those of the surrounding spectators. She felt rather sorry for La Bigottini, the beautiful and talented Parisian dancer who had become the rage of Vienna and who was emoting with her usual style the story of "Nina, the peasant girl made mad by love.'' Would nobody watch the stage?'' Jane did, resolutely.

''Madam, I wish to return home,'' Flora said through her teeth. ''I have never been so humiliated. You've made a fool of me, and I won't stand for it.''

''I'm sorry you feel that way, my dear,'' Jane said, trying for understanding. Had MacGowan been her own brother, she would surely have been ready to strangle him by this time. Indeed, she was halfway minded to do so on her own account.

''Yes, let us go,'' Petra put in. ''Is more a sensation to leave now, do you not think? They will all say we follow after him and meet him elsewhere.''

''We're staying,'' Flora said, a look of alarm crossing her face.

Petra gave Jane a surreptitious wink.

Jane tried to relax under the very public scrutiny she was subjected to for the next hour until she could make her escape to a supper party where the only advantage was that the eyes were fewer in number. It seemed a century ago that she had congratulated herself on not caring what people thought. MacGowan had made a direct hit. She cared very much for what Flora and Petra thought of her; she had hoped they looked up to her, respected her. Now she stood revealed as a silly woman, a ridiculous figure, a duenna preoccupied by romance.

Petra seemed delighted by the situation, Flora disgusted, for once, beyond the power of speech. Jane bore each of their moods with stoic patience for the rest of the evening.

She knew very well that her sudden concentration on the girls' opinion was only a cover-up for her real anxiety. Now, for good or ill, she had Archie's declaration of love to consider. He had said it to his sister, and in an offhand way, but he had said it all the same. ''My love for Lady Averham''—those had been his very words.

His love. Jane chided herself for her sentimental foolishness all the while she stored up the words in her heart, where she knew they would be her most precious treasure.

She had never wished so much for an evening to end. She was sure that she would drift off to sleep immediately, her problems forgotten for at least a night, wrapped as she would be at long last in the assurance of Archie's affection.

* * *

The event was somewhat different from the expectation. Jane turned countless times upon her pillow that night, but she came no nearer to peace within herself. She wondered, as morning dawned, if she would ever be tranquil again.

In all her thirty-four years, nobody had ever claimed to love her. Her parents had never said they did. Her little girls had been too thoughtless, her husband too cold and uncaring to grant her that precious gift. Now she had it from the man she loved with all her heart.

Jane finally gave up trying to sleep and lit the lamp. Yet reading held no charms for her either. At length she found herself at a table near her bed, in company with a pack of cards, laying out endless rounds of patience.

A night spent thus did little to convince her that the solitary existence of a widow was the most desirable thing in the world.

Pauline, when she found her mistress in the morning stolidly lining up jacks under queens, was not reticent. "The circles under madame's eyes, they are as black as the Seine on a moonless night. How can one attend the masked ball tonight? Ah, that is the answer—the mask." She bustled about, casting Jane dark looks and emitting theatrical sighs. "If there is unmasking, madame must not do it. Ah, it would be more than my reputation is worth! I had thought that the new happiness would lead to a greater bloom, but this! Naturally madame will go to bed now; that should repair some of the damage."

"Pauline, you take a good deal too much freedom," Jane said automatically. She stood and stretched. She had grown abominably stiff during the hours of losing hands. In truth, her bed, which had hardly seemed to welcome her in the night, did look enticingly comfortable in the harsh light of morning. She crossed to it, dropping her dressing gown on a convenient bench, and burrowed down under the covers.

"Before sleeping, madame will have a *petit déjeuner* to nourish the body into best looks," Pauline announced. "I shall have the girl fetch hot milk and plain bread. *Le chocolat*, that would not lead to a deep and soothing sleep."

"As you say," Jane murmured, patting back a yawn. She struggled to a sitting position. Strange, she couldn't seem to keep her mind on her worries. . . . "But today is one of my usual days at home," she cried. "I can't simply sleep the day away."

"Madame must," Pauline said. "Mademoiselle Schmidt, she will act the hostess. It is *convenable*, is it not?"

"Insofar as I could not possibly expect Lady Flora to do me the favor, I suppose it is most appropriate," Jane said, shaking her head. Naturally Pauline would know every detail of Petra's marriage plans; still, Jane could never get used to the way servants so easily learned everything. "Petra is a most practical young lady and will know just what to do. Bring me my desk, please. I must write a note to the Countess Zlotska, asking her to spend the morning here. I believe she was going to anyway, but now she must, to watch over the girls."

"Madame's absence will cause the talk," Pauline said, crossing the room to where Jane's little portable desk reposed on a gilt table, "but better the talk than that Vienna should see her looking so! What will the young man think?"

"Pauline!"

"Ah, the color, it helps. But it does not help enough. I shall see that madame has a full nine hours."

"Whatever you say, Pauline," Jane said meekly, hiding a smile. She supposed that she could hardly cause more talk than she had already . . . drat Archie for causing her a sleepless night, of all things most disastrous to the looks even of a schoolroom miss, let alone a woman of a certain age. Now she did indeed have the duty of wasting the day in sleep, for she couldn't appear in public without it. How odd that the worries of the night seemed so silly, seemed hardly to exist, when nothing had really changed and she was not one whit better off, with regard to MacGowan, than she had been when she lay down last night. . . .

Pauline was severe enough to shake Jane awake to drink the milk and eat the bread when it came, but she looked sorry to do so, and she soon drew the heavy draperies closed against the crisp bright day and left her mistress in the repairing hands of Morpheus.

16

THE MASKED RIDOTTO that evening at the Hofburg was
no torment to Jane; indeed, since one must go out, she
couldn't have asked for a more congenial entertainment.
Archie penetrated her disguise at once, of course, but all
the other guests were uncertain who she was—or, if they
knew the rules of the masquerade prevented their saying
so. Jane was thankfully anonymous for an entire evening,
free to watch Petra's new happiness as the betrothed of
Lord Foxburgh. Free, also, to observe her brother-in-
law's determined assault upon Lady Flora and to doubt
that it would ever succeed.

The next night, though, brought the Razumovsky ball,
where Jane must appear in her own guise. She nearly
shuddered at the thought after the restful masquerade.

All Vienna would be wondering what Lady Averham
and Mr. MacGowan would do next. And Jane herself was
as mystified as any gossipmonger.

No amount of thinking had served to reconcile her
mind with her emotions. She was astonished, elated, that
Archie should profess love for her; she was annoyed that
he should persist in his public attentions when she had
made her disapproval known.

Most of all, she feared him.

As the carriage rolled out beyond the town walls to
the Razumovsky palace, Jane tried to concentrate on the
coming festivities. She was dressed in her best, and she
was burning with the excitement of a kind. Yet rather
than face her lover and the speculative multitudes, she
would rather have stayed at home in bed, a good book
her only companion.

The atmosphere within the Averham carriage was
strained due to the fact that Flora refused either to look
at Petra or Jane or to speak to either of them. Petra, with

philosophical calm, ignored her future stepdaughter. Jane
was used to Flora; but she feared it would be a long night
and prayed that the young ladies would soon start dancing and be able to separate.

However uncertain her own mood, Jane had to rejoice
to see Petra's blooming looks. Betrothal certainly agreed
with her goddaughter. As for Flora, Jane spent most of
the carriage ride in scrutinizing her young guest. Was it
only imagination, or did Flora look almost feverish this
evening? There was an odd gleam in her eye, but perhaps
this was only her resentment of Jane's entanglement with
Archie and Petra's with Lord Foxburgh.

Jane had almost resolved to risk a scene and ask Flora
if anything else was the matter, when the carriage pulled
up at the Razumovsky residence, distracting her and
pitching the party into all the bustle of arrival. The three
ladies, unescorted this evening by any gentlemen, were
soon moving up a flight of magnificent stairs and on into
the fashionable crowd.

Hundreds of people graced the Russian plenipotenti-
ary's newly constructed palace this evening: the loveliest
ladies, the highest dignitaries, all the vivid personalities
of Vienna milled about in the richly decorated rooms.

Jane called out greetings to friends and managed to
deflect a score of compliments from gentlemen who
wished to walk with her. By the time she had refused,
with a smile, the fifth man's request, she began to wonder
if she was playing this game wisely. She had thought that
coming out tonight without any escort would make clear
to Archie her wish for independence. But perhaps she
ought to have arrived under the guard of a regiment. Perhaps she ought to beckon to these men instead of putting
them off.

As she, Petra, and Flora strolled through a gallery
lined with priceless statues, two tall figures elbowed their
way through the press of people and bowed before the
ladies.

"Lord Foxburgh and Mr. MacGowan." Jane held out
her hand first to the earl, then to his son. Archie was
looking magnificent, of course. Jane had to glance away
to avoid staring at him in open longing. "We are so happy
to see you," she said as Archie clasped her hand. There
was more than only social truth in that statement, and

MacGowan probably knew it. From the warmth of his gaze, he must suspect that Jane was more than politely pleased at his presence.

"Some of us are happy," Flora said with a toss of her head.

Flora was indeed angry at both her father and her brother and was too honest to make a secret of her feelings; all very well. Sisters and brothers might brangle. But such rudeness to a father was new in Jane's experience. She gave the young woman an amazed look while Lord Foxburgh shook his head and Archie frowned.

"Really, sister," MacGowan said, "you might be vexed with us, but proper conduct should still carry the day when we meet on social occasions."

Flora tightened her lips and said nothing.

Her father chose to escape the tension. Having planted a light kiss on his daughter's unresisting cheek and saluted Jane's hand, he laid claim to Petra and swept off with her on his arm.

"Oh!" Flora gave a perceptible shiver. "How I detest seeing that."

"You detest seeing your father happy?" Jane asked in a cool tone. "I would get used to that spectacle, my dear. And is it not true that you don't often have a chance to see your father at all, what with his career and your penchant for the Scottish countryside? If I were you I would enjoy his company while you are together and not mind what he does with his personal life."

"Archie," Flora said through her teeth, "take me away. I'm about to be ill."

"And leave Lady Averham alone?"

"Yes. She has hundreds of friends in this crowd. Let some one of them take care of her."

Truly, this girl was behaving in an extraordinary manner. A glance around told Jane that Flora's snappish words were beginning to attract attention. From his position behind a gilded column, the old Prince de Ligne winked at Jane. She felt extraordinarily heartened by the simple act of comradeship.

"Perhaps you do need to lie down for a bit, dear," Jane said, forcing herself to smile at Flora. "Let me go with you to find the ladies' retiring room. This is such a vast place."

"Oh, never mind, Archie," Flora snapped, ignoring Jane. "I'm quite capable of finding things by myself." And turning quickly, she dashed away through the crowd.

"Oh, dear." Jane immediately followed after. Flora must not be lost in this squeeze.

"Jane." MacGowan caught at her arm. "She's out of sight. Even if every other lady at this party weren't dressed in white as she is, you'd never spot her. We must trust to Flora's discretion."

"That settles it. I must find her." Jane moved on resolutely. MacGowan, unable to stop her, walked along with her. His arm stole about her waist.

"Sir!" Jane tamped down the thrill she felt at his touch and tried to act as though he were any man taking an unwanted liberty.

"For your protection, ma'am, in this crowd." The arm stayed where it was.

In the chamber set aside for the ladies' use, no one had seen Flora. Jane reported this disheartening news to Archie, and they searched on. Through the brightly lit ballroom, where no one was dancing as yet, into more lavish rooms of the palace went Jane, closely followed by MacGowan.

So many art objects, Jane marveled, not for the first time, as her eyes rested on an antique tapestry. How wealthy Razumovsky must be. And how very many hideaways there were in this palace where a young lady might lose herself.

Soon even Archie was beginning to look worried. "She is my sister; I ought not to have let her go," he murmured as they peeked into an antechamber and backed out again as quickly, having surprised a dashing hussar and a voluptuous lady in the middle of an indiscretion. "She could truly be in danger."

Jane's cheeks were hot from the scene she had accidentally witnessed. "She left so fast, you would have been hard pressed to catch her," she had to say in all fairness, much though she would have preferred to agree with him and lay the blame at his door. "I was the one standing next to her. I ought to have kept tight hold of her arm."

"As though she were a child? No, Jane, you have been

kind enough to shelter the ungrateful chit, but you're not obligated to do so much.''

"But as her chaperon, I must certainly keep looking for her."

"Yes. I think we'll spend the whole evening in that fruitless task. Promise me you'll give me a waltz later on, whether we find her or no.''

Jane looked into the smiling blue eyes. "I fear, sir, that you're not a considerate brother.''

"Is that a yes or a no?''

"I suppose that if I don't dance with you, you'll find some other way to make us a spectacle,'' Jane said. "But I pray we may find her. It would be beyond anything insensitive for a girl's duenna to be dancing the night away while the girl is off . . .'' Jane hesitated, unsure as to what Flora might mean to do. "Can we ask the servants if she simply ordered the carriage and went home? That would be like her.''

"I'll take care of that matter right now." Archie hailed a passing footman and spoke to him in low tones. The man nodded and sped away. "I told him we'd wait here for his answer,'' Archie then said, drawing Jane down to a velvet-covered chaise in a convenient corner, out of the way of the crowd. "For the moment we are the next thing to alone. I won't waste my chance. Jane, my darling Jane, won't you tell me what I wish to hear? We might make this our betrothal ball.''

Jane closed her eyes in sudden pain. This had come so fast. Her lover was not one for leading up slowly to a subject. "Archie—my dear one—you simply won't understand. You can't make me change my mind by wearing me down. I know I won't marry again. It has nothing to do with you. I find the state objectionable, and I can have a full and rich life without . . .''

"Without what, Jane? Without our love?'' His arm, which had not left her waist, now tightened. "You know I love you. I suspect you harbor tender feelings for me. You're afraid of them, aren't you?''

"I'm afraid of you,'' Jane said. She panicked at the mere thought of letting him know of her love. That he suspected was only natural, considering her behavior, but knowing would certainly be far worse.

"I'm sorry for that.'' Archie's voice was soft, and he

looked directly into Jane's eyes with such tenderness that she had to drop her own.

At this interesting point, the footman Archie had spoken to returned, bowed, and informed them that no young lady of Flora's description had ordered a carriage and gone away.

"She wouldn't have been able to make them understand her, in any case," Jane said, getting up. "She has only English. Now, Mr. MacGowan, where should we search next? The antechambers are certainly an embarrassing task, but I suppose we ought to continue."

"The moment we return to the real world, it's back to Mr. MacGowan," Archie teased. But he rose with her and led her on through the richly appointed salons.

"She can't have gone to the garden," Jane murmured as they wandered. "That would be folly. She's not that stupid . . . I mean to say . . . Oh, I'm sorry, Archie. Sometimes Flora irks me, and I forget you're her brother."

He only laughed and shook his head at her.

They made a silent and informal agreement that Archie should be the one to open any doors, lest Jane view anything objectionable to the delicate sensibilities of a lady. Though Jane privately doubted that she was any longer a lady, and though she had never been a frail flower, she agreed that she had as soon not come upon another hussar intimately engaged with a female.

"Our host is all that is respectable, mind you," Archie said as he opened another door, found the small room within empty, and closed it. "That military man and his lady fair were no doubt an aberration."

"Or simply put there to remind me what a fool I've been making of myself," Jane muttered, stalking on.

"Do you equate our love with the silly scramblings of a couple of—"

"We have no way of knowing their situation." Jane interrupted Archie's scoffing words in an impassioned tone. "We have nearly done as much, you and I, a time or two."

That silenced him. His jaw tightened perceptibly as he opened the next door.

They had already looked in on the ornate library, with its soaring gallery and staggering collection of rare books and scrolls. This chamber turned out to be a minor book room of sorts, fireless but lit by a branch of candles. It was cozy and gilt-trimmed, the light illuminating the precious bindings of rows of books, and it was not empty.

"Flora!" Jane cried.

The girl looked round, the bored expression on her face changing to one of vexation.

"What is the meaning of this?" Archie snapped, charging into the room.

On his knees before Flora was Anatole Bronsky. Like his fair companion, he first appeared vexed, but then his expression altered to one of cunning.

"This man has compromised me, and he is going to marry me," Flora said coldly, waving a hand in the direction of Bronsky. "We haven't yet discussed the details, but you may tell Father that it is settled, Archie."

"I'll be damned if I will! You will certainly not marry this fellow. And what do mean by 'compromised'?"

"The usual," Flora said after a moment's hesitation.

"I cannot allow my love's brother—my own future brother—to labor under such an error." Bronsky sprang to his feet. "I have done nothing to her dishonor."

"Wait," Flora said. "Being alone in a room with you is compromise enough. It's certainly so for other young ladies. Why not for me?"

"Flora," Jane said carefully, "you cannot mean that you would choose to—"

"Yes, I would." Flora folded her arms. "I've been planning this for weeks."

"Have you?" Archie asked in an odd tone.

Bronsky's astonished stare proved, at least to Jane's satisfaction, that he hadn't heard of Flora's plans before this evening.

"Yes," Flora was answering her brother. "Monsieur Bronsky and I will have a sensible, platonic marriage. I know enough things about him—"and here she stared hard at her professed lover—"to ensure that we do."

Bronsky shook his head as though it were full of water.

Jane approached the young man and laid a hand on his arm. "You poor man. I'd wager you thought Lady Flora was completely under your spell. Isn't that so?"

Bronsky's white teeth flashed. "She is, madame. She

accepts my letters. She speaks kindly to me and no other. And now she is ready to marry me."

"Perhaps you'd better talk over the details," Jane suggested. "For instance, you do know the word 'platonic,' don't you?"

At his puzzled expression, Jane translated that particular term into French and German.

"Ridiculous!" he cried at once, rounding on Flora. "Goddess of my heart, her ladyship tells a strange tale. You do not truly wish for an unnatural union, do you?"

"I wish to be left alone, and there is nothing unnatural about that. You will of course take the MacGowan name and do what I ask in exchange for the allowance I mean to pay you," Flora said, folding her arms. "Do remember, Monsieur Bronsky, that I have certain information about you which I am too polite to impart to my brother or Lady Averham."

Bronsky scowled darkly.

Jane exchanged a glance with MacGowan and was astonished to see an amused gleam in the eyes of Flora's brother.

"What can you mean, Flora?" Jane asked.

"Indeed," Archie added, "it's news to both of us, I am sure, that you're too polite to do anything."

Flora began to pace the room, her favorite activity when she was troubled.

"If you are delicately alluding to your friend Bronsky's work for the Russian government, that little stirring-up of the Poles he's been engaging in, don't bother," Archie continued. "The affair is known."

"What?" Flora whirled around, and her brows came together in an attitude of extreme displeasure.

"Impossible!" Bronsky cried. "I am an innocent man. Who tells such lies?"

"Oh, do be quiet," Flora snapped. "My files on you are complete."

Jane stared at the girl in amazement. What had been going on in Flora's life without her chaperon's knowledge? Quite a bit, it would seem.

"Don't worry," Archie said, speaking low. "Flora has had Bronsky investigated."

"Heavens," Jane murmured.

"Now." Flora stopped pacing and spoke up imperiously. "So you know about him, Archie. All very fine. You must agree he'll make me an admirable husband."

"He'll make you nothing of the sort. Do you care for this man, Flora? Is that why you're making such a fuss?"

Jane and Bronsky both looked on in silence at the quarreling brother and sister. Jane thought Bronsky looked ill.

"Of course I care nothing for him," Flora said. "That's why he'll do. He is someone I can control."

"Is that so, my fine lady?" Bronsky cried out, striding forward. He grasped Flora by the shoulders and kissed her, hard. "This for your platonistic marriage!"

Flora tore herself away, eyes cold with disgust. "That, sir, was uncalled-for."

"And this entire plan of yours is not called for." Bronsky's face was becoming very red. "You have used me shamelessly, English lady, and I shall never forgive."

There was an ominous silence. Jane held her breath, waiting for the explosion.

"How dare you?" Flora finally said through clenched teeth. "I am Scottish, you . . . you foreign devil!"

"Foreign, am I?" Bronsky cried. "My lady, you are here the foreigner. You do not belong in Vienna." He said the last sentence as though there were no greater insult he could utter.

MacGowan stepped forward at this point. "That will be quite enough, Bronsky, Flora. You are brangling like newlyweds already."

"Never shall I marry this block of ice," Bronsky stated.

"Good. As for your other activities, sir, you will know very shortly how little your rousing of the Poles has been appreciated in certain circles."

"I believe in my cause," Bronsky said stubbornly.

"Yes, but your cause isn't poor Poland and the citizens who yearn for freedom. I suspect your cause is none other than Anatole Bronsky and what he can get. Am I right?"

Bronsky's eyes flashed, but he said nothing.

"And you, Flora. I was going to beg Father to send you home, as you so desperately wish, but now I feel that another round of parties will be a fitting punishment for you. I have never seen such lack of social skill."

"Oh!" Flora turned crimson.

Jane longed to say something soothing, but she was much aware of being the unwilling observer in a family matter. She decided to repair matters as best she could from another angle and beckoned to Bronsky, who stood off to one side looking dissatisfied and noble.

"Madame?" He approached her and clicked his heels before her. Behind them Flora and Archie continued to spar, on MacGowan's side with reason tempered by only a few insults, on Flora's with barbs and name-calling.

Jane smiled and touched the young man's arm. "Dear sir, I fear this experience has opened your eyes with regard to Lady Flora's feelings."

He nodded grimly. "I will admit to you, madame, for I know you for a woman of the world, that I believed her to be deep in love with me. She allowed me no intimacy, but this I put down to the normal coldness of the English lady."

Jane smiled, glad Flora was too busy expostulating with her brother to hear Bronsky's second aspersion upon her Scottishness.

"You understand, you who are not cold," Bronsky said, seizing her hand and kissing it.

Jane wondered, startled, how he had ever come by the information that she was not cold, but hoped this was merely a general impression. "I do understand that Lady Flora somehow misled you."

"I wrote her passionate letters of love nearly every day," the young man said.

"You did!" Jane shook her head at her own lack of efficiency in the area of chaperonage. She would never have suspected that one of the young women under her roof had been receiving love letters from a young man.

"Naturally I was after her money," Bronsky admitted with a sigh.

Jane merely nodded. This came as no shock to her, and she respected him the more for not pretending.

"But this!" He ran shaking fingers through his hair. "A young lady to have me investigated and to inform me, so coldly, that she will hold the strings of the purse! That I will take her name! It is intolerable."

"I would advise you, Monsieur Bronsky, to choose more wisely next time," Jane said. "Lady Flora is not ready for marriage, and, as you have seen, her notions of the union are quite unorthodox.''

"Madame, you are most good and kind. If I were you, I would be raging at a young man who would try to steal Lady Flora away from her family, and right under your nose! You are generous, Milady Averham. I salute you.'' Again he kissed her hand, this time with more passion.

Jane drew the hand gently away just as MacGowan approached her. Following him was a sulky Flora.

"Lady Averham, Flora would like to apologize to you for intriguing under your roof, and to assure you that such a thing will never happen again," Archie said with a significant look at Jane, then at Flora.

Flora gave a tight nod.

Jane could tell that the girl was very near tears. She stepped forward and embraced her. ''My dear, this scene must have tired you terribly. Would you like to go home now? I'll have the carriage called.''

"No." Flora was stiff and unyielding, but she did not fight the physical contact. Jane surmised from this that Flora had indeed been overset. ''My brother says . . . that is, I wish to stay here.''

"Very good of you, my dear.'' Jane drew back to smile into Flora's expressionless face. ''I'll wager you're making the extra effort so that Petra and I won't have to leave the ball.''

Flora nodded, with a sidelong glance at her brother.

"Well, well.'' Archie spoke up in what Jane sensed was a touch too much good cheer. ''Let's go to the ballroom, shall we? I won't ask you to join us, Bronsky, for reasons which must be evident. But if I may escort you two ladies, I believe I just heard the fanfare for the royal personages. The polonaise will start at any moment.''

Jane, one eye on Flora, was glad to accept Archie's arm and leave the scene of Flora's attempted compromise. She was beyond anything glad that Petra was safely betrothed and Phyllida was at home with her beloved music; the art of chaperoning was evidently still a mystery to their duenna.

Bronsky soon disappeared. MacGowan and his two ladies hadn't yet gained the entrance to the ballroom when Averham stepped up to the three.

"Robbie.'' Jane had rarely been so glad to see anyone.

She knew he would distract Flora; he always irritated the girl so greatly.

"I've been looking everywhere for you, Jane," Averham said, looking at Flora. "May I beg the opening polonaise with your charming charge?"

"The polonaise is endless and boring." Flora spoke up with a special frown for her admirer.

"Ah, never boring with you for company, Lady Flora." Averham swept his most charming bow.

"Do go, dear," Jane urged. "Slow as the dance might seem to a young person, think how much more boring it would be to sit on the sidelines and watch."

"Which you will have to do for the Russian dances later," Averham put in. "Better move about while you can."

"Very well." Flora stepped from her brother's side and accepted Averham's arm. Her expression was pained. Robbie's was mischievous.

Jane watched them move away. "Oh, do you suppose they will ever come to an understanding?"

"I can't say," Archie replied. "I have rarely seen a more ill-suited couple, but he seems to be taken with her."

"And she always does give in to him at last," Jane considered. "Perhaps there's hope."

"Depends, my Jane, on whether or not you believe that every creature in the world should be married. And if you do, why are you so ungenerous in your own case?"

"Oh, please don't torment me with that. Not now." Jane did not look at him, though she still held tightly to his arm.

"I don't intend to. Will you dance the polonaise with me?"

"I may as well. As I told Flora, the only thing less intriguing than moving through those endless figures is watching them from the sidelines."

"I knew you wouldn't resist my gallantry forever."

Jane chanced a look into his eyes and had to laugh; he was so good-humored about the matter. And if his love for her was genuine, her obstinacy meant the dashing of his hopes. By rights, he should be angry with her. "You are so very kind," she said with a tremulous smile.

"Dear Jane!" The two words, murmured low into her ear, made Jane's heart contract strangely.

They said no more, but continued to the dance floor, where endless couples were lining up for the ritual polonaise. Their way took them past the seats of the Emperor Franz and his empress, the pale, tired-looking beauty Maria Ludovica. As Archie swept a formal bow, Jane sank into a deep curtsy in greeting to the royal couple.

On rising, she took a second glance at the two young ladies who were at present with the emperor and empress. Two very pretty young ladies, both small and dark . . . one of them was Petra! Well, that she should be having a royal audience was nothing wonderful. Petra had been presented to Maria Ludovica and had made a good impression.

Jane's gaze turned to the young lady who was Petra's companion. Only years of social training kept her mouth from dropping open in surprise. Standing next to Petra was Chloe.

17

Jane was dimly aware of Archie's steadying arm about her as she stared at the spectacle of her thirteen-year-old daughter rubbing elbows with royalty.

Chloe wore an apricot satin ball gown which Jane recognized; it belonged to herself. She had worn it the previous winter, which meant that at least Chloe had tried to be thoughtful by not stealing something from her current wardrobe. The dress had apparently been shortened, and not by an expert hand, but the bodice gapped in a manner which it would take a few years to set to rights.

"How did she come here? What can she be doing?" Jane whispered, more to herself than to MacGowan, who nevertheless bent to her to murmur something reassuring.

Jane nearly winced when the Emperor Franz beckoned to her. His imperial majesty would take her to task for letting her daughter run wild. And he was perfectly right; she deserved his censure.

Face flaming, Jane advanced to the imperial chair.

Chloe noticed her mother and smiled nervously, while Petra looked sheepish.

"My dear Lady Averham, I have been telling your young girls how much I have enjoyed the reports of their antics," the emperor said with a kind smile. "Nothing has entertained me half so well at my breakfast table as the accounts of the tricks they have been playing."

"Tricks?" Jane repeated the word in a dazed tone.

"Ah, they have kept it from the mama, as who would not," the empress put in, also smiling at Jane in a kind and indulgent manner.

"May I be permitted to ask . . . that is, what . . . ?" Jane was more than annoyed to find herself stammering in her confusion, quite as though she were a green schoolgirl. She could sense that Archie was standing just behind her. Good; he might catch her if she fell down in a faint. She looked at Chloe again. That gown really didn't fit at all. And that a girl barely in her teens should be parading through society in it! Would the family ever live down this embarrassment?

"We beg leave to explain this to Lady Averham, Majesty," Petra put in at this juncture, with a deep curtsy.

"Perhaps it is better thus. A family matter, not so?" The emperor reached out and pinched first Chloe's cheek, then Petra's when she rose from her reverence. "I congratulate you, Lady Averham, on your beautiful family. Young women to be proud of, and original. Ah." Again he laughed, shaking his head at Petra and Chloe in what seemed a mix of admonishment and appreciation.

He and his young empress looked at each other and exchanged another laugh, which touched Jane oddly. She knew the royal ménage did not get on. It was something that her young ladies had caused Franz and Maria Ludovica to find a moment of rapport.

"Let's take the girls back to the room we just left," Archie said into Jane's ear when they had all backed away from the royal presence. "Young ladies, follow us, please," he added over his shoulder with an unmistakable authority.

Jane looked back at the miscreants and was relieved when Lord Foxburgh hurried after the group. He reached Petra and offered his arm, which she accepted with a grateful air. Chloe walked between the two couples. Another surreptitious glance told Jane that Chloe's posture was that of a prisoner on her way to the block.

When they reached the little book room, Jane turned to the girls and said, "One of you will explain, please, what is going on. What did the emperor mean by tricks? What in the world have you been doing?" She paused and gave Chloe a hard look. "After I know that, I will hear what you are doing at this ball and in my gown."

Chloe flinched and looked to Petra.

That young woman stepped forward from Lord Foxburgh's sheltering arm. "We are sorry, madame," she began. "Chloe and I decided to have a little amusement with the house spy in the Johannesgasse."

"With Johann?"

Petra nodded. "We thought to confuse his masters by setting out ciphers and such for him to find. Only, rather than our secrets, these messages told of Johann himself." Her lips twitched. "At different times we accused him of working for the Russians, the French, the English . . . all the great powers. What we did not know," and here she exchanged a rueful look with Chloe, "was that the emperor is most wise, and his Baron Hager's methods are most thorough. His majesty knew all the time that we were the ones sending the messages, though we were most careful to write them as though they came from visitors to your salon."

"Oh, my God." Closing her eyes in pain, Jane struggled to take in the information. She had noticed nothing of the mischief going on under her nose. First Flora's intrigue with Bronsky, and now this.

"Does his majesty not have the greatest sense of humor?" Chloe burst out. "Oh, Mama, only think! He pinched my cheek. And he called us amusing, and before you got there he was even saying I was pretty, and telling me that I couldn't be as young as his agents reported. Why do people call him dry and cold? He is the most wonderful man . . ."

"I expect he would like to hear your raptures," Jane said, shaking her head. "Oh, Chloe. What has come over you? Were you always so full of mischief?"

The girl paused to think for a moment. "Yes," she finally answered, which caused Foxburgh and Archie to laugh and Petra to titter nervously.

"As for you, Petra, inciting this child to such dangerous games! What am I to do with you?"

"I am very sorry, madame, but as you see, we caused no harm," Petra said, bowing her head. "It was only a little way to pass the time."

"Only great good luck got you out of this so gracefully," Jane said. She did not mention that this was Petra's second fortuitous exit from an intrigue this Season. Truly, the girl led a charmed life.

Jane looked at Archie. "Do you see now, sir, how wrongly I have acted these past weeks? I should have been concentrating on my daughters, and on Petra and Flora. Petra has taken care of herself, thank goodness, but this evening we've narrowly rescued Flora from disaster, and now I find a girl of thirteen cavorting about in my ball gown. It's all my fault.''

"Flora was rescued from disaster?'' Chloe put in eagerly. "What was it, Mama? Did she try to elope with Bronsky?''

Petra, with a whispered word to Foxburgh and a sympathetic look at Jane's stricken face, chose this moment to leave the room on her betrothed's arm.

Jane blessed Petra's understanding. She was glad that no other eyes would witness the dressing-down every finer feeling compelled her to give her daughter. "Miss, you will find the world a much different place tomorrow morning, you may be sure. You'll go on bread and water for a month, I swear. And I believe I must delay your come-out by a full year to teach you that society is serious business—it's not an occasion for a child to dress up and ape her elders.''

Chloe's lower lip thrust out in a familiar manner Jane had not seen for some time.

"I wouldn't be too harsh with the child,'' Archie put in.

"Wouldn't you? But how am I to regulate her behavior without being harsh? Benign neglect hasn't served at all.'' Jane turned on her lover. She could feel tears in the corners of her eyes, and this exposure embarrassed her deeply. "I intend to spend all my days with Chloe from now on. Until we can engage another governess, I'll give her all her lessons, hear her practice her music, and personally escort her to bed each night, where I shall lock her in.''

"Oh, Mama!'' Chloe gasped, reddening. "You wouldn't.''

"You won't have time,'' Archie said, grasping Jane's wrist. His arms encircled her, and he bent to kiss her.

Jane started back. "Must you always act without warning, sir?''

"The element of surprise is a classic tactic. And I intend to brook no further nonsense from you, Lady Averham. You've been preoccupied, true, but it's hardly surprising, considering what we've been through together. Why, our lives have changed forever in just a few weeks.''

Jane nodded. She was unable to find words.

"Don't think you're to blame for your daughter's antics," Archie continued with another kiss. "I suspect young Chloe is simply a spirited creature, and that no matter what you do, she'll find a way to show that spirit."

"You have it exactly, sir," Chloe said with a little look of triumph. "But why do you keep kissing my mother? There's no one here to witness it. I know you only do it because you want to cause talk. Oh! You think *I* will talk. I suppose I am a sad gossip . . ."

Archie turned to the girl. "I love her, and I suspect she loves me."

"What?" Chloe's expression changed instantly to one of revulsion. "That's absurd. Mama is not that kind of woman. Why, she's my mother, and I'm grown up!"

Jane's heart sank. She had known that her girls would never approve of a romance between her and Archie.

"Naturally I heard about the three kisses in our drawing room," Chloe went on. "A joke, wasn't it? You don't have to play any more jokes for my benefit."

"My dear young lady, this has nothing to do with you," Archie was beginning when the door, which had been left ajar, opened wider.

Bronsky stood there, shrewd dark eyes taking in the scene. "I come to help you, Lady Averham," he said, bowing to Jane. "You have been good to me; now I be good to you." So saying, he turned to her daughter. "Mademoiselle, would you accept my hand for the dance?"

"Dance!" Chloe's eyes shone. "With you, the best dancer in Vienna? Oh, yes. And you may tell me what happened with you and Flora tonight. Good-bye, Mama. You and Mr. MacGowan can settle this between you. I'm afraid you'll have to be stern with him." Picking up her too-long skirts, the girl dashed from the room, closely followed by an amused Bronsky.

"She is going to dance," Jane said in wonder, putting a hand to her head. "A girl barely in her teens whose gown fits like . . . Oh, neither she nor I will ever live it down. Good heavens. I must catch her and take her home immediately."

"Jane." MacGowan's tone was commanding as he crossed to the door and closed it. He stood against it, arms folded, and frowned.

Jane gave him an exasperated look.

"Haven't you noticed that we're alone?" Archie came forward to take her in his arms again. "What if we were to seize such a delightful opportunity, as that hussar and his lady were doing in that other room we chanced upon earlier?"

"Are you mad?" Jane's eyes widened. "You've said you'll have nothing more to do with me in that way. You ended our affair. You—"

"I love you." He stopped her next words with a kiss. When he released her, he gazed deeply into her eyes. "Don't you have something to tell me?"

Jane took a deep breath. "Yes. You know it anyhow. I love you too. I love you to distraction."

"You have been rather distracted in the last days," he muttered as he bent to run his lips along her neck.

"But it changes nothing," Jane continued in desperation. A warmth grown no less exciting for its familiarity was invading her limbs, and she knew that she could win him back to her bed with very little trouble—or could she? Perhaps his were the tricks; perhaps he was trying deliberately to arouse her desire so that she would give in to his demands.

"It changes nothing? You love me, and it changes nothing?" He stopped what he was doing to laugh at her. "My own Jane, you leave me no choice but to marry you. Best if you simply give up now and admit that it will happen, for it will, you know. It will."

"No," Jane whispered, backing away.

"Are you still afraid?" He searched her face. "Can you really be afraid of me?"

"Not of you. Of marriage. Of giving over my freedom again. But I will admit I'm vexed with you." Her eyes pleaded for understanding; she suspected she did not look vexed at all. "You decide we ought to marry, and you'll brook no argument, will you? You're controlling me, as I was controlled all my life until I became a widow. Oh, I don't know what to think. The insistent lover thrilled me, make no mistake. But this! You give no thoughts to my wishes, only charge forth with your own, determined to carry the day."

"Did he love you, Jane?" Archie was close beside

her, putting his arms around her again in that seductive way he had.

The complete change of subject startled her. "What?"

"The late Averham. Your husband. Did he love you? I have the strangest feeling you're raging at him as well as at me."

She shook her head. "He bought me from my parents. He offered a title; they, a substantial dowry. I was a commodity, nothing more." She shuddered at the memory. "My parents—I'm afraid I've never really forgiven them. To them I was merely a thing. My brothers, I believe, had some reality in the family, but I? I existed only to raise their status."

She paused, amazed that she had said so much about her family circumstances. When last had she dwelt on the cheerless atmosphere of her childhood, the dragging sense of despair and hopelessness which had accompanied her to the altar at sixteen? She had been glad that Averham's career had taken her out of England so often, for she had never had any desire to mix with her relations after their betrayal of her.

She never thought about them if she could help it, and now she was talking of them, easily, fluently. She had so little pride where Archie was concerned.

"I love you," he said. "Our union would be so much more than what you had with that fool—and he *was* a fool not to cherish you greatly. We would have so many wonderful discoveries to make together."

"Would we?" Jane's question was shy, for she felt herself melting. What was happening to her? He was so very eloquent that she believed everything he said. Marriage with him sounded like a perfectly reasonable solution to this problem of mutual love. But was this only another example of her wretched tendency to bend to others' wills?

Then she thought of something new. In this case, his wishes happen to match her own. She did love him so, and marriage was what he wanted. She would be taking a chance, of course, but how many chances had she taken all by herself? This would be an adventure all her own— hers and his.

She had discovered recently that she could bear very well the speculation and titterings of her fashionable world. And she knew in her heart that Archie's and her disparity in age was nothing but a convenient excuse to deny him. Her circle was not so unsophisticated that a few years either way would make a grave difference in how a couple was viewed.

Everyone who really cared about her would be happy for her, in any case.

She stared at Archie, nearly overcome by these new ideas, which seemed so easy after all her sleepless nights.

"Your daughters' lives must wait for another Season," he said, kissing her cheek. "This is your time, Jane. Our time. Let's be together as we were meant to be. Let's not waste another moment."

Jane stayed silent for a long time, then spoke. "You're right. The risk is there, but there is always a risk, no matter what choices we make."

He laughed at her. "You say that so painfully. Don't worry, my dearest. I'm not right that often. But in this case I must admit I've seen clearly almost from the beginning."

"You started our affair," Jane pointed out.

"And I soon saw my mistake, though not before I had come completely under your spell. Don't worry, Jane. I won't take away your freedom. We'll find some way to put it in writing if we must."

Jane shook her head. "That won't be necessary. I trust you," she said, and realized as she spoke the words that she had never before given such a compliment to a human creature.

He grinned. "Now, where shall we honeymoon? Thanks to this Peace, the world is at our feet. What is your favorite place in Europe?"

Without hesitation Jane responded, "That cottage in the Vienna Woods. Or would that be too humble a spot to begin our married life?"

Archie's smile widened, and he hugged her to him. "There, you've said it, my darling. There will be no honeymoon without a marriage, you may be sure. And you may honeymoon in a cellar if you like, so long as you do it with me." Lifting her off her feet as he was wont to do when he was excited, he spun around the room with her and then set her down. They were both laughing, dizzy, and they leaned together.

The door opened, and a dark gentleman and a light-haired lady peeked in. With scandalized expressions, they closed the door quickly.

"Flora and Robbie!" Jane gasped, still unable to stand on her own. "Why do you suppose they were looking for an empty room? She doesn't even like him."

"Or she hasn't admitted it to us. Let us not suppose too hard, lest we catch them out in a worse discretion than this," MacGowan said. His hands began to roam Jane's back in a delightful pattern. "Do you know," he whispered, "we were draped about each other in such a voluptuous way that from their viewpoint we might have been in the middle of lovemaking."

"We're always in the middle of lovemaking," Jane retorted. "Even when we fight."

"Well said, Mrs. MacGowan." Archie kissed her softly on the forehead, eyes gleaming with a wicked light. "You have the makings of an excellent diplomat's wife."

Jane's face lit in mischief. She knew she could say anything to Archie. "It might be indelicate in me to mention it, but I have had practice."

His smile proved that he appreciated the joke. "I mean to give you even more practice—but not in the diplomatic arts."

And he crossed the room to the door and turned the key in the lock.